BECAUSE... VENGEANCE

DIANA L. SHARPLES

Because...Vengeance

Other novels by Diana L. Sharples

Running Lean
Running Strong

Finding Hero

Because...Anonymous
Because...Paranoid

Chapter 1

Monday...Not Exactly a Do-Over

I get up.

That's a big deal, because basically I've been unconscious for days. Pain meds are both friend and foe, numbing me against the many hurts, but also making me dull and incapable of doing simple things without assistance. The narcotic-induced, technicolor dreams were not as interesting as I expected them to be. No awakening of the muse while I slept. More like all my nightmares conspired to make my heart beat fast and soak my sheets with sweat.

So, on a day I think is Monday, I get up and shuffle to the bathroom to shower and scrape the week's worth of patchy stubble off my face.

Who is this thin, weak, pale kid in the mirror with my hair and eyes? When did I stop being myself? It was before the car wreck, I'm sure.

Every movement hurts. Breathing hurts. My cracked ribs and bruised stomach are telling me they're not ready to go back to school. The doctor warned me it would be this way, the pain gradually easing off over eight weeks or so. I have an absolute legitimate excuse to stay in bed for another day, or another seven days.

But I need to get out of this place.

Sound travels through this old mobile home like it has no walls at all. Mom must have heard me moving around, because she's got a cup of coffee and a bowl of cereal already poured for me. She jumps up from her seat at our card-table *dinette* and tries to take my backpack out of my hands.

I pull it away from her. "I'm fine."

"You shouldn't lift anything heavy. The doctor said—"

"I'm fine, Mom."

She folds her arms, gives me that parental authority look. "I can make you stay home."

"Then you'll have to stay home from work to keep me from leaving."

She's not going to do that. We need the money too much, and if she misses any more work, she could get fired.

Her warning, *"Don't get into any more trouble, Noah,"* repeatedly invaded my dreams, screeched through the gaping, fang-filled mouth of a Tibetan Yeti the color of a canary. I was too terrified to laugh.

Loser. Delinquent. Your fault. All of it.

That particular mantra never leaves me alone. It hangs out at the back of every thought and has been there since long before the crash.

Mom sits across from me while I eat. She's dressed for work in her blue smock and scuffed clogs, her hair pulled back so tightly that I wonder if it's to keep her eyes open. How many of those gray streaks have been added since we left our home in North Carolina? How many does Dad add daily with his angry texts and phone calls?

How many did I add this past week?

She places her elbows on the table and takes a slow sip of her coffee. "Something I need to tell you." Her voice is muted, like she doesn't really want to say anything. "I'm going to the police station today."

"Can you see if they have my phone while you're there?" I smile, trying to let her know I'm joking. Pretty lame joke, though, and she doesn't respond to it.

My phone may be inside the wrecked car of a killer, held at the police impound lot. Or maybe they're scanning it for evidence.

"I spoke with Jessica last night," Mom says. "She says I need to file assault charges against your father and then sue for divorce and custody of you."

Jessica is the dental nurse where my mother works. Not a person

I'd call an authority on family law.

I scowl into my coffee. A couple of grounds float around the center. The sight of them are enough to make my persistent nausea churn. Using the tip of my index finger, I push the grounds to the side of the cup.

"Isn't the restraining order enough?" I ask and then take another sip, my eyes crossing to watch the grounds.

"This is different. It means he'll be arrested."

The coffee catches in my throat and I cough. Big mistake. I manage to lower the cup to the table without breaking it as I double forward and grab my right side. Mom is there instantly, fussing and cooing useless words. There's nothing she can do. I take small, easy breaths so I don't disturb the injured places any more.

"Breathe deeper, Noah. You know what the doctor said about pneumonia."

"I'm fine!" I bark. "Just give me a second."

Mom backs away and takes her coffee mug to the sink. It clanks around enough that I can tell she's ticked off now.

I lift my head and try to breathe deeper. It freaking hurts. "I... I thought you didn't want him to go to jail."

She slides her hands along the edge of the countertop and leans against the sink, looking at the blind-shuttered window rather than at me. "The restraining order won't keep him from hurting us in other ways. And if he does find out where we're living—"

"Maybe he won't."

But he could. It's possible now. All it would take is for Dad to read in a newspaper report about how George Norwood kidnapped a student—me—and is also a person of interest in the death of a fifteen-year-old girl. Dad would see which school employed the man and read how he somehow passed a background check even though he was suspected of killing his wife twelve years ago. Who, coincidentally, was found drowned in a reservoir in Vermont. Dad could read that article, and he'd know the name of my school and what town we live in.

He just needs to be sober enough to figure it out.

"I need to take action before your father does," Mom says. "Jessica told me—"

"How does Jessica know anything?"

"Her husband is a cop. He knows."

"So, it'll be like, you file against Dad and he files against you, it's your word against his, and I don't have any say in it?"

Mom sighs at the ceiling. "Hush, Noah. I'll need your support to do this. It's going to be ugly. And I really need you to stay out of trouble."

I groan at this. Staying out of trouble isn't quite as simple as it sounds. What happened last week wasn't something I went looking for. Maybe I chose the wrong friends, but it wasn't obvious in the beginning that they were anything more than ordinary manga fans.

I wonder what will the Manganites say or do now that their friend is in jail or juvenile hall, or wherever the authorities sent him, because I discovered what he did to Hana Seoh. Will people at school connect me, with my new injuries, to the newspaper article about Maintenance Guy George? Has there been a lot of social media chatter?

I swallow several spoonsful of cereal, and try to console myself with the positives. A killer is in custody. Any one of the Manganites could have been his next victim. Or beautiful Mia Park could have been, since the guy's socially inept son was sending her threatening notes in the form of badly written poetry.

If I think about it, I can still feel Mia's kiss on my cheek and hear her saying that I'm a good person. A hero. Not a guilty, delinquent loser.

I need that. Deep in my soul, I need to receive the affirmation of a girl kissing me and thinking I'm worthy of something. I'm starving for it.

Mom might be asking a whole lot from me.

There's a knock at the front door of our trailer. Mom shimmies to the living room and peeks through the window blinds to see who's there.

"It's Simon." She lets him in.

My one and only friend in Georgia is wearing a red jacket that's too large for him. He looks like a Christmas elf with his bright blue eyes, his cheeks pink from the cold, and the slight green tint in his hair from faded Kool-Aid coloring. That's where the comparison ends, though, because Simon greets me with a lazy wave and a frown instead of his usual cheesy grin.

I stand and take one final swallow out of my mug. The grounds are gone. Gag. "What-what are you doing here?"

"I called him when I heard you getting ready," Mom says. "I thought it would be good to have someone with you at school." She comes back to my side and runs her fingers through my hair. Bring on the embarrassment. "Are you sure you're okay to go back, baby?"

I shoot Simon a warning glare, but he doesn't seem to be paying attention. He's staring at an uninteresting corner of the living room.

"I'm good. Let's go." Protecting my right side, I grab my backpack with my left hand and head for the door.

It's frigid outside. Not cold enough for ice to form, but enough that I gasp when the wind fills my fragile lungs and hits the little scratches flying glass made on my face. It's not even Halloween, and this is Georgia. So what's up with the polar vortex?

As we're rolling down the single-lane road leaving our trailer park, I lean back in my seat and close my eyes. Simon makes little noises in the back seat, soft grunts and the tiny clicks of his fingers tapping out text messages. I roll my head against the headrest to look at him. He's focused, and it suddenly strikes me as odd that he hasn't asked me how I'm feeling.

"What's going on?" I ask.

Staring back at him while Mom is driving prompts the nausea again. My head feels like it's spinning when I shift forward.

"It's Chloe," Simon says. "She had a problem at her house yesterday."

Chloe?

Simon knows a lot of people, and I'm sure he's mentioned this person to me before. I should remember but... blank.

"What happened?" I ask, covering my forgetfulness.

He's typing again, saying a lot more to this Chloe person—I'm assuming—than he is to me. Finally he stops and sniffs. "She, uh, had a break-in. Stuff stolen."

"Oh dear," Mom says, her eyes flicking to the rearview mirror.

"Yeah," he says. "They took her camera equipment that she needs for her work on the school paper."

With this bit of information, I remember who he's talking about. I haven't actually met the girl yet, but I saw Simon walking through the school cafeteria with her. Tallish, blond girl, on the cute, nerdy side of smokin' hot. If Simon is this bummed about what happened to her, then there's some relationship between them that I need to keep my nose out of.

"Wow. That sucks," I say, and leave Simon to his texting for the rest of the ride.

When we arrive at the school and wait to turn left into the lot along with a line of school buses, diesel exhaust adds to the nausea I'm already feeling. Breathe. Deep and slow. Even though it hurts.

"Honey?" Mom says, glancing over at me as we make the turn.

"I'm okay." I'm lying. Coming back to school today might have been a mistake.

Simon and I unload from the van and he puts his phone away. Like Mom, he asks if I'm okay. I nod. I need to do this. I'm moving slow toward the school entrance, but I am moving forward.

Simon sticks close to my side. Inside, girls are wearing pajamas. Carrying teddy bears. Not all of them, but enough that I gawk and wonder if I'm still stuck in a dream.

"What the?" I point at a flannel-clad girl scuffing past in fuzzy slippers.

Simon rolls his eyes. "It's spirit week. Today is pajama day."

I'm so glad I didn't remember that. Not that I would ever, *ever* get caught up in the whole Homecoming craziness. Even back in North Carolina, school spirit and sports were never my thing.

But maybe girls in pajamas will be what I need to keep people from noticing my scratched-up face and the slow pace I'm walking to keep from jarring my ribs.

Or... not. A couple of girls in regular clothes walk past us, glance at me, and quickly turn away, whispering to each other. They don't see *me*. They see the wreck I've become.

"Are you sure you're okay?" Simon asks again when I've slowed down too much.

I have another problem. One that hits me like a sucker punch. I can't remember where my locker is.

Okay, I've attended this school less than a month and I've been absent for several days, but this doesn't make any sense. This isn't like forgetting a girl's name or that it's spirit week. There are several hallways that branch off the main one by the entrance. Down one of them is my locker. But which one?

My forward motion stops. "Um."

It's just the stress from my family life and the car wreck, right? I can't be... *damaged.*

"Noah?" Simon touches my arm.

"Are we going to your locker or mine?" I ask.

He shrugs. "Yours?"

I swing a hand out in front of me. "Lead on."

Simon tilts his head a little, but only for a second. Then he continues up the main hallway. I follow a step behind.

When I was in the hospital, the police came to question me about what happened with Maintenance Guy George. I was missing pieces. Sometimes a detail seemed just beyond my grasp. Sometimes not there at all. I figured it was the pain meds. I figured it would all come back.

But now, even forcing myself, I can't remember all the details of the accident. We went flying down an embankment along the highway and nearly flipped over. But honestly, I think I only know that because people told me that's what happened.

Something trembles inside me as I follow Simon to the third right turn. He stops about halfway down this hallway. Red lockers, top and bottom, with numbers and combination locks. Even if I could have found my way here without Simon, it wouldn't have done me any good. Because that combination? Gone.

Simon tilts his head again. Like a puppy.

"Um..."

He lightly taps a finger against the lower locker beside him. Number 855. I nod and stare at it.

"Still have your class schedule?"

If I do, it's crumpled up somewhere at the bottom of my backpack.

I swing my backpack around in front of me, grit my teeth at my complaining ribs, unzip it and start digging. I find the schedule, with the locker number and combination typed at the upper corner of the paper. As I bend forward to dial the numbers, a whimper escapes me. It's better than the cursing I'd like to do.

"Here." Simon takes the paper from my hands. He dials the combination, opens the locker, and stands back to let me handle the rest.

"Thanks," I mumble.

He clasps my shoulder gently. "You'll be fine in a few days. No worries."

Simon also walks with me toward my first period—I do remember where that is, thank God. I'm grateful for his help, but it's starting to feel a little awkward.

Outside my world history classroom, I lift a hand to wave to him, but stop. Because... *she's* here.

Mia Park walks like she isn't tethered to the earth by gravity. There's a feeling of her being *above it all*. Not arrogance, but a kind of grace that elevates her. Maybe I sense this because I find it hard to drag my eyes away from her dark eyes and flawless oval face framed by flowing chestnut waves of hair.

Yes, I know. I'm totally sappy that way.

People call her Ice Princess for that graceful aloofness. But I know something else about Mia. I've seen her humble, even vulnerable. For one moment in time, I was her hero.

I straighten my back. Which hurts. Mia sees me, and her pace quickens, along with the beating of my heart.

Simon knocks my elbow and grins, and I'm tempted to knock him back a little harder.

Mia stops about four feet away and clutches her books to her chest. "How are you, Noah?"

How am I? Possibly falling in love. But she's asking about my injuries. Nothing more *interpersonal*.

I nod coolly. "It's all good. Glad to be back."

There's a movement of air to my right, and Simon is gone. The little dude moves pretty fast.

Mia dips her head slightly. "Good. I'm glad too. I spoke with Jun last night, and he wanted me to thank you for giving the police new information about what happened to Hana. The whole family is grateful."

I'm not even sure what information I gave them. Books. I found some books with evidence in them at Ivan's house and I stole them. I nod again. It seems kind of weird to say, "You're welcome," so I don't.

"I hope it helps." Another lame thing to say. What's the matter with me? What would be better for Hana's family, to believe she committed suicide or to be told that she was murdered? Did I help them find closure or open the emotional wound further?

"His family has been through so much," Mia is saying. "Someone broke into their house over the weekend."

Is that a thing? Like, people read obituaries in the newspaper and target those houses for burglaries? I chew on this coincidence for a moment, along with the other one, the break-in at Chloe's house.

"That awful," I say.

"Yes." Mia glances toward the classroom, like she really wants to go in there rather than talk to me in the hallway.

I give her a break and take a step that way. We're within arm's reach of each other now, and everything in me wants to shift even closer, while every vibe she gives off says this is just a temporary encounter.

"Jun said it was strange," she says softly. "They didn't take anything valuable. Just made a mess in the house. His wrestling trophies were stolen."

"Maybe they were looking for something specific?"

She hunches her shoulders. "Like what? A trophy? None of Mrs. Seoh's jewelry was touched. No electronics stolen."

"Maybe someone came home and interrupted the guys before they could take anything."

We're in the classroom and standing at that uncomfortable spot where we have to go separate ways to our desks.

My desk? Doesn't matter. I can just pick one.

Mia takes one step away from me. "I guess that's possible. Um. Noah... I need to tell you something."

Uh oh. Here it comes. The big blow off. This is a place I've stood before. I recognize the girl's posture, the already apologetic tone of her voice.

"I'm so grateful to you for what you did. Not just for Hana, but for me. Figuring out those notes. You saved me, and I won't ever forget that."

But...

"But, I think Jun and I—I mean, I don't know for sure. But I think he wants to get back together with me."

Of course he does. And it's not like I couldn't see this coming. Girls in Mia's social strata might like me for a little while, maybe for a fling on the dark side, but they always go back to their comfortable places. Mia and I aren't even friends, really, and maybe not even that. Now she's letting me know that little kiss in the hospital didn't mean anything other than, "Thank you."

I try and fail to take a deep breath. "That's good. I mean, if he makes you happy, then..."

What am I saying? I'm totally lying to her. I'm not letting her see that she's plunging a long needle into my heart.

She smiles, but she has a twitchy look about her, like invisible strings are pulling her away from me. I let her go and claim a desk at the back of the room.

Setting my books down proves to be harder than I anticipated, and my textbook slips from my grasp to fall to the floor. *Blap!* Everyone looks. Even Mrs. Christensen, who was busy at her desk with another student.

Hey, look! Noah the creeper is back.

The More Things Change, the More ...

"So, what are you, some kind of detective? Or just a rat?"

Todd McCaffrey walks beside me, but not close enough that it looks like we're together. He speaks across the gap without looking at me.

I choose not to answer the question. I've had a horrible morning just getting through my classes. By third period I was ready to call Mom and ask her to come take me home. But, oh yeah, no phone. And going to the nurse's office means I'd have to answer the hows and whys of my condition.

"Thing is, you got it all wrong," Todd goes on. "That girl, Hana, was a liar. I mean, I'm sorry she's dead, but she jumped into bed with Ivan and then freaked out because he didn't fall madly in love with her. She was a little slut."

If I didn't feel like I could lose my footing at any moment, I'd whirl around and punch this guy. I wasn't here when it all went down, but from what I've been told, Hana was a happy little Manganite who got caught in Ivan's web. And then someone—Todd?—spread all over social media that she was sleeping around.

She was a victim, and I would *love* to be able to nail Todd for his part in the lies that ended up taking her life.

"Is that what you told everyone?" I mutter. "With all your posts? Did you hack her accounts too?"

He laughs at this, so casual and cocky. "It's what everyone said about her. You got your information from the wrong sources, my friend. Like your precious Mia, who's desperate to change the narrative for the sake of her lover's *honor,* so she can win him back."

The emphasis he puts on that word, honor, makes it sound like a racial slur, which presses the rage button in me again.

"Ivan raped Hana. And his father kidnapped me."

"That's funny," he says. "You got another one?"

"I'm actually not supposed to talk about it," I say. "Police investigation and all that."

"Because you set him up."

I give him my own version of the cocky chuckle. "Whatever, dude."

I'm done playing detective. The police will get justice for Hana. Todd has probably posted lies about me on social media already, unseen by me because… no phone. I don't care. I'm done with all that, and with this conversation.

Holding my side for effect, I slow down enough that Todd outpaces me.

Simon meets me inside the cafeteria. He's been waiting for me. I guess to carry my tray for me or make sure I'm not keeling over. Good of him, but I need to take care of myself. I need to retain whatever dignity I still have. We go through the line and I get myself a slice of pizza.

We're heading to the table, where Simon's friends are already sitting, but have to stop while a proud wrestler with a Barbie-doll girl under his arm crosses our path. Drake Ogletree. Worse luck than a black cat.

"Whoa, milky boy," Drake croons. "What happened to you? One of those manga geeks do some *kung-fu* on your face?" He laughs like this is the funniest thing ever and tugs his girlfriend away without waiting for an answer.

"She must really love him. He's such a sweet guy," I mutter.

Simon grunts and moves ahead. Running interference for me? But at our table, the other guys are staring, and I start formulating a stupid answer to the inevitable question before it's spoken.

"Dude," Jeremy says, his mouth full. A bit of food escapes and slithers toward the goatee he's trying to grow. "You look like you tried to French kiss a leaf blower."

That's actually funnier than what I came up with, so I let it be.

Matt backhands Jeremy's shoulder. "Car wreck," he hisses. "Remember? With the janitor? Simon told us."

"Oh, yeah." Jeremy says.

"Actually, he lied," I say. "I punched a propane tank. Big explosion. It was on the news."

"Really?"

Unbelievable. But it gives me my first smile of the day.

I lift my pizza slice off the paper plate. It's soggy, so I need two hands. An extra hand flashes in front of my face and flips the pizza through the air and onto the corner of Simon's tray. Heat instantly rises to my brain and I jolt up from my seat to face the enemy.

Daniel Garrison.

Apparently allegations of cyberbullying and the arrest of his friend haven't left a good mark on the leader of the Manganites. Daniel bristles like an angry possum, his red hair in gelled clumps dangling in front of his flashing eyes.

"You're back," he says.

"Wow. That's all you got for me? Am I supposed to be scared?"

"I didn't think you'd have the guts to come back. Thought you'd run away to another state. That's what you do, right? Run away from stuff?"

The heat in my head intensifies, burning the backs of my eyeballs, which feels like a migraine coming on.

"Fight!" Jeremy yells. Out of the corner of my eye I see him stand and raise his hand. "Fight!"

Simon tells Jeremy to shut up while Matt yanks him back into his seat. And then Simon is by my side, leaning against my right shoulder.

"Don't do it, Noah. You don't need any more trouble."

Simon needs to mind his own business, even if he is totally right. I don't need to give the principal and the police any additional reasons for them to turn me over to the Department of Family and Children Services. Or worse, since I'm nearly an adult. Ivan and I could be roommates at some detention center.

Daniel is waiting for me to answer his taunt.

"I didn't do anything wrong. What happened to Hana is all on y'all's heads."

"First off, nobody raped Hana. Second, none of us wrote those notes."

"Really?"

"Yeah, really! And third, why did you break into my girlfriend's house last night?"

I wince at this completely random information. "Do what?"

"You get back at people by stealing stuff from them?"

Synapses fire like crazy inside my head, connecting what might be coincidence but look too much like a pattern. But I need to answer Daniel like I have no clue. "Seriously, I don't know what you're talking about."

Now Matt is out of his seat. "Dude! He was in the hospital! How could he even steal anything from anyone?"

Daniel leans toward the table to yell at Matt. "He stole my girlfriend's Asian ball-jointed doll. It's worth over five-hundred dollars."

A doll? This is getting weirder by the second.

I glance around the room. Am I actually here or is this one of those technicolor dreams from the pain meds? Maybe it is. I see Todd several tables away, a Cheshire cat grin on his face.

What does he know about Paisley's doll? Or is he just reveling in the fight?

Daniel whirls back toward me. There's spittle on his lips that he doesn't wipe away. "Give it back."

Simon tugs at my sleeve. "Forget it, Noah. Come on."

Dream or not, one thing I do know is that I don't let my friends fight my battles. Or tell me what to do. I jerk my arm out of Simon's grip—and then wince and sway. *Ouch.*

Daniel isn't impressed by my show of intense pain.

"Look moron," I say, facing him but holding onto the edge of the table for support. "I was in the hospital until Friday, and jacked up on pain meds all weekend, all because of *your friend's* whacked out father. If I wanted revenge, if I could even do anything about it, and if I even knew where Paisley lives, do you really think I'd go to her house and steal a stupid dolly?"

For just one tiny instant, Daniel looks uncertain. Then he shrugs. "So you got one of these guys to do it for you."

I shake my head, slow and confident. Then I straighten up. Like Wesley in *The Princess Bride,* I battle my pain to face down my adversary, so he thinks I'm stronger than I actually am. I take a step forward. We're face to face. I'm about an inch taller than Daniel. He glares. So do I.

Jeremy is on his feet and yelling again, and I know it's just seconds before a teacher rushes over to break this up.

He blinks. Twice. He's nervous.

"You really want to do this, dude?" I keep my voice low and smooth.

No surprise, he takes a step back. And when a teacher yells, "Hey!" Daniel looks toward the shout and uses it as an excuse to break our standoff. As he backs away, he points a finger at my face. "You're just lucky you're hurt right now. When you're better, it's on between us."

I want to say, "Bring it," but the teacher is here. The woman watches Daniel as he struts over to the Manganites' table next to the cafeteria doors. Paisley, the instigator, waits there for him, standing with her chin elevated, like she has some reason to be proud. Bethany, the perpetually naïve and gutless, won't lift her eyes off whatever she's eating.

I sink slowly into my seat, mostly so the teacher notices that there's an injured and innocent man here.

I won't miss the Manganites. And I won't feel sorry for Bethany anymore. She chose the wrong friends. Her sad expression doesn't touch me at all. But as the teacher moves on and I accept my soggy pizza back from Simon, that pattern sneaks back into my thoughts.

Three break-ins over the weekend. All people connected in some way with Hana Seoh. It's too much of a coincidence.

Across the room, Todd, AKA Mack the Hack, is still watching and grinning. He'll likely give me a new name on social media. Not rat or creeperboy, but thief.

Chapter  2

Monday Afternoon ... Home, but Not Alone

I have to drag myself off the school bus. Simon is working today, so I walk up the slight slope to my house alone. It's a steady, plodding torture. When I see Mom's van sitting in the driveway, I stop, my mouth hanging open, and stare.

This can't be good.

If she's home, it means something is going on. Maybe she got fired. Maybe she heard from Dad and she's packing up all of our possessions again to leave.

If she's not at work, she could have picked me up at school.

Whatever she's doing, I'm heading for my bed. My ribs are aching and my head and stomach feel like they're slogging through slime.

I trudge up the steps and turn the door knob. She has it locked still, so I drag my key out of my pocket. My jeans are practically falling off, because I've lost weight since we moved here. I tug them back up before unlocking the door.

Inside, Mom glances at me and then resumes what she's doing, which is plumping pillows on the sofa. Ratty old colorless sofa, new pillows. Red, orange, and gold, autumn colors. There's a gold and cream geometric patterned rug in the middle of the room, too. And the air smells of electrified dust, which tells me she's been vacuuming.

Either she lost her job, or things didn't go well at the police station today. Because whenever my mother gets really upset about something, she goes shopping to make herself feel better. I'm surprised she hasn't refurnished the entire trailer yet.

"What's up?" I ask.

She straightens but looks around the room rather than at me. "What do you think?"

"Looks nice. What's going on?"

"Don't leave that there!" Mom points at the backpack I'm about to drop by the door.

I don't know where I get the strength to lift that backpack again. "What happened today? Did you go to the police station?"

She grabs a rag and a bottle of Windex off the glass coffee table and moves over to the windows. "They wrote up a report," she answers, spraying the rag with the cleaner. "But they said at this point it's a matter for family court and I should get an attorney."

"The cops don't care about domestic violence?" I suspect she's not telling me the whole story.

"It happened in another state. And too much time has passed." She applies the rag to the window blinds in aggressive strokes. "Go put your things away."

What's the statute of limitations on punching a minor and causing a concussion? The way Mom is attacking the dust on those blinds, I have a feeling she didn't actually tell the police everything that happened that night. Which means she's still protecting Dad.

I'm not sure how I feel about that anymore.

I go to my room, almost dragging the backpack filled with books and instructions for homework I have to make up for almost every class. Mom's been busy for a while, because my room is clean too. The pillowcase is a different color. New. I collapse on the bed and drop the backpack at my feet. Shoes must come off. I kick them away, and one of them thumps the opposite wall. Because my room is *that small.*

I'm just about to lay down when I see my phone sitting on top of the plastic crates I use as a bedside table. Surprise! It means at least Mom did actually go to the police station. The screen is a spiderweb of cracks. I'm scared to run my finger over it. I press the side button to turn the phone on, but it's dead. Not even a flicker of life saying *feed me!* As I'm plugging it in, I hear Mom approaching in the hallway.

"Noah, how did—oh my gosh! What is... is that your feet stinking?"

I groan. "Thanks, Mom. Make me feel worse."

She waves a hand in front of her face. In a moment she'll go get the can of air freshener and saturate my socks. "I'm sorry, but, seriously, go wash your feet. And put on that nice white shirt I bought for you. We're having a guest tonight."

Save me. "Mom, I feel like crap."

"Are you in a lot of pain?"

"Yes! Thank you for noticing."

"Noah, please. I need you to behave tonight. It's important."

"How about if you do the entertaining and I'll just go to sleep?"

"A woman from DFCS is coming. She'll want to talk to you."

Crud. No way I can get out of this thing. Groaning, I set my phone down and try to stand. Try. And fail. My body is unwilling.

"Sweetie," Mom says. "I'll get your pills."

That's what I need, to be dopey from pain meds when the DFCS woman comes to determine my fate.

"No. No. I'll just go take a hot bath."

"How did school go? Did you have any trouble?"

I shrug. Pain all day. But she can figure that out easily enough. I don't want to tell her about forgetting where my locker is. It's just temporary, right? Stuff will heal and I'll get back to normal.

"Any problems with those... comic book kids?"

"Manganites. Nothing I can't handle."

She strokes the back on my head, catching my longish hair between her fingers. It sends a chill through me. "Stay away from them. We don't need any more trouble."

"I haven't forgotten," I mutter as I force myself up.

"Noah." She heaves a big sigh. "I need you to be on your best behavior tonight."

"I get it!" I move past her into the hallway. I may need to close the bathroom door on this conversation. "Seriously, Mom, it's as important to me as it is to you."

"We can't do anything that will give your father an advantage—"

"I know! Okay? I know."

She withers. Maybe not enough that another person would notice, but I've seen it too many times. The inward withdrawal of an emotionally battered wife. Arguments are difficult with my mom. Even if she's right, she gets to a certain point and then shrinks back. Self-preservation. And maybe because Dad has told her so often that she's wrong, she believes it. And if I'm right, I feel bad for making her feel wrong.

"Sorry," I say, and slink into the bathroom.

Sometimes I want to grab her and scream, "Let him go! He doesn't own you!" But I know she's damaged inside. The abuse went on for too long, before I even recognized it. My whole life, Mom poured herself into making things perfect. Not for herself, it turns out. Not because she found any pride in having a clean house. But because she feared judgment. *His* judgment. And now the judgment of the person coming tonight to... to judge us.

For me, it's different. My father typically reminds me that I'm a loser, that I'm destined for a white-trash existence with a crap job and a pack of kids, probably with more than one baby-mama. He's said it so often that I just sort of accept it. I don't have a lot of plans for my future, like many of my friends at home do. The things I'm good at, like my art, are a waste of time, according to my father. I'm slacking off when I draw. When I study comic art so I can learn to draw better. And last year when a teacher—an art teacher—told me the same thing, Dad said good riddance. I could sign up for something useful instead. The whole thing killed something inside me. My internal muse doesn't speak much now. If it makes any sound at all, it's a whimper.

So the only plan I have is to get through tonight. To heal. To graduate. And then to go somewhere else and try to figure out who I am.

The tub in our bathroom is too small for me to relax in for very long. Pulling myself out of it feels like I'm ripping every muscle in my side. I dress in the appointed white, button-down shirt and the cleanest jeans I have. They both hang limp on my frame.

A warm aroma greets me as I go toward the kitchen. It smells like a real home for a change. Mom has the table set and something is baking in the oven. She's at the counter, pouring bag-salad into bowls. Mom has discovered that if she places her cell phone in an empty coffee can, the can acts as an amplifier. She's got some soft music playing, tinny but soothing.

I walk up behind her and slip my arms around her. "It'll be okay, Mom. I'll tell this woman what happened and that it's best for us if we're far away from Dad. It'll be all right."

She drops the empty bag on the counter and rotates in my arms to return the hug... and her elbow jabs me in the ribs.

Stabbing pain, and for an instant I see only the blood vessels in my eyes. I stagger back from her, manage to find the card table with one hand, and collapse into a chair. I think the high-pitched shriek in my ears is Mom crying my name.

"I'm sorry! I'm sorry!" she says, her hands on me.

"Just give me a moment."

"Ice." She dashes for the fridge.

She prepares an icepack for me, a plastic bag of cubes wrapped in a kitchen towel. I lay my head on the table and press the icepack lightly against my side. Mom sits across from me and lowers her head to her fists, her typical posture of prayer these days.

As my pain slowly settles from a thunder clap to a slow rumble, the oven timer dings and Mom rises to serve supper. She prays over our meal, her usual short mantra, and adds a request that God will help us through this evening and the days to come. I say, "amen" like a good boy and carefully dig my fork into the chicken pot pie Mom has placed in front of me.

Later, as Mom is dipping our mismatched, garage sale dishes into a sink full of soap and water, I hear metallic footsteps outside and a knock on our door.

"Oh! Oh! She's here." Mom scrambles around to find a dish towel, but I get up and answer the door, leaving my half-melted icepack on the table.

The woman standing on our porch is middle-aged and stocky, with a no-nonsense look on her face. Her dark hair is twisted on top of her head. She's carrying a manila folder. Mine, I'm guessing. DFCS in

Georgia already has a nice thick case folder on me. Great.

"Hello. I'm Karen Dupree from the Department of Family and Children Services," she says, extending a hand to me. "Noah?"

Yep, she knows me already. Probably has my school ID photo from two different high schools in that folder. I shake her hand and step to the side so she can enter.

Right away she's scanning the trailer, the sorry living room, the tiny dining area, and the kitchen with the cracked countertop and cabinet doors hanging crookedly. Mom hurries to greet her and gestures toward our oh-so-welcoming sofa.

I've already forgotten the woman's name. Stupid concussion.

Mom and the woman take seats on the couch. I sit in the arm chair. I've never sat in this thing before. One side of the cushion is lower than the other. Ouch.

Small talk for a minute, and then the woman opens her file on the coffee table. She shifts in her seat to look squarely at me.

"How are you doing, Noah?"

Simple politeness would have me saying that I'm well, but that's obviously not the case. The way her eyes are leveled at me, with only a hint of a smile on her lips, it looks like she's not going to be satisfied until she gets the truth out of me.

Even so, I feel my entire body tense. It's an effort to unclamp my jaw.

"I'm okay," I manage.

She stares at me. Not in a reprimanding way, but like she's just waiting for me to figure out what I want to say. It's unnerving.

"I'm… okay."

"He was in a car accident last week," Mom says. "He has two cracked ribs and another concussion. He had the first one before from… from when we were in North Carolina."

Mom doesn't seem to want to spill the whole story either.

The woman nods. "Yes, I read about that in my report. But I want to hear from Noah, if you don't mind."

My knee starts jumping up and down. I can't stop it.

"Um, yeah. But I went back to school today."

"That's good. As long as you feel up to it. Do you? Feel up to it?"

"It was my choice."

"Good. Are you happy here, Noah?"

Happy? Is she kidding? My parents' marriage is falling apart and I'm living in a dumpy trailer, five hundred miles from the rest of my family and friends. Happy?

I shrug. "I guess."

She purses her lips and looks down at her file. She's not buying my strong and silent act. "I have a report here which says that, while you were in North Carolina, you fell accidentally and hit your head on a brick hearth."

I nod.

"Your father offered to take you to the hospital, but your mother did it instead, and then she took off with you. She never went back home. Is that true?"

"No," I say.

"Not all of it," Mom says, her voice weak. "Neville made me take Noah to the hospital. He didn't offer."

"Noah? Is what your mother is saying true?"

Mom is telling a half truth. Dad didn't want an ambulance because there would be questions and they might see that my fall wasn't an accident. At least, that's what Mom told me when I was alert enough to listen to anything.

"I don't know," I say. "I was unconscious."

"Why didn't someone call an ambulance?"

"We couldn't afford it," Mom says.

My fingernails claw into the arms of the chair. I don't want to unload my entire family conflict on this woman, but Mom is flat out lying. To protect Dad.

"Mrs. Dupree," Mom says, reaching over like she's going to touch the woman. "My husband has a drinking problem. I'm trying to get him to agree to counseling. Until that happens, I need to keep my son safe."

Dupree. Karen Dupree. That's her name. She keeps looking at me, even though Mom just spoke to her. "Why is Noah in danger?"

"Because he hit me," I blurt. "That's why I fell. He pushed my sister, and I got between them, so he hit me."

"I see. The hospital report says there was an accident with a skateboard."

"Who rides a stupid skateboard at eleven o'clock at night?" I say.

"Noah." Mom is withering again. She can see, just like I can see, what's happening here. Mrs. Dupree isn't here for us. The woman is here for my father. And the only way we're going to come out on top of this is to tell the truth, that my father is an alcoholic manipulator who has become more and more abusive over the years and is now violent.

"Mom. Tell her."

She shakes her head. She can't. She just can't. Because even five hundred miles away, Dad controls her.

"Okay, fine." I cross my arms tight to squash the urge to hit something, even though doing so hurts like crazy. "No, I'm not happy here, because this isn't my home. But I don't want to go back to my father. He's a drunk and an abuser. And I'm not going back."

"Were you given the choice to come to Georgia?"

Crud. No. Mom made all the arrangements and I mostly went along for the ride.

"I have the choice now," I say. "I'm staying."

"Your father alleges that you were taken without his knowledge or consent. Although there was no separation or custody arrangement at that time, the fact that he had no idea where you were for quite some time means he has a case for kidnapping."

"I didn't," Mom says, sounding like she's about to cry. "I didn't kidnap him. I only wanted to protect him."

I stand up. I'm not going to let this woman, this stranger, come in here and judge my mother. "My father is a liar. It was just a matter of time before someone got hurt. And you know what? I'm glad it was me instead of Mom."

"He claims it was an accident."

"He's lying!"

Mrs. Dupree closes her file. "Here's the situation, Noah. Please, sit."

I'm tempted to stay standing, to loom over her until she's intimidated. And then, in a mental flash, I see my father doing the same thing to my mother, to my sister, to me. I clear my throat and slowly sink back into the crooked armchair.

"Your father stated you were unlawfully taken from your home. For your mother to take you, unconscious, as you said, out of the home and across state lines means she has committed an act of parental abduction."

"I wasn't unconscious when we left the hospital."

"Were you conscious when you arrived there?"

"Um, I don't remember. I think I was going in and out."

"Then you weren't really in a position to object to where she was taking you. And that hospital..." She opens the folder again and sifts through a few pages. "In Fayetteville, North Carolina. That's quite a distance from your house in Bentley, is it not?"

Fayetteville? That far?

I don't answer. I see where Mrs. Dupree is going with this, and I'm powerless to stop it.

"When she made the decision to drive you, a semi-conscious child, to a hospital over eighty miles from your home, she put your life in danger. That's child endangerment."

Shriveled into the corner of the sofa, Mom whimpers. She's going to lose this battle. They're going to take me back to North Carolina. To my father. And she'll follow. Because she's not strong enough to fight.

But I am.

I stand up again. "She had to get me out of there. And I'm fine now. I am... of sound mind and body. I have a say in where I want to live. If you try to make me go back to my father, I'll run away."

Okay, that was a little pouty, but still true.

"I'm not here to take you back, Noah," Mrs. Dupree says. "I'm here to evaluate the situation and inform you of the status of the case. And I'll make sure to note your aversion to returning to your father's care. But I do need to inform you—both of you—that this doesn't look good to me. I'm not an attorney, but I believe your father has a legal case."

Mom wipes her face and sits up straighter. "I filed a restraining order against him."

"I don't think that makes much difference, dear."

I want to slap this woman for thinking her little endearment can make her look sympathetic after she's just given us such bad news. My arms are tense and my hands are balled up. My father's influence in me. I almost feel like I'm standing outside of myself, screaming, "Stop!" while my aggressive body can't perceive the command.

"I believe you," Mrs. Dupree says at just the right moment. "Mr. Dickerson struck your son in the heat of an argument and caused him to fall. There are also several prior police reports of drunken behavior and one DUI."

They got Dad on a DUI? That's news to me. Although I'm not surprised he didn't tell us about it.

"I'm going to file my report stating everything we talked about here tonight. But I have to be honest with you. If you had gone to the police that night, when Noah was hurt, we'd have an entirely different situation now. Mr. Dickerson would have been prosecuted and you could have filed in family court for custody of your son. But you ran. And that means you broke the law."

"What am I supposed to do now?" Mom says, the tears welling up again. "Am I going to be arrested for trying to protect my own son?"

"My advice..." She pats Mom's knee, like they're friends now. "You need to find a good family law attorney. And fast. An attorney may be able to file motions with the court to protect you and your son."

"Does my father have an attorney?" I ask, my teeth clamped tight again.

Ms. Dupree turns her head toward me again, her eyes harder than her words a moment ago. "Noah, I know this doesn't make much sense to you, but the laws are in place for very good reasons."

"Good reasons?" Heat rises to my brain, destroying every bit of politeness I'd been able to muster before. "What I see is the law taking away people's ability to use common sense."

"Noah," Mom moans.

"Mrs. Dupree holds up her hand. "Let him have his say."

Wow. Thanks. I point a finger at Mom. "She's a victim, not a criminal. And I'm a victim. But y'all have to come in here with all your laws, and things get more messed up than before.

The woman nods, like I've just spoken brilliant words. I don't feel brilliant. I want to punch something solid.

"You know," she says, "the law can work for you. There is another option."

I wait, barely moving.

"Noah, breathe," Mom mutters. "Your lungs."

I want to yell, "Shut up." But I draw air in, expanding my lungs until it hurts.

Mrs. Dupree glances at Mom.

"His ribs. He could get pneumonia if he doesn't breathe deeply enough."

"Ah." She nods and returns her gaze to me. "Legally, you're still a minor, but you are old enough to file charges against your father on your own. Even now, weeks later. If you want to have your father charged with assault for hitting you, you can do that. Although you may have to go to the police in North Carolina."

My mouth drops open and some of the tension goes out of my arms. I stare at Mrs. Dupree as I grapple with the full meaning of what she has said. Beyond her, my mother has frozen in place, waiting. The only thing that changes about her is the widening of her eyes as they fill with fear.

It's in my hands now, to do what my mother couldn't do or wouldn't do earlier today. To make a real-life, serious, adult decision on my own with long-term consequences.

To put my father in jail.

Later... Thinking

After the woman from DFCS leaves, all Mom says to me is, "It's your decision." She goes back to doing the dishes, and I go back to my bedroom. I don't bother to turn on the light. Concentrating on my homework will be impossible.

I hear Winston, the skittish dog next door, start his high-pitched barking. I raise my window blinds and I see him straining at the end of his leash, which means he knows whoever he's barking at. Otherwise he'd be under the trailer and barking. There's a movement outside Simon's trailer, and the light comes on inside the screened porch.

Simon walks home from work every night. His mother doesn't drive. I see her at the door, welcoming him. Even from this distance I can see that she's an attractive woman, not even as old as my mother, and it's hard to believe that she's disabled. Some disorder. I haven't asked Simon for details.

They have three chihuahuas that add their yapping to Winston's until the front door closes behind Simon. A moment later the porch light goes off. Winston crawls back to his resting place under his trailer.

Warm light flows from the bay window at the end of Simon's house.

I could walk over there. I could tell Simon about this decision I have to make. He'd be concerned, sympathetic. He probably wouldn't be able to tell me what I should do, but it would be good to have someone to talk to. I've got a lot of friends back in North Carolina, but not many that I can talk to about serious things. Even Stuart, my best friend, doesn't know everything about the Dickerson family drama. It's because I've always kept that part of my life separate from my social life. I wanted to be the bad-boy Romeo of South Stiles High School. I wanted to look like I had it all together and could make any girl I wanted fall in love with me for at least a few minutes. I never wanted anyone to feel sorry for me. I didn't want to be a person with... needs. It was easier that way. I could be cool at school and angry at home.

My phone is nearly fully charged, so I send Simon a text.

NOAH:	Got my phone back. It's okay if you want to ride with us to school tomorrow morning.
SIMON:	Awesome! Thanks!

I stare at the text. Two words. And I feel lonely. Because there's nothing more I can say. It's hard to break some habits.

I turn on the light, sit cross-legged on my bed, and try to get some homework done. The words I read leave my head as soon as I don't need them anymore. The problems I solve for algebra are meaningless. None of this seems to matter, because of the question that consumes my mind.

Can I have my own father arrested?

Dad.

My dad.

Who wasn't always like this.

Mom walks by my room, and her voice passes through the thin walls, telling me not to stay up too late. Then she leaves me alone again.

I hear her moving around in her bedroom. Her bedsprings squeak as she lies down and twists around. She cries for a little while. A common thing since we moved here, but now she has another reason. The decision has been taken from her hands. Even her inability to make a decision gave her some security because it bought more time. Now it's on me, and I might not delay so much.

I'm still awake when the neighbor comes home and Winston lets loose with his alarm again. I throw off my blanket and stare at the ceiling. Then I touch my phone on the nightstand, and it sends out a sphere of thin, blue light.

If I dare to put that cracked screen against my face, I could call my sister. After all, the decision I have to make involves her, too. I've only spoken to Naomi three times since I left. Twice without Mom knowing, and once in the hospital, when Mom was talking with her and let me say a few words.

I get out of bed and put on my shoes and jacket. It's tough to sneak out of the trailer without making any telltale sounds. Anything beyond a whisper will wake Mom up. The floors are creaky and the front door sometimes sticks. Moving at a snail's pace, I get outside quietly as possible and walk to the street. Everything is silent. Even Winston seems to be sleeping again because he doesn't bark at me. My pajama pants don't come close to keeping me warm, but I walk to the front of the trailer park and then pace next to the sign that says, "Oakridge Estates." Right. I don't think there's an actual oak tree or ridge anywhere in the place. Just a lot of land uneven enough to be annoying and the typical skinny Georgia pines. No grass or gardens. Just packed red clay and pine straw in the yards.

I tap in Naomi's number and hold my phone gently against the side of my face. I'm already freezing as her phone rings.

She doesn't answer. After blowing out frustration in several frosty puffs, I turn to go back home. Then Naomi's ringtone, the opening guitar riff from My Chemical Romance's *I'm Not Okay,* lights up my phone. I nearly drop it while answering. My hands are shaking, and not just because of the cold.

"Naomi."

"Noah! What's happening? Are you okay?"

Just hearing her voice rips something inside me. "Yeah. Yeah. I need to talk to you, though."

"God, Noah, I can't believe this is still happening to us. I can't believe it's lasted this long."

Five weeks. I figured it out while I was in bed staring at the ceiling. Five weeks since Dad punched me and Mom broke down enough to leave him.

"What's going on with Dad?" I ask. My key question. Is he getting better? Is there a chance for change?

"Still pissed. He came over two nights ago and demanded that I come back home. Guess he figures I'll take care of him."

Naomi has been staying with her boyfriend's family since she graduated high school last spring. She's not sleeping with Julien, she says, but Dad doesn't believe her.

"You should see the house," Naomi says. "I don't think he's cleaned anything since y'all left. There's fast food trash piling up everywhere."

"Dang."

"It smells. Like, bad. No way I'm moving back in there."

"He'll just use you." The same way he used Mom. For years. Maybe since the day they got married. "Mom won't go back to him unless he changes. That's not happening, is it?"

"Ha. No. She should stay away. Divorce him." Naomi's voice is hard, but I know what she's saying isn't easy. "I don't want to lose you and Mom, but I can't see any way out of this."

"A woman from the Georgia Department of Children and Family Services came to our place today."

"Are you serious? What are they going to do? Put you in foster care? At your age?"

"No. She told us that Dad wants to have Mom charged with kidnapping."

"Can he even do that?"

"I guess he can. Of course, he lied about what happened that night."

"So what is she going to do?"

"Honestly, Nae? Probably nothing. I mean, she's not going to have him arrested. She's asked me a few times where I'd like to go. Even said we could go to the beach in Florida."

"She's going to keep running."

"I don't want to. I won't."

"Noah, maybe you should just come home. You can stay with Nathan."

Bad, bad idea. Even if I stay with my older brother, the courts will probably consider me a runaway and force me to go back to Dad. Or foster care.

"I can't," I tell her. I'm shaking so hard now that I can hardly get the words out.

"Please, Noah. At least then he can't charge Mom with kidnapping. I can't even imagine her in jail. In prison. She's not strong enough."

"What if Dad goes to jail instead?"

"For what? Hitting you?"

"Yeah. The DFCS woman said I could have him arrested. Mom doesn't have to do it."

"He'd get bail or whatever and be out in no time. And then he'd be angrier than he already is. He'll hate you for it."

"Maybe that's a good thing. He won't be able to use me as leverage against Mom."

"Noah, he's our dad."

"Well, yeah, but a few minutes ago you were saying they should get divorced."

"Divorce isn't jail. You can't do it, Noah. It'll only make things worse."

That's really what I was thinking. Having Dad arrested won't do any good. It won't wake him up so he'll get sober, and it won't make him leave us alone. I sigh, and it comes out shaky.

"Are you crying?" she asks.

"No, I'm freezing. I'm outside so Mom won't hear us talking."

"Oh. Well... don't do it. Okay? Please?"

"If he has Mom arrested, she won't get out right away. Not for something like kidnapping. And the court will send me back up there."

"Come home. It's the only answer."

"Is that what Dad told you?"

"What?"

I know I'm getting irrational. A floaty feeling comes over me, and the anger is ready to flare up. The only thing I know for certain is that I can't go back to live with Dad. Living with Nathan wouldn't be much better, because Dad would still be able to get at me, and he'd make Nathan suffer for it, too.

Mom was smart to try to keep both of my siblings out of this situation.

"I can't come back. I can't. You know what? If he doesn't kill me, I might kill him."

"No you won't."

"You don't know, Nae. You don't know. I'm so pissed at him. And I don't know what I can do to protect Mom except to stay away."

"Well, what about us? Me and Nathan? Mom doesn't seem to be thinking about what's best for us, and I think taking you away was just thinking about what's good for *her*, not you."

Now Naomi's getting angry. And some tiny part of my brain that can still think straight is saying I should end this conversation before it breaks down into an argument. I really, really don't want to fight with my sister. I don't think I could take it, being mad at her too.

"You know what?" she says. "Just come home. Or don't. It's your choice."

My choice. And either my father goes to jail for hitting me and gets released the next day, or my mother goes to jail for who knows how long. Their battle. But my choice. They've got me in the middle of a tug of war, like I'm a possession rather than a human being. Rather than a son they're supposed to love. Naomi might be right, that if I get away from Mom, the two of them can go their separate ways and it'll be over. But I'll be the one to suffer the consequences. Like getting hit again when my dad decides to punish me for leaving him.

"It's not fair." I'm shaking so badly I have to press my phone hard against my face to keep from dropping it. The phone is the only thing about me that's warm.

"Welcome to real life, little brother."

I let loose with a blistering verbal attack on her. How dare she put me in this position. How dare she tell me what I should do so then she can blame me when it goes wrong. Which it will. How dare she add to my burden rather than help me figure out how to carry it. This is *not* why I called her.

Naomi isn't shy about throwing crap right back at me. In seconds we're both shouting. And that little rational place in my brain says a neighbor will soon call the cops about the noise.

"I'm done," I bark at my sister, and I hang up. I storm back to the trailer and don't even try to be quiet bursting in and stomping down the hall to my room. I throw myself onto my bed and shake. Uncontrollably. A violent earthquake in my soul. Mom comes to my door to see what's going on and I tell her to leave me alone.

Just leave me alone.

I tremble in my bed, and time passes. Maybe I doze a little, I don't know. Eventually the light changes at my window, dawn instead of street lights.

And I'm still alone. Thinking. Emotionally and physically exhausted.

Chapter 3

Tuesday ... Still Thinking About It

I'm still alone, getting ready for school and drinking as much coffee as I can stomach. Alone, even with my mother sitting three feet away from me. She doesn't share her thoughts and barely speaks other than the most basic of questions. Do I want to go to school today? Do I want any oatmeal?

When a ridiculous "shave-and-a-hair-cut" knock comes at the door, announcing Simon's arrival, I actually feel more alone. I can't talk to Simon. What's a sixteen-year-old guy I've only known a few weeks going to tell me anyway? *"Dude, that sucks, man."*

Or maybe, since his father was a cop, he'll say, *"Yes. Arrest the bum."*

We pile into Mom's van. Before I get in, though, my gaze snaps to stains on the front seat and headrest. Maybe down the back of the seat too, where Simon can see them. Mom tried to clean them up. Scrubbed with upholstery cleaner. But she couldn't get all of it. Brownish discoloration remains in the gray fabric.

My blood.

Shed during the trip to the hospital after my father nearly killed me.

I didn't know that Mom drove eighty-five miles before she stopped somewhere to get the gash in my head stitched up.

Insane. None of it makes any sense.

When we arrive at school, Mom puts the van in park and clasps my arm before I have a chance to open my door. She doesn't look at me. She doesn't say anything.

But I get it. The tightening of her fingers conveys her message clearly. She still loves him. She's afraid.

But I'm still thinking about it, and I don't have an answer for her.

Simon unloads and waits for me on the sidewalk. Mom and I sit here a moment longer.

"I've got to go," I finally mutter.

She sniffs, nods, and releases my arm.

My side is stiff and sore, but I slide out of the van and push the door shut without hesitation and without looking back at her. What's she going to do today? Go back to work at the dentist's office and pretend our lives aren't falling apart? While I do the same thing at school. Both of us alone, with the same problem.

Simon clasps my shoulder as I'm watching my mother drive away. "Everything okay?"

Pretty obvious everything isn't okay, but I'm not going to try to lie to him. Instead, I've got a question that came to me overnight.

"You said something last week. I've been thinking about it. It was a Bible verse. When we were trying to figure out what to do about the Manganites."

Simon rolls his eyes. "I get that it was their friend who—"

"What was the verse?"

He winces just a bit, then squints toward the street. His thinking expression. He mumbles to himself for a moment and then returns his focus to me. "Do not return evil for evil?"

"Yeah, that was it. Does it work?"

"Work? What do you mean?"

We're standing on the school sidewalk, with people moving around us as they get out of their parents' cars and head for the doors, and we're about to have a theological discussion. Never in a million years could I have predicted this. But I really want to know. Simon used the verse to determine how we should respond to bullies. My father is the king of bullies.

"I mean, does it make things better to just treat people better than they treat you?"

Simon's hair moves as his brow pinches. "I'd have to know the situation."

"In general. Come on."

He sighs and turns his eyes downward. "Do not return evil for evil. Yeah, it's about treating people better. Really, about treating them as we want to be treated."

"It's about forgiveness," a girl's voice says next to my shoulder.

I jump about a foot off the ground.

Immediately, her eyes grab me. They're the color of the ocean on a cloudy day. Her eyebrows, with a slender, sexy arch, seem natural, not styled. I hardly notice her glasses for the beauty that they frame.

Simon chuckles. "Hey! Chloe, Noah. Noah, Chloe."

I feel like I have to move back a step to take her in. She's taller than I thought. Everyone looks tall next to Simon, but I didn't know Chloe would be my height. Maybe a smidgeon taller. She's done something different with her hair since that day I saw her walking with Simon in the cafeteria. There are deep purple strands peeking from underneath the blond layers.

I'm a total sucker for purple.

She leans forward to hug Simon. When she straightens to look at me, maybe to finish what she started to say… Dang. I'm in trouble again.

I can't be in trouble again. I can't. My life is too stinking complicated to introduce a girlfriend. Even though my heart is singing a Puccini aria right about now.

She smiles at me. One of her teeth is just a little crooked, but the imperfection only makes her cuter. More real and approachable. She extends her hand to me. Long fingers, short nails. Working for the school newspaper, she probably types a lot.

"Noah, I'm happy to meet you. I'd say, 'Welcome to Agatha Cross,' but it appears you've had a rather bumpy introduction to our school already."

"Bumpy. Yeah, you could say that." I take her hand. It's soft, and her grip is light.

"He was asking about a Bible verse," Simon says.

I've hung on to Chloe's hand a second or two too long. I wonder if Simon noticed.

"I heard," she says with a little nod. "It's basically about forgiveness. Forgiveness is me giving up my right to hurt you for hurting me."

"Is that from the Bible too?"

She laughs, and it's like a bird singing. I'm quickly going to run out of similes with this girl.

"Anonymous," she says. "But I got it from Beyoncé."

A chuckle sputters out of me, although the humor doesn't last. So I'm just supposed to give up my right to punish my father for hurting me?

I'm nowhere near ready for that idea.

"Any news from the police?" Simon asks as he turns toward the school doors.

I gotta think the abrupt change of subject was on purpose.

Chloe groans as she swivels to walk by Simon's side. "Unfortunately, no."

I fall in just behind Simon.

"The police think we surprised the person when we came home from church. Whoever it was broke in through my window and left the same way. They messed up my room and got away with my camera bag, but they left my laptop on the floor by the window. They didn't get into any of the other rooms."

"So lucky that's all it was," Simon says.

Chloe moves with long, confident strides. She's wearing iridescent purple high-tops and skinny jeans. I catch a whiff of lightly floral shampoo or perfume.

I could follow her like a hound dog, just sniffing and watching those shiny shoes roll with each step across the pavement.

This feeling is nothing new. I allow myself a moment to take it in. The problem is, I know where it leads. And I hate that I can't go there. So I hang back, a pathetic voyeur, gobbling up this hint of what my life used to be, while Simon and Chloe talk about significant life events.

"Actually, there was something else they took," Chloe says. "I didn't realize it until yesterday afternoon, after the men replaced my window and I went in to clean up the mess."

"What?" Simon is eager to know. Maybe eager just to hear her speak. He squeezes closer to her as we go through the school entrance.

I don't blame him for a second.

"You'll laugh," she says.

"Why would I laugh?"

"They took a framed picture of Walter Cronkite off my wall."

"Who?" Simon says.

I do want to laugh. Because I know who Walter Cronkite is. Was. The strangeness of a teenage girl having a picture of an old television reporter on her bedroom wall overrides my caution. I move ahead so I can watch her as she answers.

Chloe rolls her eyes. "I know, I know. Why do I even have a picture of Walter Cronkite? He was a reporter and called the most trusted man in America. The photo was autographed, and my great grandmother gave it to me. She was a Washington reporter at a time when it was hard for a woman to gain respect in that job. When I told her I want to be a photo journalist, she gave me the picture and told me to study his style of reporting and do the same."

"Wow. That's pretty awesome," Simon says as I'm thinking the same. "But... who would know that a picture of that man would be worth anything? Is it worth anything?"

"Probably not. Just sentimental to me."

"So why would someone take it?" I ask, thinking now of wrestling trophies and a five-hundred-dollar doll.

Chloe slows down, looking at me like I've just asked the most important question ever.

I answer it for her. "Someone who knows it was important to you."

She stops. "Someone who knows me?"

I stop too and shrug. "Seems like the place to start."

Simon is looking at me with his mouth open, and suddenly I wish I hadn't opened mine.

"No," I say. "Not again. I'm not helping. I've got my own problems."

"Ooh," Chloe says, her lips pushed out sympathetically. "Yeah, I saw what people are saying about you online."

It's my turn to roll my eyes. I start walking again. "I haven't looked. And don't tell me. I'm out."

"They're saying you're a rat. But I know it's not true," Chloe says.

My brow pinches. How does she know anything about me?

"Simon told me what happened. I was thinking about writing about it, but then the break-in happened on Sunday and... you know."

"Reporting a crime doesn't make a person a rat," Simon says.

"I guess that depends on whose side you're on," Chloe adds. "We're on Noah's side, but those other people..."

I drop back while they're still talking. Am I a rat? Not because of getting Ivan's father arrested, but in my own family?

I stop. Chloe and Simon pass through the double doors going into the school. They walk on a few steps before Simon notices I'm not with them. I'm outside, and the door closes between us.

What Chloe said... I'm the rat who will bear the guilt of sending my father to jail, and all the court dates and legal fees, the loss of his job, the final ripping apart of my family. I'm the victim, but I will gain no victory by punishing my abuser. I've become the bully, taking revenge against my father.

Simon comes back to the doors and opens one. "Sorry, dude. I didn't realize you couldn't hold the door open."

I grab the other handle and yank it toward me. *Ouch.* "I can open the stupid door."

I move past Simon, and now I'm looking into the wide, sympathetic blue eyes of Chloe. I'm sure Simon told her about my injuries. And now she feels sorry for me because of them. She has no idea that her words about someone else just stabbed me in the heart with a truth I didn't want to consider.

I feel like telling her to stay away from me.

I'm the betrayer. I ratted out the Manganites—as I'm sure Daniel will remind me again today—and I'm about to rat out my own father.

Mia called me a hero. Funny how I suddenly feel like the furthest thing from it.

I lower my eyes and walk past Chloe. Simon catches up to me, still apologizing.

"You didn't do anything wrong," I grumble.

"What's going on? Want to talk about it?" Simon says.

"Later. Maybe later. Thanks."

I walk away from them, leaving them standing there, mystified.

But I'm the one who is really mystified. I'm a rat if I have my father arrested. If I don't, he'll do *evil* things to my mother. To stop it all from happening, I have to forgive him, and give up my right to be angry. And move back to the situation that started it all.

None of it... *none of it* makes things any better.

At least I'm able to find my locker without help today. So there's that.

Lunch... To Go, Please

The noise and drama of the cafeteria are too much for me today, along with the possible run-in with Daniel Garrison, which would make me want to kill him. And I can't face lying to Simon again, telling him I'm okay when he can obviously see that I'm not. So I grab a candy bar at a vending machine and head outside for lunch. Technically against school policy, but I need the fresh air.

There's a slight burning in my chest, which is not good news. I have to consciously think about taking deep breaths. Otherwise, my body avoids the pain by going shallow. As I stroll to the student parking lot, I tell myself, deep breaths. Deep breaths.

The leaves in the park next to the school are changing. The warm tones, along with the forever green of the Georgia pines, seem to make the sky look bluer. I could keep walking. I could leave...

I distract myself with bumper stickers. Most of them look like the cars belong to parents. I see one where a political slogan has been scribbled out with marker.

Breathe deep. Breathe deep.

The mental mantra might help keep me sane.

The sound of a feminine giggle destroys the peace. Looking up, I see Drake Ogletree in the next lane, sitting on the tailgate of a pickup truck. His Barbie-doll girl is nestled between his knees, all flippy hair and body posture meant to seduce. A pang erupts beneath my ribcage, having nothing to do with cracked ribs. It reminds me that I haven't had a girl in my arms for a long time.

But I'm not going to envy Drake. And I'm certainly not going to mess with him. The last direct encounter I had with the wrestling star, he wanted to rip my head off.

Cue the end of my walk through the parking lot. I turn around to go back to the building, to find somewhere else to do my yoga breathing exercises.

A car engine roars past in the next lane. The dark sedan with tinted windows flies toward Drake and his girlfriend and screeches to a halt near them.

Moving on. The bro-fest about to happen doesn't interest me in the least. But a loud string of cuss words stop my feet and yank my head around. I duck between two cars and crouch next to a bumper to spy.

"I know you did it, dude!" some guy yells at Drake. "Her neighbor saw you slinking around the house."

Now *this* is interesting? Drake is a creeper?

Playing with fire, I know, but I pull my phone out of my back pocket and rest it against the car bumper, aimed at Drake and his accuser. I start a video recording. If Drake catches me, I'm beyond dead.

"You're talking online about that game last year, too! What's your deal, man?" the other guy yells.

My little cracked screen shows Drake jumping off his truck's tailgate and throwing his hands wide. Universal *come-at-me* posturing. His language will force me to include a warning when I put this up on Instagram. He tells the other guy, Kevin Somebody, that he doesn't know what he's talking about.

The girl backs up around the side of the pickup, pressing her hand to her mouth.

"Lauren," the other guy says. "You broke into her house and stole some of her jewelry and tore up all the pictures she had of me."

Another break-in? And Drake did it? This is too good. I shift to a more comfortable position and keep filming.

"It wasn't me, man," Drake says, like any criminal would.

"Mrs. Janovich saw you in your letterman jacket!"

"Who? That old lady next door?"

So Drake knows the name of the woman who lives next door to this Lauren person? Where I come from this might not be unusual. Everybody knows everybody around Bentley. But here? Aren't people in more populated areas like strangers with their neighbors?

The two guys are squaring off, face to face, one jock to another, and the girl is walking around pulling her hair back. Her mouth is open like she's about to start screaming.

"Her room was trashed. That means whoever did it *knows* her."

The phone drifts downward. I'm watching the fight directly now and thinking about three other suspicious and seemingly personal burglaries.

Drake throws his arms out again. "Kevin, come on, man. I got no reason to steal her stuff."

"Maybe you're still trying to get back at her for dumping you. Maybe what you really want is to get at me! Huh? Is that it?"

Drake calls the victim, Lauren, a bunch of evil names, and now it looks like the other guy, Kevin, is ready to take the first punch.

I've been dumped by a lot of girls. Never made me want to break into their house and steal anything. Even after Madison Baker kept my director's cut copy of *Blade Runner,* I didn't sneak over to her house and take it back. I moved on. Found another girlfriend. Bought another copy of the movie from a used DVD bin at the flea market. It bugged me that Madison kept it, but whatever. Some things aren't worth fighting over.

Move on Drake.

Kevin shoves Drake's shoulders, which only makes Drake come back angrier. It's on. They're grabbing each other and throwing fists, and the girl is screaming. Someone yells from the school building, and I know people are coming to stop the fight.

Shutting down my video, I draw back between the two cars and slink around a bumper. Footsteps go thundering past. I stand and walk the other way. From a safe distance I glance back. Teachers are pulling the two guys apart. They'll be dragging them to the principal's office, and chances are I won't see Drake for a while.

It feels like payback.

My phone is warm in my hand. The video is sure to go viral, like fight videos always do.

But so what?

If Drake figures out I'm the one who posted it, he'll come after me. And then someone else will post a video of me getting my face bashed in. The only fame I'll get is when my own crushing defeat goes online.

"I need you to stay out of trouble, baby."

Hearing my mother's voice whimpering through my memory, I pause at the crosswalk as another teacher rushes past. The man doesn't even notice me enough to tell me to get back inside. I glance down at my phone, at the screen paused on the last frame of the video. For half a second I consider deleting it. But there's something that might be more important than a fistfight on this thing.

Three break-ins. I don't know what Drake might have against Chloe, but I know he hates Jun Seoh because of an altercation during wrestling practice last year. Paisley is one of his bullying targets. And now an ex-girlfriend could be his target. Seems more than coincidental. Maybe like vengeance?

Simon is going to love this.

Bohemian Sanctuary

"Drake dated Lauren Harmon last year," Simon says. "From what I heard, she cheated on him."

I grin at this. Not because it's that amusing, but because it happened to Drake.

Simon isn't working today, so he invited me to his place. We're inside rather than on the screened porch because it's freezing and blowing rain outside. We're sitting around a coffee table with our homework spread out in front of us. I'm on the couch and Simon is cross-legged on the floor. Every couple of minutes a Chihuahua looks at me and starts barking again. The high-pitched canine scream bounces off the walls of my tortured skull. That one howling bark sets off the other two, and Simon has to shush them all. Again.

Even with Chihuahua serenades, this is a better place to do homework than in my trailer, where I'd be stewing over my family drama and feeling sorry for myself. This place is a whole lot more comfortable than mine, too. It's filled with books, movie posters, shaggy throw rugs, and macramé wall hangings. Yeah, macramé. It's old and creaky, cluttered and warm, and smells like candles and incense. I feel safe here. Even with multiple yappy ankle biters.

I told Simon about the fight today. He'd already read about it online but didn't know I was there to see it. These things get around school fast, especially when they involve a stuck-on-himself wrestling star and a football player. Kevin Lofton and Drake Ogletree. Today's news boys.

At least no one seems to be talking about me and Maintenance Guy George now. I finally checked my phone today and found nothing. Granted, my social media sources at this school are quite limited.

"Kevin graduated last May," Simon says. "Guess he and Lauren are still dating."

"So she dumped Drake for Kevin?" Moving my thumb ever-so-lightly across my phone screen, I scroll through my newsfeed again. It's mostly filled with stuff going on back in North Carolina. No one is talking about me there, either. But then my thumb stops flipping over the screen when I see a familiar, Agatha Cross name. Paisley Black. Apparently she hasn't learned a lesson from her suspension. She's ranting now about some guy named Connor, who she says is a cheater.

Dang, girl. Get a life of your own, will ya?

"Hmm. No..." Simon says.

I wince. It takes me a second to remember what we were talking about. Right. Kevin, Lauren, and Drake.

Simon turns a page back in his math textbook, checking something. He's actually doing homework. "There was another guy in between them. Drake went to prom last year with Savannah Young, and now he's dating Chelsea Monroe. Savannah, by the way, used to be friends with Mia Park. So that could be another connection."

"You seriously do know everybody, don't you?"

"Sorry, just getting all the players straight."

Good for him. Now, where was I? "Anyway, the guy, Kevin, said a neighbor saw Drake breaking into Lauren's house. Drake said it wasn't him, of course, and that's when the shoving stared."

"And you got a video of the whole thing."

"Well, yeah, but it isn't very good. You can't really tell what they're saying." I watched the video when I got home this afternoon. The audio is pretty bad, and Kevin's car is in the way of a lot of the action. But it turns out that I whispered to myself during the fight without realizing it. My opinion of Drake Ogletree came through loud and clear.

Now I'm walking around with this idea that I'm going to end up someday as a voyeuristic old fart who talks to himself.

"Still, it could be evidence," Simon says.

Evidence. That word makes my stomach tighten. "I'm sure the principal got the whole story from them. Think Drake will get suspended?"

I'd like to see that. The evil in me coming out. I'd like to see Drake get what's coming to him.

"I'm not sure," Simon answers. "It was in the parking lot."

"Still on school grounds."

"And Kevin—who isn't a student anymore—provoked Drake."

"Pushed him. But Drake threw the first punch."

"We'll see. Drake's dad has a lot of pull with the school board. That's one reason the illegal wrestling move last year was such a big deal. Drake's father threatened to go to the school board and have Coach Anderson fired."

So Drake does something wrong, and Daddy can get someone else fired? Sounds like good-old-boy justice.

"Who was the other guy Lauren dated, in between Drake and Kevin?"

"Bryce Valentino."

A laugh sputters through my lips. Bryce Valentino? This guy's name just beat mine for most-likely-to-make-the-girls-sigh. Noah Rhys Dickerson doesn't stand up to the built-in Valentine. It makes me think he could be a singer of Dean Martin tunes. Or a mafia hit man.

"He graduated last year too," Simon goes on. "After being crowned prom king."

This just keeps getting better. Valentine the prom king.

"He went on to... Georgia Tech, I think."

"Dude, your brain is like a computer just storing up all this information."

Simon chuckles and shakes his head "I've lived here all my life. And it pays to have a friend on the newspaper staff."

Ah, the alluring Chloe Thomas. I saw them together after school today, hanging out for a minute before boarding buses. Any interest I might have in Chloe definitely needs to be shut down. Simon is obviously smitten. Kind of funny, since he looks about fourteen and she looks like she could be in college already, even with her purple-tipped hair and iridescent sneakers. But who am I to judge?

"So, *anyway*," I say, getting my own thoughts back on track. "Four break-ins. Chloe, Jun, Paisley, and now this Lauren girl. Could Drake be going after everyone who's on his bad side?"

"It's a distinct possibility, Sherlock."

I smirk at him. With the way details have slipped out of my memory lately, I'm happy to have figured anything out, but I sure don't deserve the Sherlock nickname.

I glance down at my economics textbook. It has definitely slipped my mind why I signed up for this class.

"What are we going to do about it?" Simon asks.

Oh no. I'm not going there again. If Drake is the burglar, I'll just sit back and watch him get caught. The cops will put this one together quick enough without any help from me. And that way, I won't get my face bashed in by an angry wrestler.

"Nothing," I answer. "But it'll be interesting to watch."

I feel a touch against my ankle. When I look down, the tallest of the Chihuahuas, brown with a black muzzle, jumps back and howls at me.

"Macbeth!" Simon growls.

"What a name. Like Winston over there." I gesture toward the road outside.

"Mom used to perform at the Shakespeare Tavern in Atlanta."

"I'm thinking of auditioning for one of the three witches in Macbeth." The voice startles me, and I look up to see Simon's mother coming along the hallway, having been on the phone in her bedroom.

She uses a walker and moves pretty slow, but no way does she look witchy or crooked. Rather, she looks like she could throw that walker aside and belt out an old Carole King tune. Mrs. Walsh is young and pretty enough to make any grown man feel the earth move under his feet.

She smiles at me and runs a hand through her wavy blond hair. "Would y'all like something to drink? I have some sweet tea, freshly brewed."

I get up from the couch to help her in the kitchen.

"Let her do it," Simon whispers.

I wobble, not quite sure I'm believing what I'm hearing. I shouldn't help his mother? When she's...

Simon stares at the page in his math book. No big deal.

What the heck?

Well, I might not be known as a gentleman by most people, but I'm not going to let a disabled woman serve me. My cracked ribs won't keep me from getting my own glass of tea, and I'll pour her one as well.

Tiny dogs block my way, barking furiously now that I'm moving around. Mrs. Walsh is settling her walker against the counter when I finally reach her. Touching her back ever-so-lightly, I tell her I'll get it.

She shakes her head. "No, no, sweetie. You go sit. Do your homework with Simon. I can manage this just fine."

Indecision rocks me, literally. My head tells me to do one thing—the right thing—while both Simon and his mother are saying something else. I take a step back and watch as she reaches up into a cabinet. She pulls down some glasses and gets some ice from the freezer. One of those old-style trays you have to twist to break the ice free. She retrieves a pitcher of tea from the refrigerator and fills the glasses. Finally she hands two of them to me.

I'm in awe of her. Her smile tells me she's enjoying being able to do something nice for me and Simon.

Just across the street, my mother is hiding from a man who forced servitude upon her. For her, pouring tea would be a duty, not a joy.

I take the two glasses into the living room, where Simon is still sitting on the floor next to the coffee table. I thunk the glasses down and take my place on the couch. Simon sighs and says thanks.

Part of me wants to smack the back of his head for not getting up himself. The other part of me has too many questions. My relationship with my mother is complicated, and I'm sure there have been times when she *served* me and I took advantage of it. Blindly. I lived in the status quo my parents had created.

I stare down at my econ book, but the words don't sink in. All day I've been thinking about the decision I have to make concerning my father. The fight between Drake and his ex-girlfriend's current boyfriend is a somewhat amusing distraction. Like watching a movie. When it's over, reality returns. And as Simon's mother moves around in the kitchen, humming to herself like she's happy to be arranging things on the counter, in my mind I see my mother doing the same sort of thing with the weight of fear on her shoulders.

My phone pings with a text from Mom. Ten o'clock, time to come home. Back to my own, less cozy, reality.

"I gotta go," I say, slapping my book closed. I stand up and drain my glass of tea. Excellent. One thing about Georgia, they do sweet tea *right*.

This time, Simon takes my empty glass to the kitchen. He walks out with me, and even follows me off the screened porch.

"You don't have to walk me home." I grin and jerk my thumb toward the trailer, less than fifty feet away.

He doesn't seem amused. "I just want to explain something. About my mom." He pauses, like what he's about to say is hard for him. "She's awesome. And some days she doesn't even need that walker. Other days she can hardly move. When she's able to get up and do things, it makes her really happy. When she can't, I think not being able to fix my dinner or clean the house hurts her more than the actual pain of her disorder."

"So by not helping her with the tea, you were actually making her happy?" I'm not sure about this line of reasoning.

Simon frowns. "She doesn't want me waiting on her if she's able to do things herself. She doesn't want to be a burden."

Okay, this makes a bit more sense, but...

"We don't get a lot of people coming around like when I was little, right after my father got killed. I think it's just been so long. Like people are all gung-ho about helping out in the beginning, but then they kind of forget. It's okay, though. We're doing okay. She's been writing plays and she still sings at church. She wants me to have a normal life. We don't have a lot but... we're okay."

I blow out my breath, and it's cool enough that the air comes out frosty. I want to ask Simon what happened to her. He said she has a *disorder*. She *used* to be an actress.

"Doing things," Simon says, emphasizing the words, "makes her feel independent. Normal. That's why I said, 'Let her do it.'"

I'm cold. I'm feeling like there's so much I don't understand. Or maybe I've understood things one way and missed all the other ways. I look across the street, to my trailer, where slivers of light sneak past the blinds that my mother keeps closed.

She's trapped. And not by a disability. Not even by a man who might come home and make her feel useless or stupid. She has accepted her life as it is and doesn't yet know how to live any other way.

It took my near death to get her to do anything for herself. Except, she doesn't yet see it as a benefit to her. She's protecting me, not herself.

I breathe out again and watch the little cloud disappear in front of my face. Needing some way to respond to the confession Simon has made, I smile at him and nod. "I'd like to hear her sing someday."

"Come to church on Sunday."

"Ha. Sorry, not really my thing, dude. But thanks." I point a parting finger at him and walk across the street.

I find Mom in the living room indulging in one of the few things Dad allowed her to have for herself. Cross-stitch. Personally, I can't imagine any more catatonic activity than counting thousands of tiny stitches to make up a picture that someone else created. Paint-by-numbers with thread. But give her another month or two in this place, and she'll have the walls covered with pretty pictures made up of a billion tiny Xs.

She barely looks up when I come through the door. I say, "Hey," and she just nods. I don't press for anything more because I'll interrupt her counting. *One thousand, nine hundred, thirty-seven. One thousand, nine hundred, thirty-eight.*

I slide my books onto the table in the kitchen and stand there, watching her as she sits next to a dim lamp, counting stitches.

One thousand, nine hundred, forty-six...

Will having my father arrested set my mother free?

Somehow, I doubt it.

Chapter

Wednesday... Is This the New Normal?

On the way to school, Mom drives past the bowling alley and Durning Mills Lofts, landmarks of a disturbing night in my life. They could have marked the last day in my life, had things gone differently. I wonder how long I'll look at them and feel this tension in my gut, the little twitch in my limbs like a residual impulse to run.

I look away, turning my head far enough to peer into the back seat behind my mother where Simon is sitting. He's got his eyes glued to his phone again, his thumbs tapping out a message. Probably to Chloe. His mouth twists to one side, like things aren't going well in the potential girlfriend department.

Best to leave him to his personal drama. I settle back against my headrest as we roll up to a busy intersection overloaded with drugstores and gas stations. We're stuck at the red light for a while. Just beyond the Walgreens is a small, squat brick building that looks like it's been there for a long time. It reminds me of some of the ancient storefront buildings at home in downtown Bentley. The crumbled brick is a mottled red-gray-brown, except for the spot where someone has painted graffiti on the side of the building. Graffiti is too generous a description for this artwork. The letters, probably done in a hurry in the middle of the night, spell out, "DEFECTIVE." Someone has a complaint against O'Toole's Formal Wear Shop.

"How long has that been there?" I ask anyone listening.

"Hmm? What?" Mom says. Cross stitching seems to have worked a small miracle in her. She was actually humming along to the country music song on the radio.

I point toward the building just as the light turns green. We roll past, and Mom doesn't answer.

I don't care about anyone's beef with the formal wear place. I care that I don't remember seeing that graffiti before. It's something I would have noticed. Why don't I remember?

"Over the weekend," Simon says. When I glance back, he's still fixated on his phone.

"That graffiti on the brick wall? It wasn't there last week?"

"Nope. Guess someone had a bad wedding experience," he says.

"Thank God," I mutter.

Mom slants me a scowl like I'm crazy. "Why did you say that?"

"No, not thank God that someone had problems. Thank God it wasn't there before. I didn't remember it being there, so..."

"Noah, are you okay?"

"Yeah. Yeah. No problem."

No problem, because for the moment my memory seems to be working okay. And I actually feel all right today. Nothing is hurting too badly. The cold weather that moved through over the last few days has left brilliant blue skies and brightly colored leaves. I can pretend this will be a normal school day, filled with promise and all that junk.

When Mom stops in the drop-off lane at school, Simon rolls the van door open and jumps out. He waits for me on the sidewalk. I'm careful getting out and not ready to sling my backpack onto my shoulder.

"It's okay," I tell Simon. "I got this. You don't have to help me."

But now I can tell by the way he's staring at the buses, even lifting up on the balls of his feet, that he's looking for Chloe.

"Simon."

"What? No. It's okay. Uh."

"Go look for her."

He blinks fast. "Who?"

"Come on. It's obvious you're into Chloe. Go find her."

His face pales. "Into her! Uh…"

"Dang, Simon."

He stammers a bunch of meaningless syllables, and I have to laugh at him.

"It's not that hard, dude. Ask her if she wants to go to Homecoming, if she's into that. If she isn't, just ask if she wants to go to the movies or something. Figure out what she likes and capitalize on it."

"No, no. You don't understand."

"It's all over your face, dude. I don't have to—"

"It doesn't matter. She likes Connor Radcliff."

Oh.

"Connor… that guy who helped people cheat on the SATs last year?"

Simon shakes his head. "I don't… I don't think he did that. It doesn't matter. She's not into me. So forget it. I don't want to talk about it."

I nod slowly. "Okay. Sorry."

Simon huffs and looks away from me. "He lives up the hill in Riverbend Estates."

Which means his family is rich. At least upper middle class. Or in debt up to their eyeballs.

"He's on the newspaper staff and is kind of like Chloe's boss. He'll probably be valedictorian next spring. He'll probably get accepted to some ivy league university and own his own news network in the future."

Simon is stacking up the cards against himself, one after the other.

"His parents are like model citizens, working for charities, taking in foster kids, all that stuff. They give money to help support Chloe's mother's riding academy for disabled kids. The dude has everything going for him."

Money, disabled kids and horses? Poor Simon doesn't stand a chance.

"And I'm guessing he's so busy being a genius that he doesn't have much of a social life. Right?" I say.

"Um. Yeah. I guess." Simon answers.

"So why are people accusing him of things? If there's no proof."

"You mean if Mr. Perfect isn't perfect?" Simon says. He starts walking toward the school entrance. "I don't want to see Chloe get hurt. But the stuff people are saying online isn't true. The cheating thing could be a serious problem later on, like when he's trying to get scholarships or whatever. Online stuff doesn't go away. And now, the latest news is, he got paid off to protect one of the athletes from bad press last year." Simon suddenly stops and faces me. "Kevin Lofton, in fact. Something about fixing a football game."

Kevin Lofton? That was... right. The guy in the fight.

What's WRONG with me?

"Does Drake play football too?"

"No. It doesn't matter. It's all lies, and I'm scared Chloe is going to get hurt by it too."

"Lies..." I run my tongue over my lips and nod.

"What?"

"The king of social media maliciousness."

Simon's eyes widen and he returns my slow nod. "Mack the Hack. Some people thought he was involved in the cheating thing too. He came out clean, though."

Todd McCaffrey, aka Mack the Hack.

"He seems to have a knack for that, then, considering he was in the middle of whatever Ivan was doing with Hana and Mia, but he's still here and Ivan is gone."

"Looks like we'll have to watch him, then," Simon says.

I hum a vague response. The last time I played detective it nearly got me killed. I'm not keen on doing it again, even if it's just to poke around on someone's social media accounts. Simon doesn't seem to catch on to my reluctance. As we head inside, he's already got that distant look on his face that tells me he's thinking the problem through.

As I'm settling into my desk in world history, Mia Park floats into the classroom, wearing a short dress and patterned leggings with knee-high boots. I'm reminded of that unrequited love thing. Both Simon and Chloe, with Connor, in a triangle of impossibility. And then there's me, watching Mia swing into her desk, still sitting as far from me as possible. She doesn't look my way at all.

I tried to tell myself so many times that I'm over her. I even thought, for a moment, that my immediate attraction to Chloe was a sign that Mia was all in the past. As I gaze at the chestnut colored hair curling gracefully down the back that is turned toward me, an empty space in me opens up, begging to be filled.

And there's nothing I can do about it.

Someday, none of this will matter. Someday, high school will be a memory, and I'll have moved on from all the drama in these loud hallways that smell like floor wax and sweat. And away from the booze-scented drama in my own family. Maybe I'll think back and roll my eyes and be thankful I survived.

But at this moment, someday feels too far away.

Someday can't come soon enough

I don't know why the Manganites choose to meet in the same hallway where my locker is located, before school, before lunch, and after school. There's nothing special about their *spot*. There's no alcove, no window, no display case they can squeeze next to. They're in the way of everyone walking by. Maybe they like the attention they get as people mutter complaints and bash into them with elbows and backpacks. Like in the cafeteria, where their table is the one *everyone* has to walk past coming in and going out.

I wouldn't care—I'd actually find it amusing—except it means they've seen me at my locker.

As I'm about to squat to open my lower locker, I glimpse them in their *spot* at the end of the hallway. Minus Ivan the Tark. I'm curious about what happened to him, but I'm not going to ask.

As if she can feel my gaze on her, Paisley looks my way, and her eyes narrow to the point where I'm amazed she can see anything clearly. Like I'm a target and she's pinpointing her laser-vision. I glance away like it's all so casual and do my careful deep-knee bend. Hurts like crazy, but there's no other way for me to open my stupid locker.

"I want my doll back." Paisley's voice has a mid-tone twang, sort of like a Siamese cat, that cuts through all other noise. Claws to match.

I finish sorting my books, close my locker door, spin the lock once, and take my time standing up.

She's standing about six feet away.

"Why in the world would you think that I'd steal your doll?" I say, keeping my Carolinian accent soft and drawn out, like I've got nothing to worry about.

"Vengeance!"

"So you admit you did something wrong that I'd want to seek vengeance for?"

"You're a creeper. You got exposed. So you went after Ivan to make him look bad. You stole some stuff from his bedroom. Then you stole my doll."

My brain tries to do the math to figure out what percentage of her statements are true. Fail.

"You know, there's something I don't understand. You and your friends bullied Hana Seoh to the point where *maybe* she committed suicide. Or *maybe* your friend's father killed her to cover up a rape. That same father tried to take me for *a ride—*" I put air quotes around this. "—to who knows where. And *I'm* the bad guy?"

"She was my friend! And Ivan didn't rape her. And I heard Mr. Norwood was just driving you home and you went crazy in the car and caused him to wreck."

"Is that what he's telling his defense attorney? I've got a concussion and some cracked ribs that say otherwise."

At this moment, considering I'm talking to the enemy, I should probably keep my mouth shut about the whole thing.

"Because of *you*," she goes on, "Ivan has been locked up and his father lost his job and everything else."

"Right. Rape and kidnapping and possibly murder didn't have anything to do with that."

Shut up, Noah. Walk away.

"What did we ever do to you?" she wails, coming closer.

People are starting to notice.

I shake my head. "Me? Nothing. I just chose the wrong friends. But it's over. Have a nice life, Paisley. I'm done."

"I want my doll!" she screams in my face before I can turn away.

"How could I steal your doll? I don't even know where you live."

"Your friend Simon does."

"I want my dolly!" someone mocks in a screechy falsetto.

Paisley whirls toward them, teeth bared. I take advantage of the moment to turn away. Just one step. Then claws close around my right bicep, yanking me back. She's not strong, but *ouch*. I whip my arm out of her grasp... which hurts even more.

"Stay away from me," I growl. "I don't have your doll and I wouldn't touch it even if I had the chance."

"Then Simon took it."

I won't allow doubts about Simon to enter my mind again. Certainly not as a result of anything that comes out of Paisley's mouth.

I lean over her, stare straight into those eye slits, and fight the tremor that's rising from the pit of my soul. I want to bite her head off. But I keep my voice low. "No. He did not."

As I walk away, she mutters something low at my back, maybe thinking she'll disable my firmness with the same tone I used. It doesn't work. But I hate myself for a moment. Although I'm not consciously afraid of her, she's got me walking the long way around to get to the cafeteria. And that ignites the rage in me again.

A mantra plays in my head with each jarring step. *I will not... I will not... I will not... do that again.*

It was a false accusation that got me trying to prove my innocence before. Not going to happen again. I don't care what Paisley says.

After School... Tipping the Balance

I'm sitting with Simon on his porch when Mom pulls into our driveway, coming home from work. She gets out of the van and slams the door extra hard. I glance from her and back to what Simon's doing in half a second.

The slightest seismic disturbance could undo the magic he's

performing.

"Bad day at work?" he says without looking up.

There's a bunch of rocks on the plastic table. Just random rocks Simon picked up as we were walking home from the bus stop. He's stacking them one on top of the other in impossible ways. He finds the tiniest flat spot on one rock and balances it on another tiny flat space on the one below it, creating a delicate sculpture.

I'm afraid to move. Breathing, even opening my mouth to answer might send the tower toppling. "Who knows," I finally say. "How are you doing that?"

"Shh!" He's got the fifth stone perched on what looks like a sharp point. He slowly, slowly moves his hands away.

It stays for two seconds. Three. Just as I'm looking for invisible fishing line suspended from the ceiling, the rock slips. This upsets the one beneath it and the one beneath that. Three rocks roll onto the table. One of them falls into Simon's lap.

His eyes go wide.

"You okay?"

"Fine!" he says, his voice pitched higher. But he hasn't got a poker face. An instant later he's grinning. "Clearly I need more practice."

"I couldn't have balanced the first two." I sigh and look toward my trailer. "I guess I should go home."

"You could come to youth group with me," Simon says. "Really, Noah, it's not bad. You can meet some new people."

"Like Chloe?" I smirk at him.

It's Simon's turn to sigh. "What is light, if Chloe be not seen? What is joy if Chloe be not by?"

That Simon's feelings for Chloe are unrequited doesn't seem to matter. Me? I'd spend a week in deep depression and then be ready to move on, easing my broken heart with some other girl's affections. I may be sappy, but I'm not hopeless. Being depressed is no fun.

Simon's offer is tempting for that reason. There will be girls. But I'm pretty sure that's not a valid, God-endorsed reason for going to church.

"Are you quoting someone again? Who is it this time?"

"Shakespeare. Not sure which play. And he wrote about Sylvia, not Chloe. But, sadly, Chloe does not attend my church."

"Pity."

Simon will certainly look up the play and be ready to give me the title and a synopsis by morning. He tries hard to be impressive. And different. I'm beginning to wonder if it's not pride as much as desperation. Knowing that his competition for Chloe is vying for the spot of class valedictorian, I think I understand Simon's motives.

I'm impressed by the rocks. I don't need to know the name of the play. Before he can start another impossible tower, I stand and knock my knuckles against his shoulder.

"I guess that means you aren't interested in youth group?" Simon says.

"Scope out the room for me, and introduce me to the interesting people tomorrow," I say.

The daylight has already faded away in a cloudy sky. The scent of rain is in the air. So I'm a bit surprised to walk into a dark trailer. Mom always keeps the blinds shut, like someone might drive by and recognize us through a window. But she hasn't turned any lights on yet. I call out, but she doesn't answer. This isn't good. Even if she's in her room changing clothes, she'd answer. So I walk down the hallway and lean my ear toward her closed bedroom door. Sure enough, I hear her snuffling.

I knock lightly on the doorframe. "Mom?"

"Not now, Noah!" she says, her voice raspy.

Every part of me wants to rip down this accordion door and rescue her. But every memory of when I've done something like that tells me it won't do any good. She has to come out on her own, when she decides she's ready to tell me something or has driven it down deep enough that she won't talk about it at all. If I force her to talk, she'll shut down further, denying that there's any problem, even blaming me for making her feel worse.

So I walk away... and hate myself for my inability to fix anything.

I sit at the kitchen table with my school books and a notebook, doing homework mindlessly. If I absorb anything, it'll be a miracle. I could probably write a paper for my psychology class about the mental and social dynamics of a dysfunctional family. I'd get an A on that.

Mom comes out of her room about an hour later and starts preparing supper. She has changed her clothes, washed her face, and brushed her hair. Pretending things are normal. And actually, this is normal for my family. We do what we have to in order to get through each day.

I clear my stuff off the table and she sets down two plates. Some kind of chicken and pasta dish from a bag that, from the smell, is loaded with garlic to disguise the fact that it doesn't have any taste on its own. I don't have the option of turning it down, even though the cloying odor has my stomach rebelling before the first bite. I don't want to present any opportunity for Mom's stifled emotions to come out again. One bite. Two. It's sustenance, nothing more.

As I'm resigning myself to it, there's a loud rap at the door.

"Middleboro Police," a commanding voice says.

Mom shoots me a look, fear and anger in a perfect storm. She doesn't have to speak. Her thought is clear. *What did you do this time?*

Nothing. Yet.

I get up to answer the door.

Cops. Four of them. Standing on our little metal porch.

"Warrant to search the premises," says the one in the front, whose fat fist probably performed the door banging that rattled the trailer.

I take a step back to let them in. Mom stands a few feet away, looking from them to me. Her wet mouth is hanging open, her hand moving to her throat.

"Noah?"

"I haven't done anything," I say. But my mind races to Paisley's accusation. I turn to the nearest cop. "I was in the hospital until just a few days ago. Ask her! I haven't done anything wrong."

The cop produces his warrant to Mom. "We're looking for stolen goods."

Mom glares at me.

Have I got *CRIMINAL* written across my forehead that makes everyone think I must be behind anything bad that happens?

"Did Paisley Black tell you I stole something from her?" I ask the cop standing next to Mom.

The other three are looking around the living room, searching under the couch cushions and in the corners.

"Did you?" the cop asks me.

"No!"

"He was... he was in the hospital," Mom says. Like now she's not certain.

One of the cops walks up to me. "I know you, don't I?"

Dear God, save me.

"Yeah," he says. "We took you in a week or so ago. You told us about the cyberbullying case."

Maybe he did. I don't remember his face.

"You haven't been up to more trouble, have you?"

"I wasn't in trouble the first time. False accusation. Just like now."

He huffs a laugh. Like this is all in a day's work for him while for me it's one of the worst things possible. "You got some enemies?"

"Yeah! Paisley Black! Same as last time. Why don't you ask her what proof she's got that I took anything from her?"

"Noah." Mom takes hold of my arm and tries to get me to sit down and let the police do their work.

I don't want to sit. I pull away from her and find a corner to stand in.

Three other break-ins, that I know of, and the cops are in *my* house looking for stuff. Do they think I might be responsible for the others, too? I don't ask. In fact, when I think of this, I keep my mouth tightly shut.

It doesn't take the police long. After all, our trailer home isn't very big and there isn't a whole lot in it. They come out empty-handed. Surprise, y'all. Told you I didn't do it. As the guy in charge is apologizing to Mom for the inconvenience—like that's all accusing me and searching through every inch of our house is, a freakin' inconvenience—I surge out of my quiet corner.

"Isn't there some law against falsely accusing someone?"

The cop stiffens. I probably came at him too fast and triggered that self-defensive stance. I breathe heavily through my nose and force myself back a couple steps.

"There is," he says. "If you can prove the person knowingly accused you of something he or she knew to be false."

So I have to be able to read Paisley Black's mind to see what she does or doesn't know to be false. And since I obviously can't do that, she gets away with totally disrupting our evening and causing my mother to trust me even less than she did before. And if I go after Paisley with my own accusation tomorrow, I'll be the aggressor who gets sent to the principal's office.

How is this fair?

The cops leave, and Mom starts cleaning up the mess. They didn't tear anything up, but all their shifting things around to look under and over and around has left the trailer looking sloppy. Mom won't let it stand that way.

I follow behind. "You believe me, don't you?"

"Don't talk to me, Noah." She slaps a lap blanket over the back of the couch. "I don't need more than one child to worry about today."

"More than one? What do you mean by that?'

"Never mind." She pushes past me and goes through the kitchen, past our partially eaten supper, to straighten the runner in the hallway.

Meanwhile, heat is encompassing my brain. Vibrating lights appear in my vision. Another migraine. Brought on by the escalating tension.

"No, no." I go after her. "Tell me what's happening."

"I have enough to worry about keeping you safe. Why must you keep making it worse? Why can't you stay out of trouble?"

"This isn't my fault! But you said 'more than one child.' Is Naomi in trouble? Or Nathan?"

She doesn't answer. She heads into the bathroom, pulls the curtain over the bathtub and shuts the cabinet. "Is it drugs, Noah? Were they looking for drugs?"

"No!" I cuss and grab her arm.

Then release her.

Worse than approaching the cop aggressively. I'd grabbed Mom the way Dad has done so many times. The way *he taught me*.

"Mom..." I stop to pull the pieces of my brain and emotions back to a calmer place. "I'm sorry. It's just that I think I have a right to know. You haven't been telling me anything. It's like you're separated from Dad and I have to be separated from the whole family."

I'm standing in her way. She can't leave the bathroom. Although I can't allow myself to touch her or to force her to do anything, I won't get out of her way. I want answers. I'll leave her alone after I get them.

She breaks. Like she has so many times before. She doesn't have the strength to stand up to challenges, and just my standing here is enough to make her crumble.

I hate this. I hate myself. I hate what my father has done to her.

But I need to know.

"Naomi called me. Your father went over to that house where she's staying and started an argument. Julien's parents nearly had him arrested."

I stiffen. "Maybe they should have."

"Is that what you plan to do?" she spits back at me.

I'm frozen. I don't want to answer. I can't.

"I'm trying to fix things!" she yells at me. "If we could all… just… *talk* to each other instead of fighting…"

"Are you going back to him?" I manage to whisper.

Mom turns her head. She can't look at me. "I don't know. But please, please, *please* stay out of trouble Noah. I can't take this anymore. I can't."

She presses the back of her hand to her brow, and I suspect she's going to start crying.

"I didn't do anything wrong." I keep my voice as soft as I can, but the anger is raging inside me. Unwanted images leap to my mind of Dad standing in someone else's house yelling at my sister. I want to yell like him. Yell at my mother.

I did nothing wrong. I didn't even ask to come to Georgia. She brought me here, took me away from my home and friends and stuck me in this stinkin' trailer in this stinkin' trailer park Simon described as the *Pit of Despair*. Because Dad nearly killed me.

And right now, I know, Mom is weighing the needs of one child against another. Which one of us will break her first?

Overnight...

I'm awakened by the sound of howling. Not Winston this time, but the wind whipping past our trailer. Something is banging. Maybe the roof, I don't know. Storms don't normally bother me, but this one sounds like it might tear our trailer apart.

The Pit of Despair reminding me in every way possible that this isn't my home.

I roll over and grab my phone from my plastic nightstand. Perusing the social media posts from back home might give me a sense that I belong somewhere. One of the first things I see in my feed, though, is a post from Paisley. She hasn't broken off all contact with me yet, and this is probably why. So she can taunt me with her cryptic, nameless posts.

> **PAISLEY BLACK:** I know it was you. Because I know you hate me and everything I stand for. You chose to take what would hurt me the most. Now maybe you'll pay for it.

What do you stand for, girl? Seems to me it's only for yourself.

I stare at the ceiling as anger runs through me. After maybe an hour—or less, since I'm not paying attention to the time—I contemplate what she said. Whoever took her doll chose to take what would hurt her the most. While that statement is debatable, since it was just a doll, even if it was expensive, there's some truth in it. The same truth that goes along with stolen wrestling trophies, a camera and autographed picture, and whatever was taken from that other girl's room.

Whoever did this is connected to all of them.

And it is not me.

Chapter

Thursday... Not Gonna Take It No More

I unload from Mom's van and rush toward the building, leaving Simon behind. My backpack bangs against my ribs, but I don't care. My head is pounding, a migraine lurking. Having had very little sleep last night, I'm not thinking clearly. I know I'm rushing into trouble. I can't stop.

Simon chases after me, calling my name, but I move faster. I don't want him involved in what I'm about to do.

Three hallways back from the entrance to the school I rush, toward the place where the Manganites meet. I unapologetically weave around other students in my way. I see Bethany ahead, smiling and giving a little girly wave to someone. I'm guessing it's Paisley. She'll be holding court in front of a science department bulletin board.

I turn the corner. Bethany's eyes go wide, all innocent and almost like she's happy to see me. That seems impossible. If there is still a tiny smidgeon of a crush for me in her heart, it'll for sure be gone in a few seconds.

I head straight for Paisley.

She lifts up her chin and scowls, like she knows what's coming. Of course she knows. She orchestrated it. Maybe she even counted on me coming to confront her.

Maybe this was a setup?

I don't have time to think about it. I get in Paisley's face. "You told the cops I stole your stupid doll, didn't you?"

Daniel is suddenly there. He growls and grabs my arm—my right arm—and tries to pull me away from his girlfriend. I jerk away.

Ouch, ouch, ouch, DANG, ouch!

It takes every ounce of strength in me to separate myself from the pain and keep yelling at Paisley.

"They were at my house last night, going through everything to look for your doll. And guess what? They didn't find *anything*!"

She looks scared now. Daniel's got me by the shoulders. I plant my heels.

"You sent them to MY HOUSE! It made my mother cry. I didn't do anything to you, but you made my mother cry. You *know* I didn't steal anything from you. Why did you do it?"

"You could have done it," she says. "You wanted to get back at me, so you took something of mine and hid it somewhere."

I surge toward Paisley, even with Daniel still tugging on my arm. "I saw your post last night," I growl at her. "Why are you doing this to me?"

I hear other voices, and Daniel finally manages to hurt me physically to the point that I can't fight against him anymore. I whirl around to ease his pull on my arm, and now I'm in his face. Practically spitting at him. "You want to fight me, Danny boy? Come on then. Let's do it. Right now."

I'm out of my mind. It feels that way. Like I'm actually standing somewhere outside myself, watching this idiot kid with broken ribs who thinks he in any condition to fight another guy.

Daniel huffs at me through clenched teeth. "Tomorrow. After school. Snake pit."

"Today! Now!"

I'm officially insane.

People gather around us, eager for a beat down. I see cell phones lifted, videos in progress. My name will be on social media again. Teachers will be here any second to stop us, and I'll get hauled into the principal's office again. Maybe suspended. Well... fine.

Simon's voice cuts through the clamor, pleading with me. But what really sinks into my stupid head is Daniel's laugh. That's what's fueling the flames.

"You're crazy, dude. Don't you have broken ribs or something? You really think you can beat me now?"

"You started this by accusing me. Now we're gonna finish it."

Chloe is standing next to Simon, her eyes round and glistening like marbles, her mouth open in amazement. And a little part of me that still has some life not ruled by my irrational fire trembles in fear. Will either of them even speak to me after this? Should I care?

"Teacher!" someone says.

Paisley slips underneath Daniel's arm as if she's so proud of her man for standing up for her.

An ounce of sense returns to me. Just one little ounce. "Tomorrow. Snake pit."

"What did you say?" The teacher has arrived, and he's focused on me as Daniel and Paisley slip away.

"Nothing. No problem," I answer.

It's the lie told by students all through the centuries of education, and I cannot think of a time when it ever worked. But we still try. My problem is I still feel the tension in my face, and my fists are clenched. That part of me that seems to float outside myself is groaning, rubbing a hand over its face, sinking slowly back to feel the hammer come down.

"You'd better not be planning a fight," this teacher says. He's a big guy. Well over six feet tall and muscular. Maybe a coach.

"No, sir." I lie.

His eyes narrow. They're lasered in on me. "What's your name?"

Can I get out of whatever punishment he's about to slap on me if I give him a fake name? I swallow, hesitate too long, and look around us. The spectators have drifted away. Simon stands across the hall, his head down. Chloe has abandoned me and him too.

I'm alone.

"Name," the teacher barks.

I can't look at him now. "Noah. Dickerson."

"Stay out of trouble..."

Maybe my father is right, and I'm a loser. All I had to do was walk into the school and not say a word to anybody, go to class, go home, do homework, stay silent and mostly anonymous.

"Saturday detention, Mr. Dickerson."

"I didn't do anything!"

My impulsive whine makes no impact.

"The front office will contact your parents."

No. Please.

Now I'm mute. Rendered silent and obedient. The teacher taps something into his cell phone—probably my name—and goes on his way.

The period warning bell rings.

End of round one.

Simon stands across the hall, his sad eyes seeking mine.

I want to be furious with him. My only friend. He did nothing to stand up for me. He stood there with his head down. I turn away from him, press a hand against my aching ribs, and head for my locker. I hear his footsteps catching up to me.

"Don't do it," he says. "Please, Noah. You're injured."

I don't look at him. "He probably won't even show up."

"And if he does, you're going to get hurt more."

"Doesn't matter," I mumble.

"How can you say that?"

Because it doesn't. I'm a loser. I didn't do anything wrong except accuse someone who deserved it. Maybe I'll get busted and thrown into juvenile hall. Maybe they'll send me back to North Carolina. Maybe my mother won't have to deal with me anymore and she can be free at last.

Maybe I deserve whatever I get.

Even if I were perfectly healthy, I'm not a fighter. I'd like to say that Mom's tears last night pushed me over the edge, but the truth is I'm angry. Beyond angry. Not just because of what happened last night, but because of this whole month. All the years that led up to this month. I'm angry because my family is messed up and I've lost just about everything I had to live in a place where my one friend just stood back and let me take the heat.

"See you later," I mutter to Simon. Abruptly I pivot toward a boys room and head for a sink. I turn the water on so I look like I'm doing something, but just stare at my face in the mirror. My angry face. I feel that weird sensation again of my consciousness pulling back. It makes me dizzy, and I sway a little. Probably another symptom of the concussion. Or I really am going insane.

The room clears out as guys head for their classes. I drop my backpack to the floor and gently pull my hoodie and shirt up on my right side. It hurts. The bruising is still there from the accident, although it's not as dark now. I yank some paper towels out of the dispenser and wet them with cold water. After folding them into a pad, I press them against my side. The cooling won't last, but it's all I've got.

I really am the king of idiots.

If I don't show up for that fight tomorrow, everyone will call me a coward. They may even say that Daniel's accusation was true. I shouldn't care about that. I should just fake another migraine and stay home from school.

But I won't.

Because I'm sick of being a coward.

The Media Center is Safe... Right?

The cafeteria is a potential battle zone. Even if Daniel stays on his side of the room, I'm feeling so raw that I don't trust myself. I need relief from this tension. I need to sketch something. I need to get back to my artistic self.

So I skip lunch again and head to the media center. My sketchbook is at home, but I'll draw on the back of old homework pages if I have to. I just want to feel my pencil skimming across the surface of some paper.

The best tables are all taken. All the seats away from the stream of traffic, secured behind bookcases and out of from the direct view of the librarian, have been claimed by groups of students involved in projects or with books spread out so they look like they're studying rather than hanging out. What's left is out in the open, closest to the librarian's desk.

A familiar face arrests me as I'm heading for a table. Chloe looks up from her conversation with the librarian and watches me go by. Surprise registers first in her eyes and then a kind of resigned sadness. I don't expect she's going to talk to me, and I'm guessing she knows I'm not here to talk to her.

I take a seat at the table and dig around in my backpack. Paper I have. Folded or crumpled at the bottom, or in my rather mangled notebook. What I can't find is my pencil. I must have left it in one of my classes. Crud. I can draw with a pen, but I'm not comfortable with it. I'm not one of those guys who can search out a line and work it in ink, and have the sketchy results look like they're intentionally artistic. I have to do the pencil before the ink.

I sigh and lean back in the wooden chair. The same kind of straight-backed seat that Principal Manning has in her office, I note. I stare at the pebbly ceiling tiles and breathe, slow and deep, even though that stretches my ribcage and hurts. I need to settle this jitteriness in my gut. It's barely tamed rage, backed into a corner and waiting for a chance to escape.

A guy walks behind my chair, shimmying between me and a book return cart so he doesn't touch either. I don't see him as much as hear his awkward movements. I feel his air and catch a whiff of dusty leather. As he claims a seat opposite me, I can't help but stare.

He's wearing a cowboy outfit, complete with chaps. Like, actual chaps that look like they've been used while riding a real horse. There's a holster at his left hip. No gun in it, of course. And he's got a bandana around his neck and a cowboy hat on his head. The brim is flat, like in old western films, not bent and twisted the way guys wear them now.

It's vintage day. The school must have waived the no-hat rule for spirit week, because I've seen plenty of hats—and wigs or wild hairstyles—since Monday. I vaguely remember Bethany with her hair straightened and wearing a tie-dyed shirt. Around the school there have been plenty of people in hippy and greaser clothes, plus the typical poodle skirts and high ponytails. But this guy chose to go really vintage. Historical vintage.

And then I recognize him. He's the tall dude whose locker is next to Mia's. What was his name? Mia said he's autistic.

He extracts a textbook, paper, and some mechanical pencils from his backpack and meticulously arranges them on the table. By his placement of things, I can tell he's left-handed.

For a second, I'm fascinated. I don't know anything about autism. There were a couple of people at my old school who apparently had it, but I never interacted with them. Like most people I knew, I steered away, not knowing how to act. Not wanting to interact.

Wrong, I know. And I get this weird feeling, seeing myself as so immature just a few months ago. Even so, as the cowboy across from me opens his textbook to read, I avert my eyes. I don't want him to think I'm paying attention. Staring, judging. I could try to convince myself that I don't want him to feel uncomfortable, but the truth is his presence is making me uncomfortable. He's not acting weird or saying anything, but I still feel twitchy, like I should move to another table.

I really am a jerk sometimes.

What *was* his name? I can't remember. Stupid concussion.

For whatever it's worth in my harsh self-assessment, the guy doesn't seem to want to acknowledge me, either.

So we sit, two strangers at a table, and I attempt to immerse myself in an ink sketch of Wolverine. The dark anti-hero suits my mood today.

The drawing isn't going well. My muse is crippled with self-doubt and angst. I'm ready to rip the paper in half and crumple it, when a deep voice across the table shocks me.

"Wolverine."

I look up at the cowboy. He doesn't look back at me. He's so focused on whatever he's reading that I wonder if it was actually him who spoke.

"You read comics?" I ask.

"Yes."

Nothing more.

"That's cool," I say, just to cap off the almost-conversation. Is that rude?

"1982, Chris Clairmont and Frank Miller produced four comics with Wolverine and invented his catch phrase, 'I'm the best there is at what I do, but what I do best isn't very nice.' They wrote that. But they didn't invent Wolverine. The first comic with Wolverine came out in 1974. He's one of the X-Men, but he also has his own comic. The All New Wolverine comes out next month."

"Wow. Yeah, that's right." Truth is, I'm not sure if everything he said is right. But I'm guessing this guy has done his research. I'm impressed. I look down at my drawing, at the sketchy, searching lines and the questionable anatomy. Every wrong line jumps out at me. "Um. I could do a better job, but I lost my pencil."

He doesn't look up. His eyes shift back and forth over his textbook. He's a fast reader.

"Do you know if the media center sells school supplies?"

The muscles under his eyes twitch. "No," he says.

"Oh. No, you don't know, or no they don't sell stuff?"

He doesn't answer.

So that's that. I just have to deal. I scrawl a few more random lines in my sketch, making the thing worse instead of better. I sigh and glance at the cowboy's stash of pencils. Six of them. And he's not using a single one yet.

"Uh, can I borrow a pencil?"

He digs into his backpack, brings out another pencil, rises from his seat, and reaches across the table to place it in front of me. It rolls a little and he stops it. A regular number 2 pencil instead of a mechanical one. He sits back down and resumes his reading. All without looking at me. He didn't seem agitated, like I was bugging him and he wanted to shut me up. His movements were all normal. Just... giving me a pencil.

He seems okay.

"Thanks," I say.

"You're welcome."

There's muffled laughter in the room, and someone says, "Yeehaw!"

The cowboy stares intently his textbook, not responding. Not that someone else might notice, anyway. But because I was already staring at him, I saw him stiffen slightly.

Just like me.

Walk on by, hater. Don't give me a reason...

"You fixin' to saddle up, Zander?" a dude says. "What's it gonna be, a mule or a giraffe?"

At least two girls laugh at this, which means the guy is going to keep laying on the taunts, because now his ego is being fed.

Zander's fingers twitch.

Tension boils in my gut.

"It's vintage day, not John Wayne day," a female voice says.

"Well, howdy, Pilgrim," another guy says in the requisite John Wayne tone. I see him in my peripheral vision, his thumbs hooked into his beltloops, his knees turned outward like he's bowlegged. "Ya gonna rustle up some dowgies for us?"

Zander is frozen in his seat. His eyes aren't moving anymore.

But I'm not frozen in mine.

I whirl out of my chair and face the people bunched together beside the book return cart. Tie-dyed shirts and Converse sneakers, about as vintage as the latest iPhone. One guy has his too-short-for-the-style hair slicked back, like that's supposed to give him the Fonzie look. Me? I'm in black. Just black. And angry. They shut up and stare at me, stuck between laughter and apprehension.

"Leave him alone."

What's it going to cost me to face down this gang of losers? Another detention? This one would be worth it.

The bolder guy straightens up, his thumbs still hooked on his beltloops. He sneers at me. "Who are you?"

"Leave. Him. Alone."

Zander is shaking his head now.

"Are you his sidekick?" This comes from a second guy in the group, who's so brave that he's standing behind the three girls.

One of those girls snorts. "Tonto," she blurts.

"You think it's funny? Picking on someone with a disability?" I say.

"Stop it, stop it, stop it," Zander says with each shake of his head.

I may not know anything about autism, but I'm guessing this reaction is not good. I reach out to tap the table in front of him. "It's okay, man. I got this for you."

Zander jerks out of his seat. The wooden chair crashes to the floor. He backs up against a bookcase. His eyes are bugging out of his head.

The others are just as stunned as I am. For a second. Then they fall against each other, laughing. And heat rises to my head.

Control, control. Think.

"You know, cowboys are a lot more vintage than the store-bought junk y'all are wearing. At least he put some thought into his clothes. So just back off. Leave him alone."

"Stop! Stop!"

Zander's voice isn't the only one saying this, but he's got his hands over his ears. The librarian rushes over, waving her hands to shoo away the group of bullies. And me. Shooing, like she's chasing flies off a picnic table. Chloe is behind her. While the librarian pushes past me to attend to Zander, Chloe puts her hands on my shoulders and urges me toward the stacks.

The librarian speaks softly to Zander, and gradually he eases back into his seat.

The haters leave, and all of us breathe a little.

"Sorry, dude," I say to Zander. "I was trying to help."

Zander just shakes his head again, and the librarian waves me away.

"He doesn't know you," Chloe says softly.

"Well, okay, but he gave me a pencil just two minutes ago."

She shakes her head. "He doesn't know if you're helping or if you're one of them."

"I'm not—I'm..." My jaw tightens again. I refuse, *I refuse,* to be told that standing up to defend a person against a bunch of bullies was a mistake.

"I know, I know." Chloe's voice is hushed. And I think she's trying to bring the tension down for Zander's sake more than mine. The librarian has squatted down next to Zander, talking to him, and he looks like he's doing deep-breathing exercises.

"It's hard to understand, but it's difficult for him to read your intentions. People have used that against him, nice one moment and attacking him the next."

"Well, that's not me!" I break away from Chloe, snatch up my backpack and paper from the table—which has Zander's eyes bugging out again—and head for the exit.

She follows. And I really don't want to have the conversation that's coming with her. We make it out to the hallway before she says my name.

"Is this how you are?" she says. "You lay into people when you get angry and push them away when they're trying to help?"

I whirl toward her. "Don't come at me with your judgement. You don't know me at all."

"I know what I see. I know what happened this morning. I know Simon is worried about you."

"You don't know anything."

Zander stands behind her, his eyes wide, his hand still holding the media center door open.

"Maybe I would if you would talk to someone," Chloe says.

I huff and throw my head back. "Spare me."

Zander says her name. Does he think I'm a bad guy again?

Chloe ignores him. She touches me. Her fingertips rest lightly against my collarbone. Her blue eyes, level with mine, are gentle yet searching. "Noah..."

It fails to soften anything in me. And that makes me feel angrier at myself. I want to leave. But whatever belligerence my father has infested me with won't let me quietly fade away.

"Chloe," Zander says.

"You're full of sympathy for people, aren't you?" I say. "For that guy standing there, for people who are bullied, and now for me."

"You say that like it's a bad thing."

"Chloe."

I glance at the cowboy. She doesn't.

"Only because you think I need to be helped," I say. "But guess what? I don't want your sympathy. I don't need you to even like me."

I'm lying! Why am I lying? Because right now my need to be in control of my situation outweighs my deeper need to be liked. This thing is the stronger, more aggressive part of my ego and I'm letting it control me.

Chloe's hand falls away from my chest. She takes a tiny step back and finally looks at Zander. I can't tell if I've hurt her feelings. Maybe she's got her own strong ego taking over. But there's a part of me, deep inside, that whimpers, knowing I haven't accomplished anything good by arguing with her.

"I'm sorry," I say, meaning it. "I just need to be alone."

She nods, once, and turns away. I watch her go back into the media center, Zander following her and talking. She leaves me alone in the hallway. Just like I asked her to do.

The loneliness that comes on me in a wave is just what I'd asked for.

Twilight... Steppin' Out

Mom's voice rings in my ears long after she has stopped yelling, long after I've slammed the front door and stomped down the metal steps outside our unhappy home.

I'm seventeen. She can't ground me. She can't make me go to church so I can *"get some morals."* She can't punish me for things that aren't my fault.

Okay, the detention is my fault. I argued with Daniel in the hallway at school, but the Saturday detention should be punishment enough.

The school called Mom, and she's fed up.

It's not my fault.

That's the mantra I play over and over in my head as I leave the trailer park and take the shortcut through the woods to wherever it will take me. Navigating the rough path in the near darkness pushes down both my inner voice and the memory of Mom's vocal one.

I don't know where I'm going. Just somewhere I can sit by myself and think. If I were still in North Carolina, I'd call Stuart to pick me up. We'd sit in his garage and he'd supply the beer. I know, I know, it's so stupid. My father is an alcoholic and I drink beer. Not often, and only when I'm in a really bad mood. Or at Nathan's house where the fridge is stocked with little else. I actually can't remember the last time I drank alcohol. Maybe at one of Nathan's parties last summer when a girl I thought liked me ran out on me, leaving me to explain to a room full of my brother's friends who thought the whole situation was hilarious.

Yeah, I really don't want beer now. I want... silence. Or at least the illusion of silence, where life goes on around me and I don't have to pay attention to any of it.

I have a couple of dollars and some change in my pocket. As I emerge from the woods, the yellow sign for Waffle House shines through the twilight.

That'll work.

I climb a rather steep, kudzu-infested slope—which I pray doesn't harbor any snakes beneath those leaves broader than my splayed hands—and reach the sidewalk that runs along the main road. When I finally arrive at the narrow restaurant I'm kind of out of breath. Mom's voice returns to my mind with a warning about pneumonia. With my hand on the door handle, I take several deep breaths and blow them out slowly.

The sizzle of meat on the grill and the clanking of plates greets me inside the building. The greasy aroma reminds me that I haven't eaten since breakfast. But I don't have enough money for food.

I take a seat at the counter, and a waitress with dirty-blond hair piled on top of her head asks me what I want and calls me "baby."

"Just coffee, please."

She delivers the cup a moment later. I wait for her to turn away before dumping sugar into it.

The place is crowded with patrons, including little kids, and the jukebox is pumping out a pop tune. A big man in a Harley-Davidson shirt leans over me to pay his bill. His arms are covered with tattoos and white hair. Another waitress stands at the end of the cooking lane, yelling out an order. Everyone seems to be yelling rather than talking, just to be heard. I'm surrounded by decibels. And while I thought it would be okay because no one would pay attention to me, I forgot about that stupid concussion. The sounds are like hammer strokes to my eardrums, and I'm going to pay for this lonely cup of coffee with a headache.

"Well, lookie here."

An unlikely whiff of Tommy Hilfiger invades the steam of my coffee, and the red and black chair next to me scrapes the floor.

Someone sits down, and when I look at him, everything inside me freezes.

"You have got to be kidding me," I manage to say.

"You know, I get the distinct impression that you don't like me very much," Todd McCaffrey says.

"Unbelievable."

"Yeah, it is. Because, really, I should be one of your best friends."

Okay, this I have to hear. "How do you figure?"

"You like to figure things out. I'm the master of figuring people out. You and I, we could go into business together. Private detectives. Dick and Mack."

"That idea is offensive on about a hundred different levels."

He laughs at this. "I know who you are, dude. In fact, what I can't figure out is why you're bothering to hide anything."

I lean back in my seat, propping my right foot against the kick plate, and take a slow drink of my coffee.

"Noah Rhys Dickerson," he says. "Formerly of Bentley, North Carolina, formerly a student at South Stiles High School, where you've got at least two dozen girls who either want to marry you or kill you."

I huff through my nose. "Easy enough to get that information by scoping out my social media contacts."

"I'm just getting started. You've got a sister, Naomi, who is smokin' hot, by the way, and an older brother, Nathan, who's a student at Dawson State University."

"Again—"

He holds up a finger. "Ah! Wait for it. Your parents are separated and you came here with your mother, and the report from that hospital in Fayetteville is sketchy, if you ask me. Sounds more like you took it in the head with a baseball bat. Pretty sure bet it was Daddy doing the swinging."

I shrug. "All you've proved is that you know how to hack into a computer network. That doesn't interest me."

"Maybe not. But stay tuned, creeper boy. You're going to see some stuff go down in the next few days."

"You going to spread some false rumors about me again?" I

straighten in my seat and put my elbows on the counter. Give him my disinterested profile.

"Not about you. Believe it or not, you're not *that* interesting in the grand scheme of things. And my information isn't false."

Snort. "Then why are you wasting time talking to me?"

The waitress takes Todd's order. Burger, just mustard.

I hate mustard.

I also hate that I'm curious enough about this guy's game that I'm waiting for him to answer my question.

"I'm mildly amused," he says. "Plus I thought you might like a chance to get back at someone we both hate."

I slant a questioning scowl at him.

"Drake Ogletree?" he says.

"I don't hate Drake. I just don't run in his crowd."

"Not buyin' it, milky boy."

He thinks he's going to get to me with Drake's favorite and unfathomable name for me. I'm not even going to roll my eyes at it. I drink my coffee. Like we're not even talking.

He shifts closer. Our shoulders touch. "I'll give you a tip. Then you watch and see what happens, and we'll talk again. I have evidence of a cover-up and, if I choose to release the full account, it will take down a key player on UGA's football squad."

"Why should I care about that?"

"Oh, I think you'll care, when things start rolling and a pretty friend of yours is in the way."

Mia?

I'm pretty sure that Mack the Hack was involved in putting threatening notes in Mia's locker, because she had information about the rape and possible murder of Hana Seoh. The police have got Ivan Norwood and his father in custody, but so far Todd hasn't had anything pinned on him. At least as far as I know.

Now he's planning something more.

My hands clamp around the nearly empty ceramic coffee cup. "Why do you do it?"

"Do what?"

I scowl at him. "You freakin' know what I'm talking about."

He smiles and waits while the waitress, apparently with a sixth sense when it comes to coffee, arrives to refill my cup.

"It's my superpower," he finally says. "My adrenalin rush. I'm the man who controls the information. I'm..." One eyebrow lifts to an unnatural height on his forehead as he touches his fingertips to his chest. "I... am your Moriarty."

What does that mean? I've heard the name somewhere. Todd obviously thinks I should know it, and I'm not going to give him the satisfaction of knowing that the concussion Maintenance Guy George gave me has messed with my brain cells.

"You're that great, huh?"

"Because of who will be taken down. This could go pretty high up the hierarchical scale. Or... not."

"Okay. If it's someone I know, why are you telling me?"

"I'm not the monster you think I am, dude. It was a real shame, what happened to that little girl. I don't like seeing girls get hurt. I think you don't either. But if I see someone who deserves to have the truth come out against him, or her, you better believe I'm going to see it done. Maybe this warning will benefit someone? Like that pretty girl I mentioned? She could have a chance to get out of the way."

"Nice monologue. Which girl?"

He wiggles those weird, skinny eyebrows at me.

"Which girl?" I growl.

"You'll figure it out. But I will tell you this. People who lie about me, who come against me, who think they're better than me, they will learn the truth. And it will not set them free. The only reason you haven't taken a hit yet is that I do find you amusing."

"You're psychotic."

"It's a lot of fun. You should try it."

I fight the impulse to roll my eyes. "So... if this thing you're talking about actually happens, how do you know I won't just tell everyone that you're behind it? That you set it all up?"

Todd touches one index finger to the other. "One, you're a liar. People won't believe you. Two." Another finger joins the first ones. "I don't know why you're keeping so many secrets, but it seems important enough to you that you might not want me telling people who you really are. Maybe you don't want Papa to find you, eh? And three, all I'm doing is conveying information. I'm not the bad guy. It really doesn't matter where it comes from. What matters is who will pay for it."

"Okay, right. So you've got secrets and you'll blackmail people with them."

"I knew you were clever."

I shake my head. "Won't work with me. You said it, I'm not that interesting. I don't have enough to lose to play your game."

"But *she* does. And you fancy yourself as a Romeo. Are you going to risk it all to save her, like you did with Mia Park?"

Does this mean he isn't referring to her?

It doesn't matter. He's talking in circles and I'm done with the game. I pick up my check and slide out of my chair. But since the cash register is right next to where I was sitting, I can't move too far away from Todd yet. No dramatic exit for me.

"I'm disappointed, Dickerson," he says. "I thought you had more grit."

The waitress takes my check. I empty my pocket for the coffee and a tip.

"It doesn't take any grit to hide behind a computer and spread lies about people," I say before turning.

"You'll change your mind when you see what happens!" Todd calls after me.

I walk home. More than once, and against my need to be in control and strong, I glance over my shoulder to make sure I'm not being followed... although I have no doubts that Todd McCaffrey could figure out my address if he wanted to. If he hasn't already.

Mom is working on her cross-stitch piece when I get there. She's not speaking to me. But her silence says more than Todd could in a whole hour.

Chapter 6

Defective...

That's the word for today, describing my life. Defective. We're driving past the formal wear store, where white spray paint still spells out the word on the side wall, and I think it's perfect.

Mom isn't speaking to me. Simon isn't very talkative either. It's a defective situation because I know how to fix it, but I can't. Or I won't. Some of both. I know what's bothering them, but I'm on an inescapable trajectory which, I know, is not going to make anything better.

Without speaking, we unload from the van at school and head toward the doors. Just before we reach them, Simon grabs my arm to stop me.

"So... after school," he says. "Is there any way I can talk you out of this?"

I sigh and give him my scripted answer. "It'll be okay. He's probably not even going to show up."

"What makes you so sure?"

"Because he put it off a day. That's a cooling off period. I'll bet he sends me a message today saying we should call a truce.

Maybe with a note tucked into the vents of my locker? That would be amusing.

"There's a pep rally today," Simon says. "Homecoming game tonight."

I knew that. I'm just not sure why it's relevant.

"Lots of stuff going on. If you back out of the fight, it's possible no one will even notice."

"I'm not a coward, Simon."

"There is a difference between cowardice and common sense."

I scowl and move away from him. "So going through with this means I don't have any common sense."

His face is stony.

Someone passes through the space I've made between us.

"You don't have to do it," he says.

I look away from him. The student who passed us goes inside, the door swinging shut behind her. I can see my reflection in the glass. Mine, not Simon's. Like I'm standing here without a friend.

"I'll think about it," I say. Which isn't a lie. All night and all morning I've thought about three things only. How to get through my mother's silent treatment. How to make sense of the conversation with Todd McCaffrey. And how to either avoid or survive the fight with Daniel.

Simon's sour expression, though, tells me he's not satisfied with my answer. Time for a change of subject.

I take a step toward the door, and he follows.

"Something kinda weird happened last night," I say. "I walked to Waffle House to get a drink, and Todd McCaffrey found me. He sat down next to me and started talking about a plot he has to take down a football player."

"More hacking," Simon says, his voice grumbly.

"Probably. The guy is nuts."

"Insane genius."

"Not sure about the genius part. Anyway, he said a girl I know was going to be targeted too. A pretty girl. At first I was thinking he meant Mia. He talked about a cover-up, and he's going to reveal it. I know it involves a football player at UGA. So I'm not sure how Mia could be involved in that. But I was thinking last night… maybe Chloe?"

Simon's eyes go wide for half a second before the sour expression returns. "Chloe can take care of herself."

"Whoa. That's totally not the response I expected from you."

He whips his head around to glare at me. "What did you expect? That I'd go running off to rescue her?"

It might be comical, this little guy with his big eyes, barking at me like he's got some muscle behind it. I might laugh… if I didn't care.

"I thought you might warn her."

"There's no way Chloe is involved in any cover-up. And the only times she's had anything to do with football players is when she took pictures at the home games. And besides that, why should I believe anything that guy says? Why should you?"

"Okay, chill. I'm just telling you what he said."

"Worry about yourself, Noah. You've got broken ribs and you're going to let some guy pound on you. Do something about that before you try to solve someone else's problems." With this he walks away.

I could easily match his strides, but I let him go.

He didn't beg me. He didn't suggest anything. He challenged me.

He also turned his back on me.

Pep Rallies are Great Places to Hide

No message comes from Daniel during the day. I looked for him at lunch, thinking he might have had a suspicious illness or dental appointment, but he was there with Paisley and Bethany. Once I caught him turning his head away real quick, like he didn't want me to catch him spying me out.

Now, during the few minutes we had of our last-period chemistry class, he's acting like he doesn't know me. Like nothing at all will happen after the pep rally today. Maybe he's going to be just as distant later. That'll be fine with me. But I *am* showing up at the snake pit. Wherever that is.

Our last class of the day lets out early so the entire student body— or those who don't manage to slip away—files into the gymnasium. I'm surrounded by red shirts, pirate eye patches, head bandanas, and students alternately whooping or talking with lots of *arrrrrs*.

I seriously don't belong here.

Nudged along by people flooding the bleachers, I take a seat somewhere in the middle, sitting among people I don't know. I'm pretty much invisible. Cheerleaders in red and white skirts and tank tops are bouncing around on the basketball court. Announcements are made over the sound system, punctuated by whistles blowing. On the other side of the gymnasium, the marching band has taken up a section of the bleachers and are getting ready to play.

With all the noise, this is not going to be a happy time for me and my concussion.

I search for Simon in the crowd and spot him along the sidelines with Chloe. She's got a camera in her hands, and Simon appears to be her caddy, or whatever they call assistants for photographers. There's another guy with them, talking rapidly to Chloe and pointing toward a roped-off section of the bleachers where, I'm assuming, Agatha Cross's beloved Pirates will soon be seated. After some grand and noisy entrance, I'm sure.

Someone near me has an air horn. The single blast, coming as the first football player is introduced, is like a knife stabbed into my brain. Time to leave.

People are standing to cheer their team. I clamber in front of them, praying to the Almighty that I don't put one of my feet in the wrong place. I make it to the aisle intact and clomp down the steps. The teacher guarding the door thankfully doesn't question me when I tell her that I'm feeling sick. Guess I must look it too. Finally I'm outside the gymnasium. Although the sounds are echoing out here as well, it's better. I duck into the boys bathroom to splash some water on my face.

Walk away.

Daniel probably won't show up anyway.

With all the teachers packed into the gymnasium, I could just walk out the front doors and head home.

"Dude," someone says.

I look in the mirror. Drake Ogletree is standing behind me. It suddenly occurs to me that I haven't seen him around since that parking lot fight on Tuesday. Now he's here, with me, alone in the boys room.

Crud.

He grins and wanders up to a urinal like it's no big deal that his presence is pushing images of doom and gloom into my head.

He unzips. "So, I heard you're going to the park later."

The park. Snake pit. And Drake heard about it.

"You look a little nervous," he says.

Why? While he's draining himself and the sound bounces around the cinderblock room, why does he have to talk to me?

I shake my head. "I'm not nervous."

"I gotta say," he goes on, "I'm impressed. Challenging a guy while you got broken ribs. Even a total loser like that geek, Daniel. You got some guts, milky boy."

Apparently having some guts doesn't relieve me of that name.

I wait to respond until he zips back up, and then I pivot away from the mirror. "Can I ask you a question?"

He laughs. "As long as it doesn't mean we're friends."

"No problem. Where is this place in the park I'm supposed to find?"

Drake's grin is so wide I'm afraid to hear his answer. "You know what? I think you can just follow the crowd."

I do a slow blink. I hadn't thought about other people showing up, especially not a *crowd*. I thought it would be just me and Danny Boy. But if Drake has heard about the challenge, then other people have too. Maybe he told them.

Across the hall, cheers erupt from the gymnasium and the band is playing what sounds like a typical school fight song. How appropriate.

"There's your cue," Drake says. "Time to get ready to rumble."

"That's so freakin' cliché," I mutter as I turn away.

So what am I supposed to do? Go to my locker and gather whatever homework I have for the weekend, like I was only going to get on the bus for home? Then walk out the door and stroll down the sidewalk toward the park? Is that how this works?

Whatever happens is going to happen. I get ready to leave, like a normal day, and then I do. Alone. I don't know if Simon is working today or if he's still with Chloe playing lovesick caddy. I don't know if he's even still my friend, since he hardly said a word to me during lunch.

People get on the buses. Or they wait for parents to pick them up in cars lined up outside the gymnasium. Or they flock down to the student parking lot. I go that way, since the park is beyond the lot.

There's a chain link fence bordering the lot, too tall for me to climb over unnoticed. I remember seeing a brown and white sign with the name of the park a short way down the main road. I start walking along the fence toward the road. No one else is going this way. Maybe Daniel isn't coming and Drake's comment about following a crowd was just a bluff.

I glance over my shoulder at the sound of voices. Drake is there with his girlfriend and some other guys who share his general jock appearance.

Drake sees me and points toward the fence. "Wrong way, Jose!"

I stop and blow out self-esteem.

Drake and his friends turn the other direction and walk along the grass next to the fence. Talking and laughing. Drake's girlfriend looks back at me and giggles.

I follow but give them a lot of space.

The fence snakes along behind the mobile classrooms and then up toward a building that looks like an old car repair place and seems to be locked up now. Here is where Drake and his crew scale the fence. I wait for them to get over—one of the girls having trouble with her open-backed shoes—before I approach the fence.

As if my body is pleading with me not to do this idiotic thing, my ribs send out agonizing pangs as I pull myself over the top of the fence. Dropping down on the other side... big mistake.

Go home. Just go home.

But Drake is watching, grinning, even waiting for me to catch up.

We head over a grassy clearing, and the uneven footing has my breath puffing as each step jars my ribcage.

There's a trail marked by nothing I can see. It leads down a hill and has plenty of rocks and tree roots to trip a person up. Like that girl with the tricky shoes. She slows Drake's group down enough that I'm practically among them by the time the ground levels out some.

Sounds of traffic from the main road fade behind us. I'm starting to wonder if I'm being led by Drake Ogletree to some deserted place where *he* is going to pound me into the ground, not Daniel. But then we come to a clearing, and I can see from the trash lying around the perimeter that this place has seen some action. There are other people already here, and Daniel is hanging out in their midst. He separates himself from Paisley and some other guys and walks toward me. Reluctantly, I think. Like he's being goaded on by the people with him the same way I've been with Drake and company.

"Didn't think you were going to make it."

"You didn't tell me what time. I came as soon as school let out."

"You went to that stupid pep rally?" he asks, like we're just here to have a casual conversation.

Casual or not, I don't like how he's making me look like a rookie. The faces of the people around us are hungry. They came here to see action, not chit chat. Even Paisley looks like she's eager for something to happen. Phones are already out, ready to make me momentarily famous on Snapchat.

I don't see Bethany. Or Simon. They're probably the only smart people I know.

And there's a face lurking in the shade beneath the trees. Todd McCaffrey. Who, now that I think of it, is probably the person who told everyone else there would be a fight today.

I had wanted to ask Simon earlier who or what a "moriarty" is but forgot. Stupid concussion. Maybe I'll get a hint at the definition in the next few minutes.

"I'm here now," I tell Daniel.

His eyes shift left and right, and that tells me he's as uncomfortable with our audience as I am. If we were here alone, would we be able to talk this out without bloodshed?

"Dude," he says, raising his hands palm out like he's the most reasonable person here. "You don't really want to do this. Look, man. You're breathing heavy already. You've got broken ribs. You'll only get hurt more if we fight."

He's giving me the option of backing out. The only problem with this is that it makes me look like a coward and he's a hero. He'll win, without throwing a punch. I'd love to walk away, but I can't let him win. Not with all these people watching. Not with Drake and Todd here. Both of them would love to see me tuck my tail between my legs and run.

Both Daniel and I are being manipulated to do something neither of us wants to do.

"Tell you what," I say. "Admit that y'all accused me of something I didn't do, and we'll both walk away."

There's a murmur, like some people are disappointed that they only came to watch a negotiation.

"Whoever broke in to my house went straight to my room," Paisley says. "It's like they knew exactly what to take that would hurt me. It had to be you."

I give her a snarky smile. "Most girls I know have outgrown their dollies."

She puffs up, getting ready to lash out at me. I need to be careful, because this thing could heat up real quick.

"That doll was worth five hundred dollars. I save up for months to buy him. And I'm sure I mentioned him to you while you were sitting at our table at lunch."

I shake my head. "Not that I recall." Even with this concussion, I think I'd remember a five-hundred-dollar *male* doll. "I don't have it. I've never seen it. And y'all have made a big mistake accusing me of breaking into your house."

"You broke into her house?" This from Drake, who I almost forgot was standing somewhere behind me. "I got accused of breaking into someone's house on Tuesday. Was it *you?*"

Oh, great. Now I'm going to be accused of stealing something from a girl I've never met. I pivot enough to look at Drake. "I haven't broken into *anyone's* house."

There's a rush of movement, crackling of dead leaves beneath someone's feet, and I raise my fists. At the last instant I realize it's Paisley. She has stuck her phone in my face. A picture of a doll dressed in steampunk clothes is on the screen.

"See!" she says.

I sidestep her. "Get away from me, girl!"

"Don't you touch her!" Daniel yelps.

"Get her out of my freakin' face."

Now people are getting excited. I take another step, but Daniel doesn't like it. He shoves me further away from Paisley. I keep my footing and lunge at him. Though my ribs are screaming, I'm able to push him away from me and several steps back.

I'm ready. Every muscle is tight. My fists are like rocks.

As Daniel is recovering from my first shove, I lunge at him again. He ducks away and slips on the uneven ground, landing on one hand.

"Come on! Come on," I growl.

No one here is on my side. No one is trying to calm me down or talk sense into me. Simon has abandoned me. Even if he were here, I wouldn't listen. The rage comes back too easily. I don't like it. I don't want it. But I can't stop it.

Daniel is scared. He's got a *support system*, but still he shimmies away from me. He says something, but I can barely grasp the words. I can hardly hear anything now.

Except the screaming of my own tortured soul.

I've become my father. The transition is complete. I've become the abuser and I can't stop.

Daniel trips again, and I pound my foot into the dirt near his face. He scrambles up, and something hard hits my left collarbone. He's thrown a freakin' rock at me. And now he's running away.

There's nothing, no impulse or thought, that keeps me from chasing him into the woods.

People are yelling, cheering, filming.

I can't feel anything but the urge to hurt someone.

This is my father. This is what he has done to me. Not shown me tough love so that I would grow up strong and respectable, but he taught me how to hurt other people. He taught me that strength over another person means power.

And I hate it with everything else that's in me.

Daniel keeps running, careening around trees, looking for some path toward freedom.

I can't.

I hate myself.

I stop.

I bend forward and press a hand over my ribs. So no one will know the real reason I've stopped.

The spectators group up around me and an expectant hush falls over them. I huff like I can't catch my breath—which is partly true—peer from face to face, and turn back toward the clearing. "Screw this. It's stupid."

Daniel yells words that sound like, "Hey! Come here!"

Is he taunting me? After he ran like a coward? No. It's over. I'm leaving.

"I found something! Paisley! I found your doll!"

Say what? It's probably a trick. I should keep walking. But people are pushing through the woods toward wherever Daniel went, and I am curious. I hang back but follow to see what's up.

He's standing next to a natural shallow pit between some trees. There's a stash of... stuff there. Some clothing, books, and the gold top of a trophy. Paisley stands next to Daniel, hugging that doll, which is missing its steampunk hat and wig.

"What the—" Drake says.

He bends down and pulls some pink fabric out of the pile. It looks like a dress that used to be fancy but is now ripped up. His girlfriend picks up a white strip of fabric and dangles it next to the dress in Drake's hand.

"Emily Schaffer," the girl says. "This is her prom dress from last year."

The white sash is dirty, but I can read "Prom Queen" written across it in gold letters.

And, I'd bet everything that broken trophy on the ground belonged to Jun Seoh.

I move forward through the other spectators and look at the stuff before my feet. Most of it is just stuff. More clothing. Some papers. A ridiculous stuffed pelican. A framed picture face down on the dirt.

"So someone stole all this stuff just to dump it in the woods?" Drake says. "And it wasn't you?" He points at me, the pink dress still draped over his hand.

"No." I squat down and use two fingers to turn over the frame, expecting to see an autographed picture of a famous reporter. The glass is broken, and whatever was inside it is gone.

"Whoever did this," I say, "has some kind of vendetta. It's personal."

People are talking, but I'm looking down at the empty frame, and thinking about where it came from. That I know the person who owned this makes the idea of a vendetta more ominous.

The frame in my grip, a random piece of glass poking into a finger, I straighten and look for Todd.

He's gone too.

Chapter

Saturday Morning… Waffle House Again

Mom dragged me out of bed earlier than necessary. She's speaking to me now, because she informed me that she got paid yesterday, and so we're going to Waffle House for breakfast. To *chat*.

I'm not a mind reader, but I've got a feeling this is not going to be a good time.

The restaurant is more crowded and louder than it was the other evening. The noise of plates rattling and people yelling over the jukebox rings between my ears before Mom even chooses the place we're going to sit. Maybe she figures this way people won't hear our conversation. But if she wants me to hear it, she's chosen the wrong place. The noise threatens to undo the good my medication is doing for my head. On top of that, my ribs hurt from running through the woods yesterday, and I've got a nice new bruise on my left shoulder from Daniel's rock.

The only open table in the restaurant is right next to the restroom doors. Ugh.

I glance at the chair where Todd was sitting. Moriarty. I looked it up last night. He was Sherlock Holmes nemesis, described by the detective as, "The Napoleon of crime." The guy was a genius and like a mafia crime boss. I remember the quote, because it rolled around in my mind for hours while I was trying to go to sleep. Moriarty was, "The organizer of half that is evil and all that is undetected in this great city."

Todd has a very high opinion of himself.

He's also hinted that he has his fingers in a lot of stuff that happens at school.

Hana Seoh. Mia Park. The hacking of my social media account. And now these burglaries.

But if so, why did he tell me?

Mom is not going to let me think about it. Nor is she going to let me engage in the universal teenage sign for *leave me alone*. The moment I put my earbuds in, she raps on the table between us and shakes her head.

I pull one of them out. "It's too noisy in here. My head. I'm just trying to block it out."

"Put the phone away," she orders.

I shut down my music and shove the phone and earbuds into the pocket of my hoodie. I lean back in the booth while the waitress takes our order. Waffle with extra bacon on the side. Whatever conversation Mom has in mind, at least there's bacon.

Mom folds her hands on the table when the waitress leaves. "You haven't said anything about what you want to do since Monday night."

I blink and put her sentence together. Right. The decision about whether to have Dad arrested.

"I don't think it would do any good now," I say.

She nods. "I agree. Good. But if that's your decision, we need to look at our next steps."

I shrug. "Stay here. You'll work and I'll go to school until I graduate."

She purses her lips. "I think it would be good if you were to talk to your father and make amends with him."

"What? No. Mom—"

"Hear me out. One of the reasons he's so angry is because he feels I've taken you away from him. And one of the reasons I think you've been getting into trouble lately is because you don't have that strong male influence."

"Mom! No. It's not like that."

"He's still your father, Noah. If you reach out to him, just talk to him, let him know that he is still your father, then perhaps he'll calm down enough that we can make some progress."

"Progress?"

Some dude at the counter is getting excited with his buddy about the Homecoming game last night. Pirates won. I wish I cared. I actually wish I'd been at the game rather than in the woods with a bunch of people I don't like, finding stolen stuff that I don't want to figure out. Mom glances at the celebrating fans and leans closer to me. She clasps one of my hands.

"Progress to get our family back together."

"Are you serious?" A squeak comes out in my voice.

"We can't keep going like this."

"You're right, we can't!"

I didn't mean for that to come out the way it did, like she's out of her mind to think about going back to him. But... she is out of her mind to think about going back to him.

"We can do better," I amend. "I admit, I can do better. But we can't do that by going back to what was worse."

"Oh. So." She leans back, and the hardness of her expression tells me I'm about to get nailed with a guilt trip. "I guess you want me to go to jail."

Yep, there it is.

"No! Mom, come on."

"Because that's what will happen if we don't do something to appease him."

"I don't want to *appease* him either. That's like giving up and letting him win."

"It's called compromise, Noah."

"How do you compromise with an abuser?"

Yesterday, for a few moments, I seriously wanted to pound Daniel into the ground. I wanted to make him pay. I wanted to win. That's what my father wants. Power over me, over all of us. That's why I have to stay as far away from him, and that atmosphere, as I possibly can.

"He's your father," Mom says.

The waitress brings our food. We both sit back and stare blankly at the table while she sets the plates in front of us. I wait until she's gone and then pick up the syrup bottle to douse my waffle.

"Ten months. That's all I'm asking for," I say.

"And then what? You'll leave us?"

"Did you ever think that maybe it would be good for you to be away from him too?"

She looks like she wants to slap me.

"I'm serious, Mom. Independence. Freedom. You can, like, rediscover yourself or something."

My attempt to make the idea look appealing falls flat. She scowls like I've insulted her.

"Eat your food, Noah. We have to get you to detention on time."

Okay. Fine. I cut into my waffle and shovel big pieces into my mouth. Mom takes out her phone and types out a text or something while she's chewing her toast. This gives me permission to take my phone out too.

Mom catches me just as I'm moving to put the earbuds back in.

"I want you to talk to your father later today. I'll tell him that you will call him."

She must have been texting him just now. I send a narrowed glare her way. "Did you tell him I have detention today?"

"No," she says, tilting her head to show she's annoyed.

Good. Because we don't need to give him any additional ammunition, although I'm feeling sure my mother has given him plenty already.

Detention... Not My First, Probably Not My Last

...But as soon as I walk into the classroom, I know this will be my most memorable detention. Because among the five students seated at desks in the classroom is Drake Ogletree, who's got his legs stretched out into the aisle and using a key to clean his fingernails, like his presence here is just a nuisance he has to endure.

I choose a desk at the back and hope he doesn't notice me.

Not going to happen. The teacher at the front glances up from a book he's reading. "Name?" he says.

So now I have to speak. "Noah Dickerson."

In a flash, Drake swivels around. "Milky boy!"

And with that, all the other students turn to look at me too.

"Silence!" the teacher growls.

I slouch in my seat and stare at some initials scratched into the desktop.

"You may do homework or just sit quietly until you're released," the teacher says, sounding as bored as I'm about to be. "No talking, no moving around, and no cell phones."

And so I sit, playing music only in my head and moving my right foot to the beat to entertain myself. I brought my homework, but being studious with Drake Ogletree sitting nearby just feels like it will open me up for more ridicule. Okay, really I just don't want to look uncool. Conforming. Even though occupying my mind with *something* would be better than staring at the room. At the back of Drake's buzz-cut head. He's not moving at all. I wonder if he's sleeping. Didn't Simon tell me something about Drake's influential father? Maybe the teacher is letting Drake skate through his detention unconscious while the rest of us suffer.

Of course, *of course,* the teacher leaves the room at one point. It's a test. He's got a camera hidden somewhere, or he's waiting just outside the door to catch us breaking his rules.

Of course, Drake turns around to talk to me.

"Everyone is talking about you online."

Great. I just stare at him.

"Pretty interesting that you were the one to discover that stash of stuff in the woods."

Oh no. Not this again. "I didn't. Daniel did," I mutter.

"But you were there."

"Doesn't mean a thing. You were there too."

He grunts and nods, like I've just made a profound point. "People think you did it, though. What are you going to do about it?"

"Nothing."

Drake glances toward the classroom door. "We need to talk. After."

"I don't think so."

"Dude. We're talking."

"Whatever."

Two girls sitting beside each other are staring at me, one with her chin in her fist, the other grinning. She lifts her shoulder, a flirty gesture, and leans over the aisle to whisper to the other girl, apparently her friend.

No. No. Don't...

She turns, her arm resting on the back of her seat. "You're Noah? The one they call creeper boy?"

"No."

But she knows I'm lying. Giggling and more whispering ensue between the girls.

"Are you really an undercover cop?" the second girl asks.

I wince at this. No doubt Todd McCaffrey's work taking off on social media. "Don't believe everything you read."

"Good. You're too cute to be a cop," the first girl says.

Drake guffaws, and the girls glance at him and shrink back into their own world.

The teacher returns, a coffee cup in his hand, and everybody acts like we were completely innocent during his absence.

I am nearly comatose when noon finally comes. My brain feels as numb as my butt, and the only thing keeping me from sliding out of my seat to the floor is my bladder crying for relief. As soon as the teacher releases us, I roll up to my feet, grab my backpack from the floor, and stagger toward the door. I rush headlong toward the bathroom, hoping I'll be able to hide in there long enough for Drake and the girls to forget about me.

It's a strange thing. I totally don't get it. But I've changed somehow. In the past, those flirty girls would have hit a reciprocal switch in me. Even if I didn't feel an attraction to them, I would have thrown myself into the game. I ponder this as I'm washing my hands, and I think it isn't so much that my personality has changed, but my goals. I'm just trying to get through stuff. I've got no connections to this place, to those girls or even the things people are saying about me online. It's all temporary. I'm temporary. It's just a matter of days, maybe weeks, before I'm gone.

In a bizarre sense, I don't really want to enjoy any of this time.

It's like a person walking the Appalachian Trail, taking only memories and leaving nothing behind. Except I don't even care about the memories.

These thoughts grip me by the throat and hang on.

Deep breath. Shrug it off. Walk away.

And I find Drake waiting for me in the hallway.

The proud stance I'd forced on myself falls away into resignation. There's no way I'm going to get away from this guy today.

He doesn't even say hello. No preamble to his intrusion on my life.

"That stuff in the woods. You got blamed for stealing that chick's doll, and I got blamed for stealing some stuff from a girl I used to date."

I'm not going to tell him I already heard this part of the story.

"Neither of us did it, but I'm thinking someone is trying to frame us."

"Hmm. Do you play football?" I ask, thinking of a conversation two days ago that I'd rather forget.

"No. Just wrestling. Why?"

I need an excuse quick. "You were at the pep rally."

"Well, yeah. Uh, I was... uh. Everyone was there."

"I just figured... never mind." I get it. He doesn't have to spell it out. In-school suspension or something like that. It's why I didn't see him during lunch all week. But the great Drake Ogletree wouldn't admit something like that to me.

He gives me a slight scowl like I've confused him. I'd love to laugh at that, but... Drake.

"Anyways, like, what we gotta do is figure out who would want to frame both you and me."

"We?"

"Right. So, some of that stuff in the woods I recognized. Like there was a wrestling trophy, and I know the guy who won it. And that prom dress, that was Emily Schaffer's. So, like, what we do is call a meeting, and that way we can figure out who's breaking into people's houses."

So much wrong with this idea that I don't know where to start.

"Um... I hate to point this out, but, Paisley thinks I stole her doll, and your ex thinks you stole something from her. Won't the people at this meeting just point their fingers at us?"

"No. Dude. You're good at this stuff. You figured out who raped that little Asian girl. You know, Mia tried to blame me for that."

"I didn't know that."

"Yeah, but..." He chuckles. "Obviously, not me."

"Clearly." Eye-rolling at this point would probably get me killed.

"So, like, we get everyone together, and you ask the questions, and we'll figure out the truth. Right?"

"I don't—"

"I'll set it up, and you do the talking. Who do I need to get? That Paisley chick?"

Probably the last person I want to talk to.

"No, Drake. I'm not sure this is a good idea."

"It's a great idea!" He claps me between the shoulders hard enough that I could cough out a lung. "I'll set it up. You just be ready to ask the right questions. It's all good, milky boy."

Maybe it would be better if he stopped calling me that. Or even if I knew why he chose that name.

Drake winks and clicks his teeth against the inside of his cheek, pointing at me as he does. Yeah, he really did that.

He struts away, and I feel like I'm in a bad after-school movie. I'm the geeky little guy who's only hope of surviving is to write papers for the popular jock.

Except, that's totally not me. Paisley's got her stupid doll back, and I escaped a beat down with Daniel. I've got no stake in this gig. I'm out.

I just have to figure out a way to tell Drake he needs a different Sherlock.

Later... It Doesn't Go Well

I'm sitting on the steps outside my trailer, ready to either let loose with a primal scream or pitch my phone as far into the woods as possible. Both would be good. After Dad finished yelling at me for ignoring his calls—I didn't dare tell him his number was blocked so I wouldn't have to deal with them every single day—he accused me of talking Mom into staying away. Like she can't possible have any willpower of her own. After all, I'm the *baby* of the family, and so as Mama's boy, I can get anything I want from her. He blamed me for being a weakling and not able to take a little poke after I smarted off to him. Of course, it wasn't his fault that I fell, because I'm just so clumsy and tripped over the throw rug in our living room.

He knew about the trouble I'd gotten into at school. Not *which* school, fortunately, but he told me that Mom is so worried that I'm acting out and I still need a male authority figure and blah, blah, blah.

Yeah, an authority figure who makes me feel like a total loser and disgrace as a son. That helps.

And finally... he wants me to come home.

Because I'm his son.

His property.

Right.

Again, the decision is put into my hands, except it really isn't. Because the only choice is what he demands.

Again, I got out of it by saying I'd think about it. He wasn't happy with that, but there wasn't much else he could say after I hung up on him.

The mutt hound next door is sitting in the middle of the space between the trailers, his long tail doing a windshield wiper thing in the dirt. His eyes are bright and his mouth is open, almost like he's smiling. He wants the treat I usually have for him whenever I come outside.

"I got nothing, Winston."

At the sound of his name, he scoots forward to the end of his leash. His tail makes a new clear spot in the pine straw.

I groan and get to my feet, clomp down the steps, and slowly walk toward him. He's still kind of skittish when I'm at my full height, so I sink to the ground, cross my legs, and hold my fingers out for him to sniff. He can barely reach me. His chain must be wrapped around something under the trailer. I inch forward until I can slip my hand over his head. I tickle him behind the ears. Winston lowers his chin onto my knee and lets out a doggy sigh.

"We're both trapped, aren't we boy?"

I'm tempted, so tempted, to unclasp that leash from the collar that's almost choking this little guy. Set him free. He'd probably freak out and run off to shiver under a bush somewhere, and then starve to death.

It's me who wants to be free.

"Want to come with me, Winston? Become a hobo? Hop a train going wherever and live like no one can tell us what to do ever again?"

Yeah, dream on. But the dream draws me in. Maybe I could find a one-room cabin in the mountains where I can cut my own wood and grow my own food.

But I'd have to have a girl with me. Because... girls.

Actually, right now I'd settle for someone of any sex who'd listen without judging me.

I'm so... so tired of being angry.

Winston rolls his eyes up to look at me, his tail no longer wagging. I inch forward again but startle him. He jumps away. It takes a minute of talking softly to him before he comes back. I stroke his head, lean forward gently, and press my face against his furry shoulder. He stinks like the underside of that trailer, but he's warm. And he accepts me. Maybe his doggie brain instinctively knows that sometimes a guy just needs a hug.

Yeah, I'm totally sappy that way.

He gives me more. A shy little lick on the cheek.

With the one dog I had as a kid, before Dad got rid of him, I'm no expert in canine behavior. What I do see is that Winston's low posture and that little lick are an act of submission. He's still afraid of me, but he knows that if he's low, quiet, and sweet, I won't hurt him.

That's sure not the way I've dealt with my father. I've stood up to him, argued with him, ignored him, and gone my own way as often as I could. I even let his example influence me to drink beer sometimes, even though I know very well how alcohol has ruined him. And yesterday, the way I wanted to hammer Daniel, even when common sense told me it was wrong, was all my father's influence. All the things I hate about myself are his teachings.

I want to walk away from it all. But I can't. Not yet.

I give Winston a final pat on the head and wipe my face with my sleeve to get the clinging fur off. Are dogs supposed to shed that much? I go inside our trailer, where my mother is waiting to hear how the phone conversation went. She probably heard part of it. The yelling part.

She expectantly looks up from her needlework.

Saying nothing, I leave my phone on the table and walk to my room, slide the accordion door shut, and sit on my bed.

Trapped. Not by this place, or by my parents arguing over which one of them has control over me, but by myself. By my broken spirit.

I need to find a way, somehow, to get myself free.

Chapter 8

Sunday... When the Desperate Go to Church

How old was I the last time I went to church with my mother? I honestly can't remember. Since coming to Georgia, she has asked me every Sunday to go with her to this new place she found. Today she invokes parental authority and demands that I go with her. Church as punishment. Not sure that's what the Good Lord had in mind. But I don't have the energy to fight her.

I'm still angry. I want to be left alone. I sure don't want to meet anyone new or pretend that I'm a polite young man who has come to worship. Mom doesn't understand. Sulking validates all the pain I've been made to feel. She's determined, though, that church will be good for me.

"If we go back to North Carolina, do you think Dad will let you go to church again?" I ask as we're rolling along the main road through town.

That was mean. It's not a simple question, but my way of making a point. Mom won't have freedom if she goes back.

The fact that she doesn't answer tells me she caught my meaning.

The church is a typical white-steepled building with well-maintained bushes and some harvest decorations around the brick-framed sign that says, "Grace Community Church." The people going inside look like a mix of generations and backgrounds. I guess this is what makes Mom feel comfortable. The assumption that she'll fit in and no one will judge her. I'm not so confident of that for myself, so I plan to keep my mouth shut while we're here.

The altar is a few steps higher than the floor and carpeted in deep maroon. There are chairs instead of pews, upholstered in tan. It's all very last-century looking.

A few people stop Mom to say hello, and a couple of women hug her. I shake hands when they reach for mine. Welcome, welcome, welcome. Mom leads me down the center aisle and toward the front where—I remember now—she likes to sit. I'd rather be in the back. For a quick exit.

Someone calls my name, and my heart stops. Who could possibly know me here? Who do I know that I would want to see here? I turn to see Chloe jogging up the aisle toward me. She's got her hair pulled partially back so the purple streaks underneath are visible. She's still in jeans, but is wearing a flowy, off-white top that's probably too delicate for school. And knee-high black boots. Oh, how I love girls in boots...

She hugs me.

Because I guess hugging people you barely know is acceptable in this church.

"So cool that you're here," she says.

We both glance at Mom, who gives me a tiny smile and moves on, probably quietly ecstatic that I'm actually talking to a Christian girl.

"Yeah," I say, and flip my thumb toward my mother. "Mom's been coming here for a few weeks."

"So... you're okay? After Friday?"

"Oh. Yeah. No problem."

She breathes out. "That's good. I was worried."

She was worried about me? Just Christian caring, right? I'm the friend of her friend, so...

"Um, yeah. But something else did happen that I need to tell you about. I mean, it might be connected, or not, to the break-in at your house."

Her eyes widen. "Seriously?"

"Maybe." I glance at Mom, easing down a row of chairs to take one toward the middle. Very polite of her to make room for other people so they don't have to crawl over her. It also means I need to get down there so I don't have to crawl over people.

Chloe touches my sleeve. "Let's talk about it after."

I nod and give her a smile I don't want to feel, but do. A sensation sort of flutters in my chest, wanting to rise up and take hold of my thoughts. Having a girl smile at me, say she cares, touch me in that gentle way like I'm a person who is worth being around. It doesn't take much more than that for my heart to go all soft and wimpy and for common sense to take a back seat.

I need to protect more than myself and my friendship—if it still exists—with Simon. I need to protect Chloe from the drama that is my life.

I walk down to the third row and join Mom in the center, right where the pastor is going to look down at me and see me cringing under his holy scrutiny. What's that line from the Ten Commandments about coveting your neighbor's wife? I'm pretty sure Simon would apply that to girlfriends, or even potential girlfriends.

Stop. Just stop. I barely know her. And I have other things I need to be thinking about.

The lights go down and we stand while a band plays popish music I've never heard before. People around me raise their hands. Mom bounces on her toes a bit, probably so happy that I'm with her. Or she's actually singing to Jesus. I should totally get over myself and consider that as a possibility. I know she has actual faith. Dad has tried to squash it for a long time, but she still has it.

This time and this place might actually be her only source of freedom.

The lights come up for the sermon, so I pull my phone out to see if I can find some of the posts Drake mentioned yesterday. Mom thumps my wrist to make me put the phone away, but not before I catch something very interesting. Two friend requests, one from Drake Ogletree, the other from Todd McCaffrey.

I manage to get through the sermon without falling asleep or having a great big load of guilt dumped on me. I even caught myself smirking at one of the pastor's jokes. At the end, though, the man calls for people to come up to the altar for prayer, and my mother clasps my wrist.

"Let's go," she whispers.

"Up there?"

"Yes."

"No."

"Come on."

"You go."

She does, squeezing past me and joining the dozen or so people at the front. I watch for a few seconds, then plop back down in my seat.

I so don't belong here.

It isn't that I don't believe in anything. I'm not an atheist. I just don't think it works the way I was told in Sunday school years ago. Even so, I hang my head and think some words.

Hey, God, do you see me? This loser, this disgrace of a son, this unworthy lump sitting in your church? Do you see me? Do I matter to you at all? Are you there? Can you give me a little bit of direction here? Please?

Yeah, that'll impress him.

"After" is a pot luck luncheon in the downstairs fellowship hall, and Mom wants to introduce me to all her lady friends. Gag! Be polite, Noah. I nod my head and smile and gradually make my way to the long tables where potato salad and tuna-noodle casserole await. I see Chloe sitting at a table with some other younger people, which will give me the opportunity I need to wander off and away from the muttered conversation I already hear behind me.

"Nancy's son. What a nice looking young man. But didn't she say he was in some trouble at school?"

I don't want to know what my mother has been confessing to her new friends.

I load a paper plate with a piece of fried chicken, the white potato salad rather than the yellow potato salad, and some red Jell-O. Then I head toward the round table with people my own age.

Chloe rises from her seat and hugs me again, kind of sideways so she doesn't bump my food. She has saved a seat for me beside her. I'm barely settled before she starts introducing people, gesturing toward each one.

"Jordan, Miles, Kirsten, Leigh and Lianne—don't worry, people always get them confused—Ariadne and Iris."

I nod at each person, but my gaze stops at the girl before the last one, whose name has already slipped away from my impaired brain cells. Her long red hair looks like it couldn't be tamed with a brush the size of a rake, but she totally owns it. The strands waft around her delicate face like a halo, and her eyes shine like gems in the midst of a cloud.

I make myself look at the next girl, and then at Chloe, but I really, *really* want to ask the redheaded girl to repeat her name. I want to know if her voice is as wispy and light as everything else about her.

Sappy, I know.

"So, tell me what happened?" Chloe says, angling toward me so she speaks softly.

"Happened when? Oh! At the... place. Yeah, we found some stuff in the woods that was stolen. Paisley's doll was there, and a dress someone said belongs to the prom queen."

"Emily Schaffer?"

"I guess, yeah. It was all in this pile in a shallow hole in the woods. I didn't see anything valuable, though, other than the doll. And I guess the dress cost a lot. But nothing like jewelry or your camera. I did see a frame with the glass broken out, and I thought maybe it could have been that picture you told me about."

"Walter," she murmurs.

"Right. But the picture was gone. Anyway, someone just dumped all that stuff there. It was all damp, so I figure it must have been there since before that storm Wednesday night."

"Did you keep the frame? I'd be able to tell if it was mine."

I shake my head. "Drake Ogletree took over the whole thing. People were arguing about it, saying we should call the police, but Drake wanted to take it all to his truck."

Chloe winces. "Why would he do that?"

"He said he'd get the stuff back to the people it belonged to."

"That's not *too* suspicious."

"Right? But then he told me that he's going to call a meeting, and *I'm* supposed to ask all these people questions so I can figure out who the bad guy is."

"Duh. It's Drake!"

I chuckle. "Yeah, it sure looks that way, but I'm not entirely certain. He doesn't strike me as smart enough to pull off a kind of hoax like that. I think he just wants to be the one in charge, like he's going to be the hero and fix the problem."

"Except you'd be the one figuring it out."

"Nope. Not going to happen. I'm done playing Sherlock."

It's her turn to awkwardly laugh. "I don't blame you."

"Anyway, I thought you'd want to know, just in case it's connected to what happened at your house."

"Thanks. I guess I'll have to talk to Drake Ogletree to see if he has anything that belongs to me."

"Ooh. Sorry about that."

She shrugs and parts her lips to answer.

"Hey Chloe. Where's Connor?" a girl at the table asks.

Uh oh. I think Chloe and I might have been leaning a little too close together for our conversation. That girl's sarcastic tone suggests she's about to remind somebody that Chloe is *taken*.

"I don't know," Chloe says innocently. And she straightens in her seat to look around.

So the great future valedictorian attends this church too?

Poor Simon.

Poor me, if this dude hears that I'm making moves on his girl... which I'm not. Or I don't intend to.

I look across the table at the girl with red hair and smile, just to show that there's nothing sketchy going on here. She returns a shy smile before glancing away. She wasn't the one who spoke. Right next to her, a girl with short, dark hair wears a grin as snarky as her question.

"I haven't seen him today," Chloe answers after her search of the room.

"Convenient."

The blond girl next to her light backhands her arm. "Lianne, stop it."

A soft blush rises to Chloe's cheeks.

Time to come to her rescue. "We know each other through a mutual friend at school," I say, waving a finger between myself and Chloe. "I didn't know she comes to this church, but since this is my first time, it's nice to know someone a little bit."

"Did you just move here?" the redheaded girl asks. Her voice isn't wispy. It's a soft alto, deep for a girl and... sultry. Like my sister's voice.

I wish I could remember her name. There was an instant of thinking it sounded beautiful before it was gone.

"About a month ago."

"Where are you from?"

"Middle of Nowhere, North Carolina."

She grins. "Is that the actual name of the town? Like Between, Georgia or Toonigh? "

I grin back at her. "You might have to Google it to find out."

She doesn't pick up her phone, which is sitting beside her half-empty plate. "Play fair. I gave you actual towns."

I chuckle. "Bentley. And it really is in the middle of nowhere."

"So no movie theaters or shopping?"

"Nope. Not much to do unless you want to hang out at the Piggly Wiggly."

The other girls laugh at this.

"Hey, Piggly Wiggly is an actual place! Half the people I know got their first jobs there. Great bologna from the deli counter."

"So, are you like, a farm boy?" the snarky one asks.

"I'm an anomaly. I'm the artsy guy destined to graduate high school with a sign pinned to the back of my gown. 'Will paint for food.'"

The three girls are digging this banter, but Chloe is giving me a placid look.

"But you're here now," she says softly.

"I am. Gives me more options for street corners to stand on with my sign."

"Stop."

I shrug and shake it off.

Casual conversation fills the rest of our time at the table, and I catch myself paying closer attention to everything the girl with red hair says. A cure for my embattled crush on Chloe? Maybe. But since this other girl doesn't attend the same school as me—I learn through listening—I'd have to come back to church to talk to her again. Or connect on social media. Not very likely if I can't remember her name.

Mom has never liked to be among the last people to leave a place, and never, ever the first. She slips out in the middle, unobtrusively. So I'm not surprised when she motions to me that it's time to leave just when I was starting to feel a bit comfortable. I mutter to Chloe that I'll see her at school tomorrow, cast a wordless but hopeful glance at the beauty across from me, and rise to dump my plate in a big trash can.

Mom and I are about to walk outside, leaving through a lower exit to the back of the parking lot, when Chloe jogs to catch up with me.

She slips her hand under my elbow. "Can I talk to you a second?"

Mom sees this and nods, smiling and happy that the nice Christian girl wants to talk to me, and says she'll meet me by the van.

Chloe walks with me through the exit door, and afternoon sunlight gleams down onto her blond hair, glowing like a halo. Her somewhat shy smile seems just as angelic. In my typical sappy way, my breath catches in my throat.

But-but... Simon. And Connor. And the girl with the pretty name I can't remember.

I need to get out of here fast.

"I just wanted to say, I'm sorry about what happened in the library. With Zander."

Oh. That.

I shrug. "It's all good."

She shakes her head. "What you did that day, and what you said here today, about holding a sign on a street corner... the two things don't match. You're better than you think you are."

I shake my head gently. "You don't know me, Chloe."

"You keep saying that, but we judge people by their fruits. You tried to help Zander. And instead I sort of chastised you for it. I'm sorry for that. I was trying to explain how things are for him, and I sort of messed up telling you... you're a good person."

I suck in my lower lip as a cringy sort of feeling comes over me. It's like she's seeing through me to something deeper than my actions the other day, but every impulse of my being says she's wrong. I'm not the person she thinks I am. I'm not worthy of this compliment. I'm used to girls telling me that I'm cute or sexy or have nice eyes, whatever, but this is... awkward.

Chloe is looking at me, like she's still peering beneath the surface, and I have to turn away. I mutter, "Thanks," and shuffle along the sidewalk, watching my feet. Which I never do.

Shake it off, get back to the place where I'm surface cool and cool with it.

"Noah?"

"No, it's good. I know. Zander has got that... thing, and I don't know anything about it. It's cool."

"Aspergers," she says, strolling with me. "I don't know that much either, but he really is a sweet guy. I think if you got to know him, you would like him."

"He likes comic books."

"And westerns."

I glance up, and she's smiling. Comfortably. And I can grin back. "Vintage, authentic, westerns."

She shakes her hair back. "The others are just so phony."

"Totally phony. And cliché."

"Cliché is of the devil."

"The dictionary definition for cliché should be evil."

"Vile, foul, nasty thing. But..." She raises a finger. "I do love a well-worn cowboy hat."

"Ah. Not in my wardrobe, I'm afraid. But I do have an awesome fedora at home."

"Wear it next week."

Whoops. It's at home in North Carolina. And she's thinking I'll be back at church next week.

Maybe I can use my concussion as a convenient excuse at least for not wearing the hat. As for church... I just don't know.

"That girl," I say, to change the subject. "With the red hair? She had a really pretty name, but I can't remember it exactly."

"Ariadne Harris."

"Ari…"

"Ah-ree-ahd-nee. Harris."

I repeat it three times in my head. "Very pretty."

"She's a good friend of mine. We go riding together."

"Riding?"

"Horses."

Why does it seem every gorgeous girl I meet lately is into horses? Isn't this place a suburb of a big city?

"Would you like to come out and ride with us sometime?"

I've never ridden a horse in my life. Even though we were surrounded by farms. It was never really my style. But… "Yeah, maybe." I gesture toward the parking lot, where I see Mom waiting for me next to our van. "Gotta run. See you at school."

"Tell Simon I said hey if you see him."

Hey, as in just friends, or hey, as in she's interested? I fight the impulse to ask. If it's just friends, it would be totally awkward, and maybe she would renege on that offer to ride… horses. Am I really even considering that?

I wave and head for the van.

On the way home, we stop at the grocery store for Mom's weekly shopping. At home, I'm getting out of the van, I hear a screen door creak and slap its frame. Simon crosses the street toward me. I haven't spoken to him since Friday morning. I can't tell from his expression if he's still mad at me. He looks kind of sad. Simon helps carry our groceries in, making Mom very happy with my newest best friend. With all the bags inside, Simon taps my elbow and twitches his head toward the front door. I go back outside with him.

"Got a text from Chloe," he says.

"Oh, uh, yeah. Turns out my mother's new church is the same place Chloe goes. They did this potluck thing today, and I sat with her and her friends."

Simon's eyebrows shoot up beneath his bangs. "She didn't say that, but… you went to church?"

"Shocking but true."

"Well, her house was broken into again."

"Again?" Potential relationship drama dissolves to nothing.

"They got in the same way. Broke out her new window. Messed up her room and took her computer, but didn't go to the other rooms."

"Dang, Simon. This really is looking like a vendetta."

"It totally does. She's really upset. Worse than last time, because it does look personal." He holds his phone up. "She said she feels violated. We've got to help her, Noah."

I want to argue that we're not qualified to do this. It should be up to the police to investigate. But I know Simon is going to pull me into this. And I know it isn't going to take that much pulling.

"It is personal," I say. "So... Who has a grudge against Chloe? Who hates her?"

"Drake Ogletree," Simon says. "It's got to be him."

"Hmm. I'm not a hundred percent convinced. I'm guessing Todd McCaffrey is at least involved, if not responsible."

"What does he have against Chloe?"

I shrug. "Journalistic integrity? He said something about people telling lies."

Simon shakes his head. "Chloe doesn't lie."

"If Todd thinks she does, then in his head she does. Why do you think Drake would want to hurt her?"

Simon gives me a half-cocked grin. "Journalistic integrity? She reported on the wrestling thing with Jun last year."

I clear my throat and glance at my trailer. "Better start a new suspect chart, dude. I'll be over in a few minutes."

Simon nods, pivots like a drum majorette in a parade, and takes a few steps. Then he stops and pivots again. "I'm glad you're okay. And... I'm sorry I wasn't there for you Friday."

He's sorry? He has no reason to be.

I wave him off. "I saw you helping Chloe at the pep rally. It's no big deal. I'll fill you in later. I wave, sparing him the explanation that looks like it's about to spill from his lips, and plod up the steps of my trailer. Moving on. That's what matters to me. And now, coming up with an excuse to tell Mom that won't tip her off that I'm playing Sherlock Holmes again.

Social Media Blitz

The conversations Simon and I find online are full of speculation and arguments, and lacking in facts. But it is, as Mack the Hack might say, mildly amusing.

Lauren Harmon:	I don't care what you say, the lady next door saw a guy in a letter jacket coming out of my house, and it wasn't **Kevin**!
Drake Ogletree:	Not me! You think your all that, but your not. I'm over you, girl.
Steve McGarrett:	Pardon my butting in, but I think you need to look at motive to find your suspect.
Lauren Harmon:	His motive is revenge because I dumped him. Who are you anyway?
Drake Ogletree:	I'M OVER YOU!!!
Chelsea Monroe:	Get over yourself, **Lauren,** Drake is with me now.
Steve McGarrett:	Exactly. No motive.
Lauren Harmon:	WHO ARE YOU?

"Hawaii 5-0," Simon says.
"Todd McCaffrey," I say.
Simon nods.

Kevin Lofton:	Motive! Right! What motive would I have to break into my own girlfriend's house?
Lauren Harmon:	Besides, we were together when it happened.

Scratch Kevin from the suspect list. Not that he was on it to begin with, until Drake started his online rant saying that it could have been him.

Chelsea Monroe:	Maybe Kevin's trying to make himself look innocent while he breaks into other people's houses.
Drake Ogletree;	I didnt do it!
Kevin Lofton:	Oh, please. That's ridiculous, Chelsea. Besides, how would I have Drake's letter jacket?
Drake Ogletree:	How you even know it was my jacket? That old lady don't see so good.

Even with auto correct at his disposal, Drake is inherently illiterate.

Steve McGarrett:	Evidence, my friends.
Lauren Harmon:	Shut up Steve! Whoever you are. I'm blocking you right now.
Chelsea Monroe:	Besides, if Drake took your stuff, why would he turn around and give it back to you?
Kevin Lofton:	Because he's guilty!
Drake Ogletree:	We found it in the woods. Everyone is getting there stuff back.
Kevin Lofton:	YOU found it, you mean. How did you know it was there?

"Good point," Simon says, whispering as if these people could hear us talking as we read their messages from two hours ago. "Drake was there at a rather convenient time."

"Yeah, but Daniel ran into the woods and found the stuff. Drake wasn't the first one there."

"Why was he even at the snake pit at all?"

I shrug. "He wanted to watch me get the crap kicked out of me."

"Dude is not right in the head."

Drake Ogletree:	I didn't. I was there for a fight. Anyone could put it there.
Chelsea Monroe:	That's true. I was with him. So there, Lauren.
Drake Ogletree:	Someone is setting me up.

"Quite possible," I say.

"I don't know," Simon says. "He took all that stuff with him. Which means the police never saw it. Looks to me more like he's covering for himself now that he knows Lauren's neighbor saw him. Could just be coincidence that Daniel ran that way."

I grunt at this. It is logical. But my gut says it's Todd. Who was also there to watch the fun.

Chelsea Monroe:	Is that guy, Steve still following?
Lauren Harmon:	I blocked him.

"He'll be back," I mutter.

Chelsea Monroe:	He said we need evidence. There's no evidence against Drake.

"Circumstantial, maybe. And a possible witness," Simon says.

Drake Ogletree:	We need a meeting. Everyone who got robed needs to meet ant figure this out.

"Do ants wear robes?" I ask.

Simon giggles.

Lauren Harmon:	So you know everyone who had stolen stuff? Really, Drake?
Drake Ogletree:	You, Emily, and that weird manga girl.

"And Chloe," Simon says.

I don't tell Simon that Drake already asked me to be at his *meeting* to *ask questions*. I told myself I wouldn't come within a million miles of Drakes meeting, but it might be kind of entertaining, watching these populars point fingers at each other and get nowhere.

Lauren Harmon:	Why did you take something from her, Drake?
Drake Ogletree:	I didn't!

Drake follows with a bunch of expletives that a couple of "church-going" guys like me and Simon shouldn't be reading. I laugh at it. Simon rolls his eyes.

The rest of their conversation degenerates from there, with the same kind of half civil half hateful chatting.

"Were these people friends once?" I ask.

"All in the jock and cheerleader crowd."

"Any football players?"

"Kevin. But he graduated."

"College?"

"I don't know *everything*, Noah."

"So look on his profile page."

Simon's fingers flick over the screen of his phone to bring up the page and a selfie photo of a smug-looking guy wearing football gear and a red jersey. Under his arm is a helmet with a black and white emblem. G for Georgia.

"UGA," Simon says.

"Bingo."

Home Again?

It's suppertime, but the trailer is dark when I get there, and nothing appears to have happened in the kitchen since we got home, in spite of the fact that Mom said she might make orange chicken, one of her best recipes. She could be resting. She could have changed her mind. But a snuffle and a cough from her bedroom tells me it's not that simple.

The accordion door is halfway open. I go and peek into the room. Mom sits on the edge of her bed, pinching the bridge of her nose between her fingers.

"Hey. You okay?" I ask.

She gets migraines sometimes. I didn't appreciate that before like I do now, since I've experienced them so much with my concussion. Like you're going blind and your head is about to explode. I wonder if it would be okay for her to take some of my medication.

She sniffs again and raises her head, shakes her hair back from her face. "We're going out to eat."

"Okay..."

We can't afford it. She'd be the first one to remind me of this. So something isn't right.

"What's going on?" I ask.

"I have some decisions to make," she says, standing.

"About?"

"Us. All of us. This family. Get your jacket and let's go."

I follow her to the living room, where she snatches her purse up from the corner of the couch where it lives.

"Mom. What's going on?"

"Get your jacket. Come on."

"Mom..."

"Your sister moved back home. She had a fight with Julien, and his parents said she couldn't stay there anymore. I don't want to talk about it, okay? I have a lot of thinking to do."

I go to my room to get my jacket, but it's like I'm walking through wet glue, the air choking and smothering me, my limbs slogging through goo.

Naomi has moved home.

Leverage to make Mom want to go back too.

Chapter  9

Monday... And So It Begins

I stand at the bathroom mirror, shirtless, looking at the hideous green bruise that covers the middle right side of my torso. A deep breath tells me I'm not finished healing inside either.

My father didn't do this to me, but I want to blame him anyway. I wouldn't be living here if it hadn't been for him. I wouldn't have been in that car accident with a man who might have intended to kill me.

I also want to blame my sister for the situation I'm in now. The last time I talked to her she said she would never go back home. What kind of control does Dad have over all of us?

Last night my mother cried out in the open. She said leaving him was the worst mistake she'd ever made. We should have stayed, she said. We could have worked it all out... she said.

All the blood that night, all the yelling of so many nights before, all the escalating dysfunction of the years leading up to that night, and now, *"we could have worked it out."*

I wish I could have held her and told her everything would be okay. But I couldn't. Because I know it won't be.

I always thought my sister was so much stronger than me.

I can't go back to North Carolina. Not now. Not this way.

It would be the worst mistake of *my* life.

After throwing on one of the five shirts I own and one of two hoodies, I leave my room to find Simon waiting for me, acting all jittery, pacing next to our front door.

"What's up?" I ask, like a greeting rather than a real question.

"Another break-in," he blurts.

I widen my eyes and slant them twice toward my mother, trying to signal Simon to shut up. Too late.

"A break-in? Where?" Mom says. "Not here in the trailer park, is it?"

We've never assumed this trailer park was a safe place to live, but evidence of its lack of security will definitely give Mom another reason to leave.

Simon purses his lips and then turns more casually toward Mom. "No, ma'am. It was on the local news report this morning. There's been a bunch of break-ins up at Riverbend Estates. This one happened at the home of a city councilman, Anthony Valentino. His son used to go to our school."

"Oh. Did you know the boy?"

"Not personally."

"So why is it of such concern to you?" She looks from Simon to me, scowling.

I shrug. "It isn't to me."

"It's just, um…" Simon says.

I help him out. "There's been a bunch of break-ins, people at school. Everyone is talking about it online."

Mom takes a sip of her coffee then presses a fingertip to her lips. "Last week… didn't you say something about a friend of yours who had a break-in? Simon?"

"Yes, ma'am. Chloe. Someone stole her camera."

"And you think all these break-ins are connected?"

"Um. Chloe is my friend, and…"

"That's the girl you were talking to at church yesterday, wasn't it, Noah?" She levels a glare at me. "Tell me this doesn't have anything to do with you."

"I just said—"

"The police came here looking for stolen property. Now, you tell me right now, to my face, that it doesn't have anything to do with you."

"It doesn't! I told you, that was Paisley trying to blame me after someone stole her doll."

"And does she live in the big subdivision too?"

"Honestly, Mom, I don't know where Paisley lives."

I'm certain there's a connection. Paisley's doll was in the pile of stuff we found at the snake pit. What I don't want Mom to figure out is that I know anything about it. And that Simon and I spent a couple of hours yesterday afternoon scouring social media for information and making charts with lines and circles trying to figure out what the connections are between Chloe, Paisley, a prom queen, Drake, and Todd. All those lines and circles kind of added up to a big zero in the end. No clear motives. No evidence, other than Kevin's accusation and Todd's cryptic monologue.

"I promise you, it wasn't me," I say firmly.

"Fine. So, the police will figure it out, especially if it involves a government official. You—" She jabs a finger toward me. "Are not to be involved at all. Do you understand? Noah?"

I sigh and spread my arms. "It's got nothing to do with me."

Grabbing my backpack, I lead the way out to the van and hiss a warning to Simon as we're getting in. It's not that I *want* to play Sherlock again and figure out who's breaking into people's houses. Paisley's got her stupid doll back and, besides Chloe, I don't know any of the other people who lost stuff.

And, again, I've got enough problems of my own to worry about.

As we're heading out of the trailer park, I think about something Simon confessed to me yesterday. He'd actually been waiting for me to come home when he received the text from Chloe. He'd been beating himself up since Friday for being unable to convince me not to fight with Daniel, and for not going with me when it happened—or didn't happen. Years ago, when he was in middle school, he and that guy Zander were friends. A detail that doesn't surprise me at all, because Simon's that kind of caring person. But he's always been undersized, and when some kids were mercilessly picking on Zander, Simon ran away. He was scared and abandoned a friend who needed him. They haven't been friends since.

He felt like he did that again when he volunteered to help Chloe and Connor at the pep rally, even though he knew I'd be facing Daniel.

After confessing this, it didn't matter to him when I said I can take care of myself and the fight amounted to a lot of nothing—apart from finding the stolen stuff. What mattered to Simon was that he let me down.

I told him it's no problem. But Simon's nothing if not loyal. And now he's really worried about Chloe, that someone is trying to hurt her.

I can't let Simon deal with this alone.

As for Mom's warning... if we find any connection between these break-ins, we'll just tell the police. No big deal.

When we get to school, Simon is eager to find Chloe. I follow him to her locker, and she's just walking away from it. She sees us coming and jogs our way, and then I'm stunned as she crashes into me with a hug. She breaks away quickly and hugs Simon as well, but I catch a hurt glint in his eyes.

Maybe she's just a hugger. It doesn't mean anything, right?

She lingers in Simon's embrace, and I breathe out relief. As she lets him go, she dabs at one of her eyes. "Did he tell you?" she says, looking at me.

"Yes."

"Noah says it's got to be personal," Simon says, pulling her attention back. "If we can find a connection between you and the other people, then maybe we can figure out who's doing it."

"Personal." She sniffs, and her smile is sarcastic. "Yeah, I'd say so. Whoever it is brought my picture back."

"Walter Cronkite?" I ask.

She nods. "Yes. And all ripped up."

"Drake." Simon growls. "He had all that stuff."

Except that the photograph wasn't in the picture frame. Even so, my mother is right. The police need to be in on this. Because ripping up that photo and returning it looks like more than vengeance. It looks like a threat. Although Simon has a lot of good reasons to think Drake is behind it all, I have lots of doubts. To me, a ripped-up photograph of Walter Cronkite looks like the vindictive work of a psychopathic hacker. I just need solid proof.

"Do you live in Riverbend Estates?" I ask Chloe.

"No. We live near the county line, north of here." she says.

"Does Paisley?"

Chloe is confused, and Simon shrugs cluelessly.

"Why?" Chloe asks.

Simon tells her about what he heard on the news this morning.

And just a few seconds into his report, she gasps. "Valentino? As in Bryce Valentino? Last year's prom king?" Suddenly she looks a little pale and she presses a hand against her mouth for a moment.

"What's wrong?" Simon asks.

"It's... it's probably nothing. I mean, I don't even know him personally. But... I need to look into something. Guys, if I can get my mother to give you both a ride home this afternoon, can you meet me in the media center after school?"

"Sure," Simon says before I have a chance to open my mouth. "I don't have to work today."

"Ah, yeah. I can," I say, although it might be better if I let Simon have all the space he needs with this girl. But I really want to know why the name of last year's prom king made her look like she just realized she forgot to study for a test. Plus, getting access to a computer would make the *other* research I started last night a lot easier.

I give Simon some space now, waving to him and the girl of his dreams and heading to my locker. As I'm making my way around other rushing students and a loud argument between a couple of girls, my thoughts are on that picture of Walter Cronkite. I looked him up on my phone over the weekend. Old dude. At least he was by the time I was born. He'd been a reporter during World War II and the moon landing. He reported on the murder of John Lennon. People trusted him so much that they called him Uncle Walter.

If someone would tear up that photo and then go back to the scene of the crime to make sure Chloe got it back in pieces, he was trying to make a point.

Todd McCaffrey said something like people who lie about him will pay for it. Did Chloe write something about Todd for the school newspaper? She probably wrote stuff about Drake, and about Kevin, since they're both athletes. And she probably reported about the guy who was crowned prom king. But did she lie?

I sit down in my first class and notice Mia taking her seat at the front. She glances at me and gives me the smallest of smiles. Is she with that guy Jun now? Do I even care?

A Psychological Game...

I'm pretty good at poker. People have a hard time bluffing me or telling when I'm bluffing them. I can spot their "tells" very soon after we sit down at the table to play. I observe, and I'm patient. I can also bury my excitement when I figure out something about them.

That same kind of anticipatory excitement simmers inside me as I walk into my psychology class. I've been waiting for this all morning, even plotting out what I'm going to say. I pretty much missed the lectures in both world history and algebra because I replayed the conversation at Waffle House, analyzing Todd's bluffs, calls, and raises and planning my response.

Todd doesn't disappoint me. He's waiting at my desk at the back of the classroom. And he's grinning. Like me, he's ready to play.

"Have you considered my proposal?" he says, stealing the first hand.

I open with a bluff, playing like I don't care. "Did you propose something?"

"In a manner of speaking. There could be some profit for you in the game."

Profit? As in selling stolen goods? That kind of profit? Somehow that seems too mundane for Todd.

"Really. What's in it for me?"

"You need me, Dickerson. I've got connections."

Other students trickle into the room. What I really want from Todd is for him to show his hand, but with other ears close by, he's going to play it close to the vest.

I set my books down on my desk and rub my chin like I'm considering his offer.

Todd moves closer to me. "Your mother needs a lawyer, right?"

For a split second my dispassionate façade drops. How could Todd possibly know that? This private detail goes beyond hacking. Unless... he's just guessing.

Some guy catches his foot on the leg of a desk and staggers, dragging the desk with him. I use this to glance away.

"I got connections," Todd says, while other people are laughing at the klutz.

I chuckle. "Do you? What, your uncle's girlfriend's sister's boss?"

Todd hesitates. Just a half second, enough to tell me that he hasn't got the hand he's pretending to have.

"My associate," he says. "It's his father."

File this away. Don't, don't, don't forget it! Todd has an *associate*.

"Hmm." I nod my head once.

Mr. Danson enters the room, so I'm going to have to go all in on this conversation or cut it off midway.

"I need more, dude. You're going to have to tell me what's in it for me and what you intend to do."

He lifts his shoulders like the answer is simple. "I told you. Profit. Connections. And you get to use that smooth manner of yours to make friends and influence people."

"I need more than cliché's here. What's the game we're playing?"

"High stakes truth or dare."

The final bell rings, and Todd edges away toward his desk.

"Who's the target," I say just loud enough for him to hear.

He grins. "We're friends, right, Rhys Le Guin? Keep your eyes open."

I know exactly what he's talking about, but the idea of accepting the Facebook friend request Todd sent me over the weekend makes my skin crawl. He's a hacker. I really don't want to give him access to more of my personal life.

Doing so, though, will also give me access to more of Todd's activities, which could be very useful. He's practically inviting me to take a front row seat.

Rhys Le Guin is my own sort of fake account anyway. One I created so I could be online and my father wouldn't find me. If I do what Todd wants, I'll have to shuffle my contacts around, maybe make yet another account so I can talk to my siblings and close friends outside of Todd's reach. I work on that during lunch.

I pull my phone out as I'm sitting down, tuck it under the desk so the teacher won't see. Moving my thumbs quickly over my cracked screen, I open the app and accept the friend request. Drake's too. Then I put my phone away without looking at Todd.

But I can feel him staring at me.

He might think my acceptance means I'm folding, that he's pulling me into his game, but I'm really raising the stakes in mine.

After School… Research

Chloe and Simon are already in the media center when I arrive, just pulling a second chair over to a computer so they can both see the screen. I stand behind them as they're sitting down.

"So, what are we looking for?" I ask.

Chloe twists around to look up and me and quickly touches a finger to her lips. There are still plenty of people in the room, a little more active and noisy now that the last bell has rung. Chances are none of them are paying attention to us, but Chloe's hush warning must mean she's got something specific in mind, and not a general search for social media chatter like Simon and I did over the weekend.

"Pull up a chair," Simon says.

"Actually, I have some research I need to do too," I say. "I'll sit at another one. Just let me know if you find something you want me to see."

Doing personal research at home on my phone with the cracked screen was not optimal or a great idea, because Mom could pick up my phone and discover something. So I slide over to another computer two machines down from Simon and Chloe.

Which, conveniently, gives Simon some space with his girl.

That thought tugs at me for a moment, and a face comes into my mind. Ariadne, with her cloud of red hair and her pink lips, curved just slightly in the little smile she left in my heart.

Oh, how I wish I had the luxury just to dream about that smile for a while and think that maybe I'd see it again. That maybe someday it would rise up to light her eyes as she says my name.

Or that it would happen that way with *someone*.

"Newsletter archives," Chloe mutters. "And then we'll search for Drake and Kevin."

"And Todd McCaffrey," I add while logging on.

Chloe turns a questioning look toward me.

"He's in this. Some way, somehow. He's practically daring me to figure out how."

Simon whispers to Chloe what I told him about Todd's claim to be my Moriarty, and how we suspect he was the mysterious Hawaii 5-0 detective in the online argument between Drake and Lauren over the weekend.

"If there's an argument to be had," Chloe says, "it's a good bet that Todd will be lurking around. If not starting it and then watching while everyone else fights."

"Have you ever written an article about him?" I ask.

"No. Not directly, anyway. But he's been involved in things that I wrote about."

I point toward their computer. "Start there. Look for anything that he might take offense to and consider a lie about him."

They get to work, and so do I. First, I open my Facebook account, just to have it ready if I need to jump to an *innocent* screen. Then I open a browser.

Freedom.

The word has been in the back of my thoughts for days, but almost like a ringing in my ears since Mom's outburst last night. But I want to look up a more legal term, one that my bruised brain struggles to spell right on my first attempt.

Emancipation.

If I were free, I wouldn't be in the middle of the arguments between my parents. I wouldn't be a bargaining chip or a tool they use to hurt each other. It almost worked for Naomi. But I want to be stronger. And I want it *now*.

Google finds the right spelling for me, and I follow up by searching for the laws for Georgia and North Carolina. Question number one: can I do this without having to go back to North Carolina?

I click on a website for Georgia, and as I read down the requirements and processes, my heart beats faster. My fingers, hovering above the computer mouse, tremble. I try to wet my lips, but my mouth and tongue are dry.

It's one thing to think about something, another to actually take this first step.

I can back out. Close the tab and forget the whole idea.

But I push myself to read.

There's a list of requirements. I need my birth certificate. How can I get that without asking my mother? And wouldn't it still be back home? We didn't exactly pack anything before we left.

Ability to manage his or her financial affairs.

That means getting a job. I can do that. I smirk at the notion that Simon could set me up at Grumpy's. Would they pay enough there that I could keep living at the trailer?

Ability to manage his or her personal and social affairs.

Hmm. I wonder if they'll look at that little car accident I was in during an attempted kidnapping. Or that I was hauled into the principal's office three times during my first two weeks at this school.

Names of adults who believe that emancipation is in the child's best interest. Physician, psychologist, school counselor, teacher, lawyer, cop...

None of the above. I got no one.

Maybe Principal Manning? Or that woman from DFCS?

Who am I kidding? There's nothing about this idea that looks feasible, and nothing about it that won't break my mother's heart into a million pieces.

There's a movement to my left and I jump. I click, and the page is gone. Simon is standing there, looking startled at my reaction. But then his big eyes droop a little, and I think he might have caught a glimpse of the blue heading on that webpage.

"What's up?" I say. "Find something?"

He holds his phone out to me. I take it and look at the photo it displays. Drake Ogletree and a guy who looks slightly familiar to me. He's got one arm resting on the shoulder of the other guy and points at him with his free hand.

"What's this?" I ask.

"Drake and Kevin Lofton. This picture was in the school newspaper with an article talking about the people running for prom court. Kevin ran against Bryce Valentino for king, and Drake supported him."

"Okay..."

"Which means they were friends, even though Kevin dated Drake's ex-girlfriend and even took her to the prom."

"They're not friends now."

"Right. You have to wonder why."

I shrug. "Maybe they had an argument at the prom. Or over the summer."

"Connor and I were at the prom," Chloe says, leaning forward to look around Simon. "I don't remember any arguments. I saw them all sitting at the same table."

Chloe was at the prom with Connor? Poor, poor Simon. Unless her phrasing—they were *at* the prom rather than they *went to* the prom—implies something else. Maybe on assignment for the school newspaper?

Pieces click together in my head.

"Prom. All these burglaries could be connected to the prom. The news said someone broke into the house of the guy who won prom king, and the queen's dress was in the stash found in the woods." I move over to Chloe's computer and lean my hand on the desk to look at the screen. "It would be a pretty big coincidence if everyone who had stuff stolen also attended the prom. The police might not put that together right away until they start asking people if they know the other victims."

Chloe shakes her head without looking at me. "They didn't ask me about anyone else."

"What exactly did they do at your house?"

"The first time, they only took a report. We thought it was just a random break-in. A crime of opportunity, since no one was home. The second time, they took pictures and looked for more evidence."

"Fingerprints?"

"No."

"I'll bet they took fingerprints at Valentino's house," Simon says, his tone dark.

Implication, the police would do more for a city councilman whose house was trashed than for an ordinary person. On the computer screen in front of me is a newspaper article about the break-in at Councilman Valentino's house "up the hill" in Riverbend Estates. The house photograph on Chloe's screen looks like a freakin' mansion.

I rub my forehead. "Tell me again, does this Valentino guy play football? Is he going to UGA?"

"No and no," Chloe says. Her voice is soft with a tiny tremor.

I look down at her. "Are you okay? What are you thinking?"

She turns sad eyes toward me. "I'm thinking that I almost don't want to go home today. I'm thinking that I can't sleep in my own room because someone was in there. The idea that it was someone who knows who I am doesn't help at all."

Simon slides back into the seat beside her. "We're going to figure it out," he says, his hand on her shoulder.

She glances at him and up at me again, her eyes starting to tear.

I nod. I'm in.

We give her a moment, the three of us staring at that rich family's house. And then Simon says, "Our prime suspects are the two guys who haven't been victims. Drake and Kevin. And they're blaming each other."

"Which has all the signs of Todd McCaffrey's meddling," I add.

"He is a meddler," Simon says. "And that had to be him trolling the conversation the other day."

"That guy is a thorn in my side," Chloe says.

Bingo. But I want to hear her reason.

"We can hardly post anything in the newspaper without him saying we got it wrong, somehow. He got kicked off the newspaper staff his sophomore year because he was trying to use it to spread gossip and false information."

"Now that's interesting," I say.

"I'll show you," she says. She clicks away from one website to another, showing the Pirates' logo at the top of the page. The story she brings up has to do with the Homecoming game last Friday night. She scrolls down to reader comments, and there is Todd's name in all its glory, all caps and including his nickname.

TODD MACK MCCAFFREY: I wonder how many of the opponents' players had bets on this game?

"What does that mean?" I ask. "Who cares about the other team's players?"

"He's referring to something that happened last year," Chloe said. "Kevin Lofton was accused of taking a payoff to cheat on a game, so the Pirates would lose."

"Kevin Lofton? *Our* Kevin?"

Chloe shakes her head. "It was a misunderstanding. Jun Seoh thought he heard him talking in the locker room. But Kevin was cleared."

"Jun Seoh!" I catch myself since I practically yelled this. "Oh, man. That's it! That's a motive. Dang!" I thump my forehead lightly with the heel of my hand. "Stupid concussion. I forgot. Jun's house was broken into too. Mia said his wrestling trophies were stolen, and there was at least one trophy at the dump site last week."

"And Drake took them all," Simon says.

Chloe looks confused. "It was just a misunderstanding. We didn't even write anything about it. But Todd found out somehow, and he posted some things on social media."

"He told me he was going to take down a football player from UGA. That's got to be Kevin."

"Seems like that would give Kevin a motive to do something to Todd, not the other way around," Simon says.

"So Kevin is breaking into people's houses?" Chloe says. "It still doesn't make sense. Yeah, maybe he'd want to do something to Todd for spreading lies, and maybe Jun, although I think Jun apologized for it. But why me? Why his own girlfriend?"

I hate that I might have to consider that Drake was right about something.

"Look at it the other way," I say. "Todd is trying to make Kevin look guilty, or Drake, or both of them. He's breaking in places and making it look like they did it. That's why he said, 'look at the evidence.' Why would he even say that if he didn't know what evidence was there?"

I look around the media center. There are fewer people around than when we first got here, but we still need to keep our voices down.

"Give me a minute," I say, and fall back into my own seat. I pull out my phone and log onto Facebook as Rhys Le Guin. I don't have all the connections at this school that Simon does, and if Todd is using different aliases to carry out his current scam, I won't be able to find those posts. But he wanted me to go on his personal page. There had to be a reason. Like he invited me to find something.

I'm scrolling slowly down his posts, almost all of which tempt me to click on them to see the entire conversations because he's clearly into inciting debate. Then I find this thing that looks like a meme, but is too specific and too obscure at the same time to be something Todd merely shared from another source.

CHEATER-CHEATER
STILL A PUMPKIN EATER
WHETHER PIRATE OR BULLDOG
THE HALLOWEEN GAME LOG
WILL RECORD A LOSS
BUT YOU WILL WIN

It's horrible. Clearly Todd doesn't have Ivan around anymore to help with poetry. And Halloween is next Thursday, so there won't be any football games. Wrestling matches? I have no clue. I wonder what Drake would say about this. No one has bothered to comment on it, though.

I show it to Chloe and Simon. They both scowl at it like it doesn't make any sense, but then Chloe nods.

"This is about Kevin," she says. "And I remember that Todd posted something at Halloween last year about a pirate wearing a mask."

"So... how is Drake involved in any of this?" Simon asks.

"Maybe he's not. Maybe Todd is using him as a fall guy."

Simon shakes his head. "I think it's between Drake and Kevin, and Todd is just stirring things up the way he always does."

"But why?" Chloe asks. "I mean, obviously Todd is messing around, but why would Drake be breaking into people's houses and blaming Kevin?"

"He'd need to blame someone," Simon says. "Why not someone who was accused of cheating? And he's using Todd to bring up the cheating thing again, to make sure Kevin looks bad."

"So you think Todd and Drake are working together?" I say.

Using my new connection with Todd, I send him a quick private message. One I'm sure he'll understand.

NOAH: Kevin Lofton?

It takes only seconds for him to respond.

TODD: Nice try.

I show this to the other two. They're on the edges of their seats as I type in another message.

NOAH: Who then?

TODD: Play the game. I'm not a cheater.

"Cheater," Chloe whispers. And she's got that look on her face, like something personal is worrying her.

During lunch today, I told her about my conversation with Todd. But not everything. Not the part where Todd hinted someone else would go down besides the football player. Someone who lied. I remember how scared Mia was when Ivan was putting threatening notes in her locker. I don't want Chloe to be afraid like that. Not unless I know for sure that she's in any danger.

Of course, having her house bedroom broken into twice is doing more damage than anything I'm withholding from her.

"What do you know about Todd," I ask her softly, extending my hand to almost touch her.

Simon is looking at me. Not in a jealous way, but expectantly. I let him see me take a deep breath, like I'm waiting too.

Chloe's eyes are turned toward our hands, hers on her knees, mine just an inch higher. "Nothing for certain, other than what you already know. But... he said he's not a cheater." She twitches her chin to indicate my phone still in my other hand. "I don't think he's telling the truth."

I snort at this. "When does he ever tell the truth? The guy lives and breathes fake news."

She shrugs, apologetically it seems.

"Tell me..."

"The thing is, I don't know any of this for certain, and I don't want to speak falsely about someone."

"But..."

"Connor."

"Is he the one telling people that Connor helped people cheat on the SATs?"

She jiggles her head, no. "I mean, he might be. I don't know. And Connor wasn't involved in that, but he was investigating it. And he suspected..." She juts her chin toward my phone again.

I nod slowly to indicate that I understand. "Which... gives him—not Connor, but *him*—a motive."

"Yeah, but," Simon inserts, "that doesn't have anything to do with stuff getting stolen. We could be talking about two completely different things. Maybe a football player was involved in the test cheating. In that message Todd said nice try, not good job."

Chloe hisses softly and glances around the room.

"I'm just saying," Simon adds.

He could be right.

I rub my forehead, wishing that my memory of that conversation with Todd was clearer. Did he ever mention anything about stolen property? I can't remember. Could my desire to help Chloe, and to nail Todd with something—*anything*—mean I got the whole thing wrong?

"Okay. Prom. That seems to be the connection. Was Paisley there too?"

Both Simon and Chloe return blank stares. They don't know.

"I can look through the pictures Connor and I took for the yearbook, but I don't know if I'd even recognize her," Chloe finally says.

"Hmm. Guess I'm going to have to ask her," I say, smirking.

"There's something else I need to tell you." She pauses, looking down at her knees again. "I shot some video when they named the prom king and queen. We were posting things on the school's Twitter account so people who didn't go to prom could see."

Chloe stops herself again. My mind wanders a bit. If she was taking pictures at the prom, maybe she wasn't there with Connor as a date. Maybe it was just work.

"I posted a video of Bryce receiving his crown. I didn't check it first to make sure it was even good. I just... posted it."

"Why is that a bad thing? Was he making a goofy face or something?"

"His zipper was down," Simon answers.

A laugh bursts through my closed lips. I put my fist against my mouth to stop it.

Neither Chloe nor Simon are laughing.

"It got worse," she says. "People started teasing him. His father complained to the school board. I got fired from the newspaper and yearbook staff for the rest of the year. I'm on probation this year, and if I go on an assignment, I have to work with Connor."

"That seems pretty harsh. It wasn't your fault his pants were unzipped."

"I didn't check the video first. That was my fault. And then people saw the video online and shared it. It's all over the place now."

"Ooh." I feel a stab of sympathy for the guy.

Simon is rubbing Chloe's shoulders.

"He graduated, and no one talks about it much now," she says. "I thought I'd never have to think about that night again. Now..."

I sigh. "Well, at least we can assume this Bryce guy didn't take your camera and computer, since his house was broken into too."

"I really don't want to see him again. If Drake puts a meeting together, he'll probably be there."

"You don't have to," Simon says.

Chloe shifts away from him and stands up. "Yes, I do. If this is how we're going to figure out who's behind the break-ins, then I need to be there. That doesn't mean I like it, though."

Brave girl.

Rather than frowning from being rebuffed, Simon looks up at Chloe with adoring eyes.

Chapter

Tuesday... Drake Versus Lunch

Chloe, Simon, and I are forming a sort of huddle at the table in the cafeteria. We can't help it that Jeremy and Matt are listening in, so we explained the situation in as little detail as possible. Jeremy is curious, but Matt rolls his eyes and reminds us that someone is going to get into trouble again.

Chloe reminds him that someone already has. Her.

We're looking at the messages on Chloe's phone. Last night she sent texts to some girls she knows who were at the prom.

LAUREN HARMON:	Yes! How did you find out about that? Someone stole some of my jewelry and my prom dress. It was Drake. My neighbor saw him leaving my house.
CHLOE THOMAS:	Anything else stolen in the house?
LAUREN HARMON:	Some stuff Kevin gave me. A big pelican he bought for me at the beach after prom.

"She loves pelicans," Chloe murmurs before tapping her phone to bring up another message.

"There was a stuffed animal at the snake pit. I think it was a pelican."

EMILY SCHAFFER: I didn't know anything happened until Drake brought my dress to me. Mom came home one day and found the back door open, but we just thought it was my little brother. My closet door was open too, but I didn't think anything about it then.

"Interesting," I say. "He made a mess at the other places. Maybe whoever it is actually likes this girl?"

"She was the prom queen," Chloe says.

JENNIFER DURBIN: No. What's going on?

Nothing to see here. But Chloe doesn't immediately click away from the message.

"She went to the prom with Mark Romero. Since he was the team quarterback, I thought I'd ask her.

MIA PARK: Jun's house was broken into. His trophies were stolen but nothing else was touched. Drake told me they were found in the woods, and he gave them to me to give to Jun.

I feel a momentary pang at the sight of Mia's name. The perpetually hormonal part of my brain says I should ask Chloe if she'll put in a good word for me. But no. Mia's got her wrestler back, and I'd rather ask Chloe about the redheaded girl currently of my dreams.

"We already knew that," I say, so Chloe will move on.

JASMINE MALONE: Not at my house, but someone stole my trumpet out of my car. My dad is making me pay for it!

"That could be related or not," Chloe says. "She's good friends with both Emily and Lauren."

"Nothing saying this person has to do everything the same way each time," Simon says. "Did you see a trumpet case at the pit?"

I shake my head. "I didn't see anything that looked expensive."

"Except prom dresses. And that doll." Chloe points out. "I sent messages to some other people, but they haven't answered yet. I don't have any connection to Bryce, but I did text the girl he went to prom with, Holly Pelletier. She hasn't gotten back to me yet. Did you talk to Paisley?"

I've been procrastinating on that. I glance toward the Manganites' table, but I feel as physically capable of getting out of this chair as I would trying to lift a Hum Vee.

"Something I thought about last night," Chloe goes on. "Todd was at the prom. Since you think he might be involved, maybe we should check with the girl he was with?"

"Todd actually got a girl to go out with him?" I say.

Simon knocks on the table and we both look at him. He's staring toward the center of the room... where one of our prime suspects is strutting toward us. Drake looks angry. I scoot my chair back a little and get my feet planted firmly on the floor, just in case I have to jump up and run.

Drake inserts himself between Jeremy and Matt, and Matt falls on the floor trying to get out of his way. No one laughs. Drake slams both hands on the table, seeming not to notice Matt's bailout.

"My championship ring is gone!" Drake barks. "And I can't find my letter jacket. Someone is setting me up, and I'm fixing to whomp on whoever it is."

I put my hands up. A risky move but... "Whoa, slow down a moment. When is the last time you saw your ring?"

"You ain't gettin' this, milky boy. If someone took my jacket, that means they could-a impersoned me when they broke into Lauren's house."

"Impersonated?" Jeremy says.

"Yeah, whatever. Look, we gotta figure this mess out."

"When did you last see the ring?"

"Yesterday. I don't wear it during wrestling practice."

"So it was here? At school?"

"Right. And whoever took my jacket must-a got it out of my truck."

"When's the last time you saw that?"

"Weeks!" he booms. Like this proves something.

What it kind of proves to me is that Drake isn't careful with his stuff. But the missing letter jacket is interesting, since Lauren said that's what her neighbor saw.

Or Drake could be covering up by saying, now, that his jacket was stolen. Why didn't he say something earlier? Like at the snake pit?

"I'm callin' a meeting. Starbucks, tonight. I'm callin' everyone."

How does he know who *everyone* is?

"So who do I need to talk to? That manga chick?"

He's talking to me, staring right at me. Waiting for me to answer.

"Yes, and Lauren Harmon," Chloe says. She's standing behind me, her phone in her hand. "Emily Schaffer, Jun Seoh, Jasmine Malone, Bryce Valentino, and me."

Drake's face pinches. "Half those people ain't even at this school anymore."

Less than half, but it's probably not a good bet that Drake can do math.

"You might want to talk to anyone you know who was at the prom last year," Chloe says. "That's the only connecting factor we've been able to find so far."

Drake points at her. "Prom. Right. Except I didn't go to the prom. So why me?"

No one has an answer for him. In fact, I think we all just assumed that he was there, being that he seems to enjoy being the center of attention.

"Whatever," he says. "You'll figure it out. I'll ask around. Anyway, y'all be at Starbucks tonight at seven. Sharp. Right?" Drake grins, smacks the table one last time, and turns away. Jeremy swivels around in his chair to watch him stomp away, and Matt comes crawling back from wherever he hid.

Simon starts a slow hyperventilation. "I have to work tonight."

I reach across Chloe's empty chair to squeeze his shoulder. "Don't worry about it. He's not going to come after you for not showing up at his dumb meeting. I doubt anyone will show up. Particularly the dude's ex-girlfriend and the *two* guys who have dated her since."

"My mother has an unbridled passion for Starbucks," Chloe says. "She can take us there."

"Seriously?" I turn in my seat. "You want to go?"

Her face is as serious as I've ever seen it during our short acquaintance. "I'm not going to let him, or anyone else, scare me from getting to the truth."

As we're leaving the cafeteria, Simon grabs me by the arm. "You've got to go tonight. Please. Make sure nothing happens to her."

I kind of think that Chloe can take care of herself, but I don't say it. Simon's love for the girl is so desperate.

Tuesday Night... Meeting of the Social Elite

After supper, when there's less than an hour before Drake's meeting is supposed to start, it hits me that I'm going to a coffee shop to converse with people who are *way* above my station in life. Populars. Jocks and cheerleaders. Teenagers with money.

Why did I even agree to this?

And what am I going to wear?

I never used to worry about what these kinds of people thought of me. I was above them, in the sense that I didn't play the social butterfly games. People either liked me or they didn't, and I was okay with that, as long as there were girls among the ones that liked me. I think I'd convinced myself that at least people respected me for knowing who I was and what I wanted. Of course, most of them didn't know the truth, that I was very good at putting on an act of artsy indifference. And if my self-confidence cracked a little, hey, emo angst is an acceptable part of the artistic personae. But there's another truth I didn't realize until I came here, and maybe not even until tonight, that even when my family life was at its worst, there was a feeling of security in being around the familiar places and faces. Even if everything I said was hiding a lie, I could find people to hang out with who accepted me. My brother and sister, my buddy Stuart, and a girl or two.

Starbucks with the populars? I'm going to stick out as an intruder, if only because my clothes don't have designer labels.

I've got on the pair of skinny jeans I wore my last night in North Carolina. And I've got the white button-down shirt I wore to church on Sunday. It hasn't been washed yet, but it doesn't stink. I leave it untucked. The weather has warmed back up a little, so maybe I won't freeze without a hoodie.

If I had a scarf or some cool shoes. A military jacket. Something. At least my hair looks okay.

I walk out to the kitchen, and Mom checks me out.

"You look nice." There's a rule. Mothers have to say that occasionally. "So Chloe is picking you up?"

"Her mother is."

"Vivian. Yes. Very nice woman. She and her husband run a day camp with horses for disabled kids."

"Yeah, she told me. Said I could go there and ride sometime."

"Have you ever been on a horse?"

"Nope."

"Well, that should be... um. Noah. I'm not quite sure about this."

"About what? Me riding a horse?"

"No. This relationship with Chloe."

"We're just friends."

"We may not be staying here much longer."

She's been saying this kind of thing since we moved here, but now it sounds like more than just a casual warning. I can't tell what she's thinking by looking at her, and I don't want to start this discussion when I know Chloe is on her way. Not when I want to be sharp for whatever is going to happen at Starbucks.

So I respond with a sigh. "It's just a meeting, Mom. For my psychology class. Chloe offered me a ride, and that's all."

Headlights flash against the windows and Winston starts his frantic barking. I say bye to Mom and hurry outside, so no one has to get out of the car to knock on the door. Mrs. Thomas drives a huge crew cab pickup, which is awesome that a woman drives a hefty vehicle like that. She probably needs it, working with horses and all. But as I settle into the back seat, I kind of feel like I'm sitting in a place of power and security.

Too bad it doesn't seem to make Chloe feel the same way. She's pretty quiet as we head for the main road into town. This is the same way Mom drives me to school in the morning, so even though it's getting dark, my eyes flick to the familiar landmarks, the bowling alley, the loft apartments, the drugstores and the formal wear shop. The graffiti is gone from the side of the building now. Must have taken some major scrubbing or they've painted over it. As we roll past, a man is locking the front door of the store for the night. The windows are dark, but I can see the shapes of manikins in tuxedos and gowns.

I lean forward between the front seats to talk to Chloe. "Someone painted defective on the side of that store. Did you see it?"

She rolls her head left against the headrest. "I sort of know the daughter of the man who owns that store. Maddie O'Toole."

"Did they ever figure out who tagged their building?"

"I don't know. Hmm." Her thumbs dance over the screen of the phone she's already holding in her lap.

"You don't have to look it up for me," I say with a little laugh.

"Just thought of something, is all."

We ride past the high school. The parking lot is well lit but empty for the night. Across the street is Grumpy's. I peer out the side window to see if I can catch a glimpse of Simon at work. The place looks pretty dead, but there's a car at the drive-thru window. Some other dude is leaning out to give the driver a drink and a bag.

About half a mile further on, the town becomes more congested. A couple of shopping centers and a bunch of restaurants are clustered around the Interstate. Even a movie theater with sixteen screens. If I hung out in this area over the weekend, I'd probably run into just about every student from Agatha Cross.

The Starbucks is tucked in between some boutique shops I know my mother would love to visit if we had any money. Mrs. Thomas parks across from the coffee shop and leads the way inside. Doesn't look like Chloe was exaggerating about her love for this place.

Drake has commandeered one of two black leather sofas sitting in a corner of the store, and a few people have joined him. Faces I don't recognize.

I sent a message to Daniel earlier, to tell Paisley about the meeting. My little act of cowardice, not wanting to face her. She'd probably look at me like she'd just sniffed dog poop on my shoes. But I'll be totally stunned if she shows up.

Naomi's boyfriend—I guess he's her ex now—works at the Starbucks in Rocky Mount. I've been there with her enough times that I'm familiar with the menu, the scents, and the flavors. I know just what I want. But when Mrs. Thomas asks me what I'll have, like she's going to pay for it, I balk.

"It's okay," Chloe whispers near my ear.

"Um. I can pay."

Mom gave me a five for the night, maybe happy that I was going out with a good person to a decent place.

"My treat," Mrs. Thomas says. "Go on. Tell her what you want."

I nod thanks, and approach the barista... a cute girl with dark hair sticking out at accidental angles around her cap.

I give her my best flirty smile. "Grande nitro cold brew, please."

It works. She nibbles her lip for a second as she's marking the information on my cup.

Still got it.

Chloe orders a pumpkin frappaccino with a mountain of whipped cream and drizzled syrup on top. We pick up our drinks, and her mother retreats to the back of the room with a hardcover book she brought along. I go to the self-serve counter to add sugar to my frothy coffee. Then Chloe and I approach the domain of the social elite.

"You made it," Drake says with a smirk.

We have to pull more chairs over, which automatically earns us a few scowling glances from other customers who probably thought they would enjoy their latte in jazz-infused peace.

No friendly introductions are made. Drake's people already know each other and they probably don't care about me. Chloe leans close to me and points each one out, telling me their names.

Jasmine "Jazzy" Malone is dark haired and lithe, sitting close enough to Drake that I'm thinking his daytime girlfriend wouldn't be happy with the situation.

Lauren Harmon arrived with Kevin while we were getting our drinks. They're sitting as far from Drake as they can and still be in the group.

Emily Schaffer is the definition of a prom queen, which means she could be a fashion model with every bit of her polished to perfection. From her waving, highlighted blond hair to her hot pink toenails poking out of peek-a-boo ankle boots.

Next to her, perched on the overstuffed arm of the couch, is a girl in jeggings and slouchy leather boots as shiny as her wet-look jacket. I think Simon pointed her out to me in the hallway at school one day. Her last name is Matisse, which I remember only because of the famous French artist. But as she looks over at me and purses her lips in a way that's both alluring and slightly disturbing, it comes to me that Simon had another nickname for her. Black widow spider? Something like that. The two girls look like total opposites of each other, angels of light and dark.

"Finlay Matisse," Chloe whispers.

I nod. Despite Simon's warning, I think I'd enjoy trying to peel back the layers of attitude in that girl.

The front door of the store opens and Mia Park, the dream girl I know I'll never have, walks in from the twilight. She's holding hands with an Asian guy I'm assuming is Jun Seoh. Thus cementing my feeling that she's totally out of my reach. The guy has a hard look about him, but it's more like he doesn't want to be here than he's typically unfriendly. The bad blood between Jun and Drake is pretty evident in the way the two of then share barely a glance and then act like they no longer see each other. Jun and Mia sit near me, and she leans toward me to give my arm the lightest touch and whisper hi.

"We're still missing a few," Drake announces.

"So what's this meeting all about?" Kevin asks. "You think you've got it all figured out who took Lauren's stuff? Or are you trying to make yourself look innocent?"

"This may not end well," Chloe whispers.

I take a sip of my drink and nod.

At least Drake doesn't jump out of his seat and charge the guy. "I told you, dude, it wasn't me. Someone stole my letter jacket and wore it to make me look bad. So you can stop accusing me."

"Same old Drake," Jun mutters.

I catch Jun's eye and give him enough of a smirk to show I totally get what he's saying.

"Okay, look," Jazzy says. "Let's put all the crap between us aside and work together to figure out what's happening. We all know each other well enough, except..." She waves her fingers toward me.

"Noah," I say. "Rumor has it that I'm from the Georgia Bureau of Investigations, which would be very helpful right now, but unfortunately it's not true. I'm here because Chloe was robbed and I'm trying to help her."

I thought that bit of humor might break the ice with this group, at least get me a smile from someone, but they're all staring at me like I'm an alien in their midst.

I am, in a sense.

"You said some people were missing," Lauren says, turning back to Drake. "Who's still coming?"

"Bryce said he'd be here," Drake answers. "And that other girl, Violet? Paisley? Some color?"

Lauren rolls her eyes and her head. "You're so daft."

"You like it," he says.

I wish I could laugh at them. "Paisley Black. I wouldn't count on her. She's got her doll back, so she's probably done."

"Doll?" M'lady Matisse says with a sneer.

A single nod and a confident smile is all I'll give her.

Chloe scoots forward on her hard, wooden chair. "What I'd really like to know is if there have been more burglaries we don't know about. If we hope to establish a pattern, then we really need as many pieces as we can get."

Clearly, in my mind, we've just established which of us is the smartest person in the group. Chloe crosses one leg over the other and takes a sip of her drink. Whatever intimidation she felt earlier about being here is buried now.

"You're with the yearbook staff, aren't you?" Matisse says.

Emily touches her friend on the arm and whispers something, after which Matisse has an ah-ha moment and grins.

As I'm trying to decipher that look, a dark sportscar flies past the front windows and slides into a parking space almost without slowing down. LED taillights forming two sides of a triangle tell me the car is expensive.

"There's Bryce," Jazzy says, and she stands to move away from Drake.

Probably to prevent world war three. Although how that's going to be avoided with the mix of ex-girlfriends and athletic rivals in the room, I'm not sure. What brings us all together and is the only hope for civility is that somewhere in the world is a person who has bunched all of us together in his enemy camp.

Except for me, of course. I don't have a stake in this battle. I might be the only one who has a hope of keeping a cool head. How weird is that?

Bryce, like Drake, looks like a typical jock, although Simon told me he wasn't one. He's buff. His hair is even buzzed like Drake's. But he's matured and has a trendy, shadowy beard. He's walking fast, and I tense up as he comes in, ready to move if this is the approach before an ambush. I clasp Chloe's wrist, just in case. She glances at me and doesn't seem worried at all. Maybe this is a sign that all is well, so I make myself relax.

Bryce walks right to where we're seated, delaying or forgoing a drink. "Want to tell me which one of you losers trashed my parents' house?" he says.

But he's smiling, and after a second, a couple of people chuckle awkwardly.

Drake eases back in his seat, his arms stretched across the back of the couch. "Hey there, green bean. Glad you could make the party. How's Tech?"

The dude's smile falls, and for an instant I think he's going to launch himself at Drake's throat.

Drake seems to be fond of food insults, although I don't know what green bean is supposed to mean. I don't even know what he means by milky boy.

Bryce grabs another chair and practically flings it into place.

It appears everyone is here now, in this group of people who are talking in whispers and glaring at each other. Chloe makes a movement like she's about to stand to address them, but I can't let her do it. I'm not a hero, and I know she's capable and strong, but none of these people, except for Drake and Mia, know me at all. They've got no reason to hate me. And, by helping Chloe, I'm also helping them.

So I stand up.

And get hit by my own wave of idiocy. What am I doing? What am I supposed to say right now?

"Uh, hey, y'all. Like I said, I'm Noah. You don't know me, and I wasn't even at Agatha Cross last year when all of you were there."

I notice Kevin's face is half scrunched up. Matisse's lips are parted, like she's about to laugh.

"These burglaries, I've been trying to put all the information together, because it's clear that they're connected. Someone has a reason to target all of you. And I think it might also be connected to the prom last year. So, like, maybe we can just go around, and each person say what happened to them and when, what was stolen or damaged, and we can see where that takes us."

I'm shaking inside like I'm standing in a snow bank with no shoes, but I glance down at Chloe. She reaches into the backpack she brought along and pulls out a spiral notebook and pen. Ready to take notes as I lead this investigation.

"Who *are* you?" Kevin asks.

"Just helping out. You know. Like, I'm impartial, so..."

Drake laughs. "Okay, fine. I'll start." He stands up. "Hi, everyone. I'm Drake, and I'm a victim of a robbery."

Only M'lady Matisse snickers at this.

There's a face in the window behind her, peeking around an advertising poster. Spying on us. I'd recognize that Spock-like haircut anywhere.

"Todd's here," I mutter, hoping Chloe hears me.

Someone else does. Kevin cusses and says, "I hate that guy."

And with that, just about everyone turns their heads to look. Todd ducks behind the poster, but it's too late.

Bryce stands and pivots toward the door. "Creeper. I'll take care of him."

Todd's appearance took something out of me. Is he spying on me or the group? I wish I could take pleasure in what I'm seeing through the window as Bryce talks the creeper down and sends him scurrying across the parking lot, but the feeling that I'm being followed is choking me. How did he know I would be here tonight? Did one of the people here tell him?

"Sit down, emo boy," Kevin tells me. "I'll tell you what happened."

I remain standing, hoping it makes me look like I have some authority, even as my knees feel a little rubbery.

"*This* guy—" he points at Drake "—broke into my girlfriend's house and trashed her room, tearing up her pictures and ripping up her prom dress. He stole her jewelry and the stuffed animal I gave her, and then had the audacity to give it all back when he, so-called, found it in the woods. He's just trying to make himself innocent so we'll think he didn't do it. But he's been ticked off at Lauren ever since she dumped him last year because he's so jealous she couldn't even talk to another guy."

Bryce comes back just as Lauren is dabbing a knuckle against her eye. Fake tears.

"It was terrible," she says. "My entire room was destroyed. We called the police. They said it had to be someone we know, because why else would he go into just my room. And then my neighbor said she saw Drake walking across our yard. He was wearing his letterman jacket. His name on the back."

"It wasn't me," Drake says. "Someone stole my jacket out of my truck. They must be using it so y'all think it's me."

Chloe writes in her notebook.

"Someone broke into my car, too," Jazzy says. She extends her hand like she's going to touch Drake's thigh but stops short. "They took my trumpet. I had to take money out of my savings account to buy another one, because we have halftime shows and a concert to perform. Whoever did this had to know that I would need that trumpet."

Or it was just a crime of opportunity. She should probably check the local pawn shop. But I'm not going to suggest it right now. They're talking, and I want to keep them on track.

"Our house was broken into while my mother was out shopping and my dad was at his law office," Bryce says.

Note, Bryce's father is a lawyer. That could mean their break-in might have nothing to do with the others. Could be an angry client seeking revenge. Or just someone targeting their fancy-schmancy house.

I glance down at Chloe's notebook, and she's still writing.

"I'm at Georgia Tech," Bryce goes on, "staying in the dorms. So I get this call from my mother, who's freaking out. She says the cops are at our house, and someone busted in the sliding door off the deck, and they've torn up stuff all over the house. So I come home, like ninety miles an hour up the Interstate, and I see the house looks like a hurricane blew through it."

Note, it sounds like Bryce's house was more damaged than the others. That sets it apart from the others.

"The cops are still there, walking around and looking for evidence, fingerprints and stuff. So I do what I can to get my mother calmed down, and eventually I go upstairs to see what it looks like up there. My bedroom is messed up, but for some reason the other bedrooms are okay. There's televisions, computers, jewelry, all that stuff, but it's all okay. Except for my room."

Scratch that earlier note. Whoever broke into Bryce's house has a serious grudge.

"And so I look all around, try to find whatever is valuable, and I can't find my high school class ring and the crown they gave me when I was made prom king."

Class ring. Prom crown. One crazy expensive, the other probably a couple of bucks from the party store. My junior year, they handed out brochures for class rings. I didn't even ask my parents for one, because I knew my dad wouldn't pay big bucks for something he'd say I'd just lose.

"Did you have your own tux? Was it okay?" I ask, assuming this rich kid would have his own.

He shakes his head. "I do, but my girlfriend wanted me to wear white, so I rented one."

Drake mutters something, and Bryce's pleasant manner drops again. Like a bowling ball. He whips his head around and glares at Drake, who just smirks back at him. Yeah, there's some kind of tension between these two.

I remember what Chloe said about his zipper.

"Where did you rent it from?" I ask, on a hunch.

He takes a breath and chills. "O'Toole's. A mistake I won't make again. Their stuff is garbage."

Garbage... like *defective?*

"Anyway, I spent the rest of the weekend helping my parents clean up the mess. And then I found out there were other robberies. Drake messaged me to be here today, that it might be someone in this group. So... here I am."

"You lost your class ring, dude?" Drake holds up his naked right hand. "I lost my championship ring from two years ago. The *championship!* So, like, someone had to know what that ring was for, right?"

But Drake lost his ring during wrestling practice. Which means one of the other wrestlers could have taken it from his locker.

Jun shakes his head. "You didn't really deserve that ring anyway. You were a lightweight two years ago. The squad carried you."

Drake bristles at him but doesn't get up. He looks bigger than Jun, but I'm guessing Jun's got better moves, since he was supposedly the star of the squad. These two have locked horns plenty of times before.

Jun taps himself in the chest. "My place was broken into two weekends ago. That was, like, three weeks after we buried my baby sister. Who would do that, huh? Break in and steal stuff from a family that's grieving? It had to be someone who knows me, because all they took were my trophies."

"I gave them to your girlfriend," Drake says, pointing at Mia.

"You gave them back, because you stole them!" Jun yells. He lurches up from his seat and Mia grabs his arm. "You've hated me for years, because you could never best me. And when I got the scholarship to Oklahoma State, you took me out of competition with that illegal move. You got benched for it, and it cost us the championship last year, and now you're out for revenge. Admit it, Drake! It was you!"

Mia is doing everything she can to keep Jun from leaping over the coffee table and doing an illegal move on Drake right now. Even Kevin stands up to get between them.

Drake looks a little nervous as he raises his hands. "It wasn't me, dude. I promise you. We found a bunch of stuff in the woods by the snake pit, and I was just there to see it. You can ask milky boy, I mean, Noah. He was there. He knows everything that happened."

Which is probably the real reason Drake wanted me to be here. I'm actually his alibi.

"You found it because you knew where you stashed it," Lauren says.

Drake spreads his hands wide. "Weren't you listening? Stuff was stolen from me too!"

"You're just trying to make yourself look innocent!"

A barista appears in our midst, telling us to keep it down. The guys settle back into their seats and the other girls in the group have their chance to talk.

Emily Schaffer didn't even realize her prom dress was missing until Drake's girlfriend, Chelsea, called her to say they found it. But two weekends ago her brother found the back door jimmied open, and someone had used her lipstick to scrawl an ugly epithet on her mirror.

And then we come to M'lady Matisse, who has been looking fairly amused this whole time. She crosses her legs and props her elbow on the top knee, like this is all so casual and entertaining. She flicks a finger at Drake. "When you brought Emily's dress back, she called me and told me everything. And I thought there was something shady about it. I thought, who would rip up a prom dress and sash? Maybe... one of the girls who didn't win?"

I lower myself down next to Chloe and say, "Who's she talking about."

Chloe licks her lips and doesn't answer. But when I look up again, I find Matisse with her head tilted and a smug smile directed at...

Mia.

Did she run for prom queen last year? She never mentioned...

But it couldn't be her. She's not like that. She's not malicious or vindictive or...

Really, I don't know her much at all.

She's holding onto Jun's arm, her mouth as wide open as her eyes.

"I'm not saying you did it," Matisse adds, "but it does give you a motive. And then maybe you broke into Jun's house because he broke up with you. At least, you told me a couple of weeks ago that he broke up with you. Was that a lie, or..."

Emily hunches her shoulders and tucks her hands between her knees. She's not adding anything to this accusation.

"Mia?" I say softly.

She looks at me like she just realized I was there, then jiggles her head. "It's ridiculous. Emily, I was happy for you when you won. You know that. And I was really upset when Hana died. Why would I do anything like this? Why would I want to hurt Jun's family after they've been through so much already?"

"It is ridiculous," Jun says. "Look, we've all got some reason to be mad at someone else, but that doesn't mean that any of us are guilty."

"I wasn't finished," Matisse says. She flicks that long finger at Jun this time. "You told me that Kevin was taking a bribe to throw a football game last year."

"I was wrong. End of story," Jun growls.

"Not the end of the story. Because Kevin was benched for that game, and the team lost anyway."

"So?"

"You seem to like sending people to the bench."

Jun throws up his hands. "Oh, come on! Are you going to say now that *I* broke into people's houses?"

"No, no. Follow me now."

I edge closer to Chloe. "Are you getting *any* of this?"

"Um," is all she says.

"What we have to do," Matisse says, "is look at the person who has the most motive to get revenge against... all of us! And Bryce, you have provided the answer."

"Me?" Bryce says.

"You got into an argument in the bathroom right before they named you prom king."

He scowls. "How do you know that?"

"Oh, come on," Kevin groans.

Are all of these people connected by immature drama? I've got *so* much I want to ask Chloe and Simon later.

"Who was it?" Matisse asks. "Who did you argue with?"

He stares at her, but then his eyes shift toward Kevin.

"Kevin," Matisse says, with firm finality. "Kevin, who ran for prom king against you and lost. Kevin, who was mad at Jun about the bribery accusation. Kevin, who took Lauren away from you after she left Drake to be with you. Kevin, who so wants to blame Drake for the break-ins, when he could easily have broken into his own girlfriend's house because he knew when she wouldn't be home."

And Kevin, who is a football player at UGA. I'm hesitant to thank Todd for this information, even in my head. But it might explain why he was lurking outside. Not spying on me, but on Kevin.

"Are you freakin' crazy?" Kevin says, baring his teeth like an angry dog. "I'm like Bryce and-and Jun. I'm away at college."

"But you come home every weekend," she says. "And everything we've talked about happened over the weekend."

He throws his arms up, but then reaches across Mia to slap Jun in the arm. "What about you, man? Why aren't you in Oklahoma, anyway?"

"I came home to take care of my mother!" Jun says, followed by a *marvelously* descriptive phrase of pure hatred.

I'm ready to take Chloe's hand and get out of here. "I don't think we're getting anywhere with this," I mutter to her.

I barely hear her hum for the argument that explodes between Lauren, Kevin, Jun and Drake.

And it occurs to me... maybe this is just what someone planned.

Maybe the real thief isn't even here. Maybe Bryce chased him away.

But these people all know each other pretty well. They're not spouting Todd-like rumors or fake news. There is truth in their words. It's just colored by their hatred for each other.

Their voices are getting louder and this meeting has fallen apart. I stand up and clear my throat.

"Y'all?"

No one is paying attention.

"Hey," I say a little louder.

I glance down at Mia, who shakes her head. Her boyfriend is on his feet too, arguing with Kevin.

All this noise... I feel a slight tension behind my right eye that could be the first signs of a migraine. I sit down and rub my temples. While the guys are on their feet now, Mia notices my discomfort because she reaches out to touch my knee. I give her an uneasy smile.

"What's going on here?" Chloe's mother is standing behind us. And all around the room other customers are casting dirty looks our way.

Chloe rises to stand beside Mrs. Thomas. "High school drama, Mom. That's all this is.

I couldn't agree more. And the sudden appearance of an adult in their midst seems lost on the combatants.

Bryce, who has been mostly silent this whole time, gets up from his chair and puts it back at the table where he found it. He's done.

A whistle cuts through all the noise in the store. It's the barista at the counter, and when we're all looking at him, he points toward the door. "Out. Now."

"Waste of time anyway," Bryce says, heading for the door. "I should have been studying tonight."

"We didn't get anything figured out," Drake says, and he jumps up to follow Bryce.

"Yeah, run away, Techie," Kevin says. "At least you don't have a two-hour drive back to your dorm like I do!"

It looks like the *party* is moving to the parking lot. Two by two our disruptive crowd moves through the door, their voices never settling.

Chloe covers her face and groans.

I edge closer to her. "Don't go out there. Just stay here."

Her mother protectively wraps her hands over the top of Chloe's shoulders as the three of us watch the continuing melee in the parking lot. There's some minor shoving and more yelling. The barista says something about calling the cops. But in a moment more, it's over. People retreat to their cars, girls flipping their hair and guys flipping obscene gestures. Unless there's some road rage about to happen, they're all leaving angry and dissatisfied.

But I'm not sure the meeting was a complete waste of time, like Bryce said. There were moments I wished I could have nailed down a statement or asked more questions. Clues were dropped, accidentally or unknowingly. And I can't wait to talk to Simon.

"Can I have those notes you took?" I ask Chloe. "I'm going to catch Simon when he gets home from work tonight."

She rolls her eyes and gives her head a shake. "Seriously, Noah, this was nothing more than a public flame war. I don't know how we're going to get anything out of it."

"We'll see," I say, taking the notebook she reluctantly hands me.

As we're walking out, my phone pings in my back pocket. Text from an unknown number, and my spine stiffens at the sight of it. Last time I got one of these, I had no clue who sent it. Now, reading it, I know exactly who somehow managed to get my private phone number.

UNKNOWN: Having fun, Sherlock?

Somewhere, not far from this parking lot, a hacker is watching.

Happiness is... When the Problems All Belong to Someone Else.

That's a pretty self-serving attitude, but I'm naming and claiming it for one night. I left Starbucks feeling as revved up as if I'd just watched a WWE grudge match. There's just one thing that bothers me... Todd might have been right that I'd enjoy watching the drama from a safe distance.

At home, I sit in the lopsided chair near the front window of our living room with the blinds cranked open so I can see when Simon comes home. Mom is in her room talking on her cell. Maybe with Dad, because her voice sometimes swells to a whine and then recedes to near silence. Typical of their arguments.

Simon finally strides up the road toward his house. His drawn-up hood and oversized jacket make it seem like he actually weighs more than a hundred pounds.

I jump up from the chair and fly to the door. "Going to see Simon!" I yell, forgetting that my father might hear my voice through the phone five hundred miles away. I don't care. Let him think I actually have a life apart from him.

I catch him on his screened porch. He puts a finger to his lips before opening the door to his trailer.

Mrs. Walsh is still awake, although she's wrapped in a blanket, watching television. She smiles up at us, looking like she could doze off at any moment, and tells Simon there's a plate for him in the microwave if he's hungry. He grabs it but doesn't take time to heat it up. Looks like the filling from chicken pot pie poured over noodles. Simon shovels in a forkful as we're walking down the hall.

I don't judge.

Surprisingly, Simon's room is bigger than mine. He's got his own television in there—old tube type, not flat screen—and lots of shelves filled with comic books and science fiction novels. His bed even looks larger than mine, even though it's still a single.

I stand in the middle of the room and survey all the bounty that surrounds me. "Can I come live with you?"

"Are you serious?" Simon says. His question is so sincere that it catches me off guard.

"Um. I was joking."

He breathes out and laughs. My joke wasn't that funny.

I sink down onto the floor, cross-legged, Chloe's notebook and my sketchbook in my lap. "Okay, might just take a miracle to sort out, but I think we can do it."

"That good, huh?" Simon sits down opposite me, also cross-legged, and shovels more creamy-veggie-white meat-noodles into his mouth.

I gag a little bit. But at the same time, I get this happy feeling, like we're two little kids sitting on the floor playing with action figures or cards. There's a sense of rightness, kind of like a desire for what could have been if I lived in a house where it was okay to have friends over.

I push the feeling aside. It's too late. Across the street my mother is probably still arguing with Dad. I have no doubt that she's not coming out on top of the debate.

I open Chloe's notebook. Her printing is hard to read, probably because she was writing fast to keep up with everything going on. Abbreviations that she would probably extrapolate at a glance, but Simon and I have to sit and ponder. But with the help of her notes, I make a list in my sketchbook of all the people who were at the meeting and what I learned from each of them. And I write down what I thought their words implied rather than what they said outright. Hints and omissions. Unintended connections. Simon makes a few corrections and editorial comments along the way. If I were to take the time to draw this out in a chart, with lines between all the connections, it might look something like a spiderweb.

Simon eats it all up faster than his supper.

"All the guys were blaming each other," I say. "They all seem to have motives. So, assuming the person who did it was actually there at all, here's what I've got. Starting with Drake, Kevin thinks he did it because he's jealous about Lauren. Jun and Drake had that illegal wrestling move thing, which cost the team the championship last year."

"Makes sense that Drake would steal his trophies," Simon says, eating all this up faster than his supper.

"Right, but I don't see what motive Drake would have for all the other stuff. That girl, Jazzy, was practically sitting in his lap when I got there. Why would he steal something from her?"

"Chelsea won't be happy."

I grunt at this. "And why would he break into Bryce's house or do anything to Chloe? And can you really see Drake stealing Paisley's doll?"

I thought that last bit was funny, but Simon gets that distant look on his face that says he's thinking.

"Following. Continue," he says.

"Okay. Jun accused Kevin of cheating last year, and Kevin had to sit out a game until he was cleared. Jun apologized, and even said at the meeting that he was wrong. So I can't find any motive there."

"But he *is home* from Oklahoma. That gives him opportunity."

"Right, but I really don't think it was him. More like either Drake or Kevin would have more reason to do something to him than the other way around."

Simon nods slowly.

"Kevin is one angry dude, though. And he's got a reason to be mad at all three of the others."

"But what about the girls? Why would he target them? Especially his own girlfriend?"

"I was thinking about that on the way home. Maybe he's trying to make it look like someone else is responsible."

"So you think it's Kevin?"

"I still think it's Todd. I think he's playing around to stir all these guys up and laughing about it the whole time. But if I had to eliminate Todd, yeah, I'd say Kevin."

"What about Bryce?"

I shrug. "He seemed okay. He didn't want to be there, but he was the only one that didn't argue with anyone else. He doesn't like Drake, but other than that, he was just... there."

"Um..." Simon pulls at his lower lip. "I actually know why he doesn't like Drake."

"Tell."

"Did Drake happen to call him green bean?"

"Oh, yeah! He did. He seems to have this thing about food names."

Simon shakes his head. "There's more to it." He gets to his knees and fishes his phone out of the pocket of his jeans. "There was a video when Bryce got crowned." He starts searching.

"With his zipper down? Chloe said she took a picture."

"Video," Simon says. "But there was more than one. Give me a minute."

"Did Drake shoot it?"

"Too many shares to tell where it came from. Here it is."

He hands his phone to me and I start the video. It's just a twenty-four second clip shot from an angle that's too low and close to the stage for any complimentary images. Bad audio of someone announcing that Bryce Valentino won. He comes to the stage, bends low so a girl can put a sash over his shoulder and the crown on his head. Then he straightens, looking like some kind of dignitary in his white tux. He throws his arms up and his chest out, giving a victory yell.

And then I see it. His zipper is all the way down, and he's wearing bright green boxer shorts. Bright, bright green. And a bit of the material is caught in the fly of his trousers.

"Green bean!" I yell, and then fall backwards on the floor. I'm laughing so hard that I can't get a full breath of air and my ribs immediately start aching.

"Calm down, Noah!" Simon says. "You'll hurt yourself."

I can't help it. Even though my cracked ribs are screaming, it feels so good to laugh this way. I haven't done it in so long.

I bring myself out of it. Slowly. Yeah, it freakin' hurts. And when I'm able to think again, it occurs to me that I would be totally humiliated if something like that happened to me. I'd never want to show my face at school again.

And maybe, maybe, I'd want vengeance for it. Against Chloe, for posting the original video. Against whoever posted this second one. And against anyone who called me that name. So maybe this dude has a motive too. Matisse said something about an argument in the bathroom with Kevin before Bryce received his crown.

Maybe in the heat of the argument, Bryce forgot to zip?

Maybe he blamed the place that rented him a "defective" tux?

I straighten, stretch my back, and draw in a deep breath and let it out. Yeah, I'm going to pay for rolling on the floor laughing.

"Bryce's rented his tux from O'Toole's Formal Wear," I tell Simon. His eyes widen.

"And, if his zipper wouldn't stay up, think he'd have a reason to paint *defective* on the side of the store?"

Simon hums and nods his head slowly.

"Can you send that video to me?"

He's on it before I finish my request.

"They all have motives," I say. "We just have to figure out which of them has the strongest motives, and then figure out how we're going to prove it."

Simon finishes with his phone then ticks the names off on his fingers. "Todd, Drake, Bryce, Kevin, and Jun. My guess is still Drake."

"And my bet is still on Todd. But if I had to change it, I'd say Kevin. Although Bryce is looking pretty interesting right now."

"What did Chloe think?"

"We couldn't really talk about it in the car with her mother there. We'll find out tomorrow."

"Or... now!" Simon's thumbs move over his phone again. Less than a minute later, he holds the phone up for me to see Chloe's answer to his text.

CHLOE: It's Kevin. And Lauren is in on it.

Chapter

Wednesday... Time Out for Real Life

Mom and I are stuck in traffic heading south on I-75 to see the doctor who wants to check on how things are going with my concussion and cracked ribs. I told Mom I didn't need to go. The medication they gave me is working pretty well most of the time to prevent the migraines I was having before, but my laughing fit last night has me hurting today, which Mom could see as I shuffled around the trailer this morning. I might have moaned some during the night, too.

She's not happy. About anything. She's missing work, which wouldn't be a problem if she weren't on notice for taking time off... because of me. Because I can't just lay low in the way she thinks is possible for a normal high school student, which means no friends, no activities, no life. I'm supposed to be as miserable as she is.

She's even blaming me for the traffic, because we wouldn't be here if I hadn't gotten myself involved with those manga kids.

The radio reminded her of that while we're sitting behind a tractor-trailer belching exhaust at us. Local news, *"George Norwood, the former custodian at Agatha Cross High School in Middleboro, Georgia, is being arraigned today in state court on charges of kidnapping a student."* No mention of my name, thank you, Lord, but also no mention of whether he had anything to do with Hana Seoh's death. They must still be investigating that.

As Mom falls into an angry silence, I put my earbuds in and look again at the video Simon send me. I've watched it a couple of times and thought I heard something, but I want to be sure. The audio is wretched, but there's a laugh, low and close to the microphone, that could identify the person who recorded the moments on his phone.

It sounds like Todd. At least... I want it to be Todd. I want that so much that I have to doubt my objectivity. I need to be certain, so I listen to the video again, keeping my phone screen against my thigh so I won't be tempted to watch and get distracted by the sight of Bryce's boxers.

It takes us half an hour more before Mom finally pulls off the Interstate. She follows the GPS directions on her phone to the doctor's office. We're late, because Mom had no idea the traffic would be so bad.

We have to sit in the waiting room for almost an hour, since we missed our appointment time. Mom glances down at my cell phone while I scroll through Todd's social media posts, looking for that video to see if he posted or shared it. That I'm passing the time on my phone seems to annoy her. She sighs loudly, and I feel like I have to apologize for being alive.

I clear my throat and flip back to where I started this search, to a cryptic message Todd posted this morning. I'm certain it's related to our "meeting" at Starbucks last night.

Todd McCaffrey: When the wolves come to brawl, the mouse sneaks away unnoticed.

I get who the wolves are, but who is the mouse? Todd himself? Since he didn't stay around to see how things worked out, it has to be him.

Finally a nurse calls my name, and Mom comes with me out of the waiting room. First task, I step on a scale.

Good grief! I've lost over twenty pounds since we left North Carolina.

Mom stares at me with her mouth open. I shrug as I get off the scale. The nurse makes a note but doesn't say anything. Probably because she doesn't realize the significance of the number she wrote down. And she doesn't see how suddenly I'm quaking inside.

What's *wrong* with me?

Okay, I know my appetite has been off since we left home. But... twenty pounds?

Despite the internal quaking, all my other *vitals* seem normal, and the nurse asks me to remove my shirt before she tells us the doctor will be right in and slips out the door.

The bruise over my cracked ribs has faded to a big blob of sickly yellow and gray. At the sight of it, Mom sucks air through her clenched teeth and tries to touch it.

"It's fine, Mom. It's healing. Just still looks nasty."

"Noah," she says, her eyes going sad. "Honey..." She lifts her hand higher to touch the new bruise on my shoulder, which is still dark. "Was this one there before?"

"Bumped into someone's locker door at school," I lie. I drop my shirt and hoodie into a chair and pull myself onto the paper-covered examination table.

Mom heaves a sigh, shakes her head at me, and finds a magazine in a little rack on the wall.

After about twenty minutes, during which time I start shivering, Dr. Johnson comes into the room to have a look at me. He has me lay back on the table so he can touch my ribs. Scale of one to ten, what's my pain like? When I'm sitting still, maybe a four. After last night, a six. He touches my new bruise too and asks about it. I give him the same lie I told my mother. He asks about my headaches and I tell him about loud noises, which he says is to be expected. He says he wants to get some new x-rays of my ribs and he'll send the nurse in with a portable machine.

He turns away from me and gestures toward my mother. "Mrs. Dickerson, might I have a word with you in private?"

That's weird. And from Mom's slightly scowling expression, it seems she thinks so too. But she gets up and follows him out of the room. They close the door, and I'm alone.

Sitting up again, I look down at my torso. Bruised and thinner, even paler but that's probably because the summer tan is gone. Still, this skinny frame, the ribs just starting to ripple along my sides... it's not me. Not how I ever pictured myself.

Something bumps the door and the nurse comes in pushing a machine on wheels. Big adjustable arm with the camera on it.

"Dr. Johnson will be right back to take care of the x-ray," she says. "But I want to ask you a couple of questions before he comes."

"Okay."

"These are just... required by law." She comes to my side, smiling gently. "Is everything okay at home?"

I shrug.

"Do you feel safe there?"

She's peering straight into my eyes, looking for any reaction. I notice this too late to realize if I've made any little twitches or blinks. But all I can think of is... I wish someone had asked me this question back in North Carolina.

"Yes, it's fine," I say. Which, I realize, is no lie. There's stress at home, and a lot of things I wish were different, but for the first time in a long time, I don't come home from school wishing I had somewhere else to go.

I wonder if the nurse believes me. I give her my sweetest smile, reserved for adults to make them think I'm a nice boy, and finally she nods and tells me again the doctor will be right back.

Dr. Johnson returns with my mother, and in a few minutes of technological wonders, he's got his x-rays and is satisfied with what he sees. He tells me to avoid strenuous exercise or lifting anything heavy and to concentrate on deep breathing exercises once an hour to make sure my lungs stay clear. He wants me to keep taking the migraine medication, since it's working for me.

As we're leaving, I ask Mom what the doctor wanted to talk to her about.

"The bill, of course. Our insurance isn't going to cover all of it. And I seriously doubt your father will happily write a check to a doctor in another state. So just stay out of trouble. Can you do that for me please, Noah? Just stay out of trouble?"

I don't have to answer. The argument continues in my head. My fault. Not my fault. I'm a victim. Except when I'm not. All I can do is wait until one voice is louder than the other and then figure out what to do about it. Or I can drown them both out with the drama of other people's lives. Until more drama comes into mine.

I wonder if the doctor really wanted to talk to my mother about that bill? Doesn't he have other people to do that sort of thing? Maybe what he did was give his nurse time to ask whether there was any reason for that new bruise that they should know about.

I can't lay the blame for that one on anyone buy myself. Except Daniel, of course. But I was stupid to be in the way of that rock.

Back to Our Regularly Scheduled School Day

Psychology class is in full swing by the time Mom checks me in for the rest of the day. I hand Mr. Danson my hall pass and turn toward the back of the room, where I see Todd sitting next to my usual desk. I trudge back there and slide into my seat, hoping the next fifteen minutes will go by fast.

"Didn't think you were going to make it," Todd mutters as the teacher is writing something on the whiteboard. "You okay?"

Is that any of your business?

I nod once without looking at him.

"Have fun last night?" he says at the next opportunity.

"Loads. How about you?" I say.

He huffs. "I wasn't invited to the party."

Mr. Danson looks over his shoulder to see who's talking, and we both go silent and inconspicuous.

When class ends and I stand to leave, Todd steps right in front of me and even shifts the same way when I try to go around him.

"Did you learn anything?" he asks.

I don't want to engage him but a jab flies out of my mouth anyway. "Probably only what you already knew."

"Ooh, probably not, Sherlock. But keep digging. You might find enlightenment."

"Too bad you couldn't be a mouse in that room, eh?"

He chuckles at this. "Good one, but wrong again."

"So why don't you tell me what I'm missing?"

"What fun would that be?"

I've got no patience for this. "You think this is fun and games, dude? Why don't you try talking to some of those people whose houses were broken into? How about Chloe, who's afraid to sleep in her own room now. Think that's fun?"

He hums and nods. "Right. About Chloe. You might not want to believe everything she says."

"Why not?"

"She sees truth with a certain lens that doesn't fit every situation."

"What kind of lens?"

"All truth is relative to individual definition."

It's my turn to chuckle. "So if I pushed you in front of a school bus, would it be true or false that it would hit you?"

Big mistake. He seems to be enjoying this and I want to walk away. "It would be true for you that you might enjoy pushing me in front of a bus. It would be true for me that getting hit by a bus isn't my preferred way of dying."

"But it's true that you would be dead. Hypothetically."

"Hypothetically dead?" He laughs again, and I wish I had my phone recording this moment.

"You know what? Never mind. Truth is more than just opinion, and I intend to get to the truth."

"Good luck, milky boy," he says as I'm walking away.

I roll my eyes. I don't even like milk.

Heading for the cafeteria, I see Bethany walking just a few steps beyond me. I have this feeling like I should apologize to her. Or give her a chance to apologize to me. She was sort of dragged along by her friends into the situation that landed me in a car accident. She could have ended up a victim if I hadn't stepped into the role.

I call her. She glances back, stops, and turns her eyes toward the ceiling like she'd really not bother with me but hasn't got much choice.

"Hey," I say, catching up to her. "How's it going?"

"What do you care?" she says.

"I care. Just... you know."

"*Chuh!* Right."

"Listen, um... Can I ask you something? Just curious. Did Paisley go to the prom last year?"

She scrunches up her face like I'm crazy to ask. "No. Why?"

"They found a prom dress at the same place they found her doll. Just thinking that the break-ins might have something to do with the prom."

She shakes her head. "Noah, the last time you got involved with trying to figure something out, you ended up in the hospital. Are you a glutton for punishment?"

I sigh. "No. And I'm on the outside of this thing, so I think I'm safe. Just trying to help a friend."

Bethany rolls her eyes like she doesn't believe me.

"Why do you think someone would steal her doll?"

"I don't know. She posts pictures of him online sometimes. Dolls creep me out, so I don't pay any attention to it."

"Hmm. Well, if you think of anything, can you let me know? Or Simon?"

"Sure. Whatever."

I spare her an awkward parting by saying thanks and striding away.

Chloe and Simon are sitting together at our table, looking over her notebook, which I left with him. I want to join them, but remembering the sight of my skinny torso, I make myself get something to eat and load my tray with more than usual. Fries and a burger. Which I tell myself I'm going to finish.

Simon has made another chart, combining Chloe's notes and the list I made last night into his more organized format. His grid is filled with names and details written in tiny letters. Some of the blocks have been colored in with yellow highlighter.

Chewing my burger, I study the chart while Simon explains.

"Each block represents a possible motive, what each person has against the others, according to what we know, and the highlighted blocks are the ones with the strongest motives."

"Not very happy people," I mumble around bread and rather dry meat. I do a quick calculation. Bryce has six highlights while Drake has only four. Interesting.

"I told him he should add Finlay Matisse," Chloe says.

"Is she even involved?" I ask.

"She hates all of these people, except for Emily. She's in one of my classes, so I asked her what she thought. She said they're *all* guilty of something, including me."

"That doesn't help us much. I did wonder why she was even there last night."

"Probably just to watch certain people squirm," Simon says. "Like Mia, since she's dating her ex."

"You've got to be kidding me. Don't any of these people date outside their little group? Are they, like, royalty that only has relations with other royalty and creates little inbred tyrants?"

Neither of them laughs at my joke.

"There's one other person who isn't on the list," I say. "Paisley. We need to find that connection."

"Drake. That's it," Simon says. "He's always bullied the Manganites, for some reason. Maybe since he'll talk to you now, you should ask him why he does that."

"If he thinks I'm going to accuse him of taking her doll, he'll turn on me in a second. Or he might take a few seconds to figure it out."

"Y'all are so mean," Chloe says with a playful huff.

"Hey, you wanted to throw Finlay under the bus a moment ago," I counter.

"All right, yes. I admit it. But only because she called me a parasitic paparazzi."

"Ouch."

Chloe toys with her salad. "She's not wrong. Not entirely, anyway. I did post that video of Bryce."

"No. Uh uh," Simon says. "You took down as soon as you saw what was wrong with it. And you didn't have anything to do with the video that went viral. That was someone else's doing."

"I wish we knew who posted that," she says.

"Was Todd McCaffrey at the prom?" I ask.

Chloe looks puzzled for a moment, then shakes her head. "I don't know. I don't remember seeing him, but then, I didn't have any reason to pay attention to him."

"What we need is a spy into that clique," Simon says.

I drop a fry to hold up my hands. "Oh no. Not happening. I'm not doing that again."

"I wasn't suggesting..."

But I'm not listening to him now. Across the cafeteria, near the windows that overlook a soccer field, Mia is sitting with her friends. Of all the people at Starbucks last night, she and the prom queen, Emily, seemed the most reserved and mature. Now that I think about it, that makes me wonder if they were able to give their full stories.

"Back in a bit," I say, getting up and abandoning the last of my lunch.

As I approach her table, a little bit of the fascination I felt for Mia a few weeks ago returns. A twinge of hopefulness at the sight of her chatting and nudging her luscious hair back over her shoulder with a graceful hand. I'm hoping she'll look up, see me coming, and smile in greeting.

She does neither. Not until I'm standing next to her table and I say her name. Then her arched brows rise in mild surprise.

"Noah?"

"Can I talk to you for a moment?"

"Sure." She pushes away from the table. It seems her chair doesn't even scrape the floor.

I circle the table and we move together toward the wall, for privacy.

"What did you think of what happened last night?" I ask her.

She sighs. "Wow. That was crazy. I just hope it all stops after this."

"You think it will?"

"I don't know. But if whoever stole those things was there last night, maybe he'll realize he made his point and stop."

That's a naïve hope, but I understand the source. I'm sure Mia doesn't want to get involved in another mystery either.

"Do you think the person was there? I mean, tell me what you think."

"Well, I know it wasn't Jun. After the funeral, he went back to Oklahoma. He only came home again after the burglary. His poor mother is having such a hard time. He has to give up his scholarship because of it, and he might start somewhere closer to home next semester."

"So it couldn't have been him because—"

"Because he wasn't here. And why would he break into his own house?"

"Why would any of them, unless they're doing it to make themselves look like victims."

She blinks, then slowly nods. "It wasn't him."

"I really didn't think so. If you had to guess, though, who would you say?"

She shrugs one shoulder. "None of them, Noah. Honestly, I think there are bad feelings between them, but they're not criminals."

I sigh and look back toward Simon and Chloe. Mia is probably right. Bad feelings and anger could be motives, but not proof. And a lot of the motives are too weak for that person to seek revenge. Plus, there are too many pieces missing.

"It has to have something to do with the prom, though. If nothing else, almost all of the people involved were there."

Mia blinks, watching me, waiting for me to say something brilliant maybe.

I got nothing.

"Why would anyone have anything against the girl who got prom queen?" I ask.

"Emily. I really don't know. She's pretty nice."

"But she hangs out with that other girl."

"Finlay. They're next door neighbors."

"Ah."

"Except..." Mia taps an exquisite index finger against her perfect lips.

Focus, Dickerson.

"At the dance, Bryce had a... problem with his... pants."

"They were unzipped. I heard about that."

"He was supposed to dance with Emily after they were crowned.

She refused to dance with him until he fixed himself. I would have done the same thing. But I think that was when he realized that he had a problem. He looked pretty embarrassed."

"And everyone saw it?"

She nods. "Someone posted a video."

I tilt my head. "Do you know who posted it?"

"Um... I think it was that hacker guy. Mack."

"Todd McCaffrey?" I say, the pitch of my voice rising involuntarily.

"Yes, him. I'm almost positive. I remember seeing him there because he wore a lavender tuxedo and a top hat to match his girlfriend's dress. He walked around filming people on his phone."

Todd McCaffrey had a girlfriend? "Who was he with?"

"Oh. I'm... not sure. I can't really remember, Noah. I'm sorry."

"It's okay." I point two fingers at her. "Thank you! Big help. Thank you."

As I hurry back to the table where Simon and Chloe are waiting, I pull out my phone out so they can listen to that video. Not watch... *listen.*

Wednesday Afternoon... Riding the Bus Home Alone

Simon is working again today, so I'm standing by myself in a line of strangers waiting to get on the bus. Although I'm alone, I feel pretty good about things. After some quick speculation during the last minutes of lunch, some surreptitious texting the rest of the afternoon, and two minutes standing together in the grass near the school entrance, the three of us have developed a theory. And Chloe and Simon are finally seeing what I've suspected all along.

Todd McCaffrey is using his social media machine to stir up old animosities between a group of populars in order to divert attention away from himself so he can take revenge for past assaults on him.

Simon told me that Drake and Todd have a long-standing hatred ever since Todd humiliated Drake in an algebra class.

Todd might have posted the video of Bryce with his zipper down, we can't be sure, but he definitely posted the one where Emily backed away from him on the dance floor and he had to zip his pants. And the name "Green Bean" later showed up on Todd's feed.

Todd never bought that Kevin Lofton was innocent of taking a bribe to lose a football game. Although he never came out and said it was or wasn't true, he posted enough to keep the question out there.

And, Chloe reminded us, Todd was a "suspect" in the SAT cheating that took place last year. Never proven, but enough to give Todd a reason to take revenge on Chloe... pointing out her *hypocrisy* in having a photograph of the most trusted man in America.

The other girls, they were the tools he used to make the guys look bad.

And the final piece of the puzzle, provided by Mia and confirmed by Simon. Todd was dating Maddie O'Toole, the daughter of the man who owns the formal wear shop. They broke up right after the prom.

Graffiti on the building? That might just be the clue Todd wanted me to find, pointing to Bryce, another one of his red herrings.

And the wolves fought with each other while the clever little mouse got away.

I glance down the line of buses and see him getting on another bus, unaware that I've figured him out. Moriarty no more.

I can't wait to get settled in my bus seat and send him a text. *Heard you look good in lavender, but you saw green.*

Someone calls my name and I whip my head around the other way. Bethany is running toward me, her manga-style pigtails bouncing. I hesitate, then step out of line. Maybe she'll only need a second or two to tell me whatever would prompt her to even speak to me again.

She stops in front of me, huffing a little. "I was thinking about what you said... about the prom? And Paisley's doll?"

"Yes..." All ears now.

She holds up her phone. "I remembered this."

I gawk at the image on her screen.

Bingo.

A big fat honkin' bingo.

It's the doll wearing a white shirt and pants, not exactly a tuxedo, but clearly an imitation, because the fly of the pants is open and a bright green fabric is hanging out. Comparatively a lot more than what that poor schmuck Bryce revealed to the world, but this photo was obviously meant to capitalize on the guy's misery.

I do hope he's having a better time of things in college.

"Can you send this photo to me?" I ask Bethany.

"We're not friends anymore."

"Crud." Yeah, Bethany cut all ties with me when I accused her best friends of writing threatening notes to Mia. I pull out my phone and glance at the bus driver, who doesn't seem at all convinced that what I'm involved in is important. I quickly open Facebook. Already logged onto my Rhys account. My thumbs flying, I send Bethany a friend request.

"What are you going to do with it?" she asks, peering at her phone suspiciously.

Behind me, there's a hiss and a bang as the bus driver closes the door. If I jump over there and knock on it, maybe he'll open it for me. But... but...

"And, uh, do you think you could give me ride home? Please?"

Bethany rolls her eyes. "Fine. But what do you need the picture for?"

"Evidence for a possible motive." I take a step away from the bus, which starts pulling out of the space at the same time.

Bethany falls in beside me. "So, what? You think the prom king stole Paisley's doll?"

"Not him. But someone who wanted to make it look like he did."

"Noah, this sounds like a bad B-movie."

I chuckle at this. "It does, doesn't it? But I want Simon to see this. We're going to put together as much information as we can to give to the police, and that photo," I point at her phone still in her hand, "gives us the connection we were missing."

"Are you planning to become a detective or something after you graduate?" she asks. "You'd be good at it."

I laugh again. Not sarcastically, but because I feel pretty good. "Not hardly. But thank you."

I never imagined that I'd be riding again in Bethany's little white car with the Hello Kitty tape on the backs of the mirrors, but here I am. It's awkward. We don't have anything to talk about, and we're not friends. And I realize, as we're getting close to the trailer park, that I don't really want her to see where I live. Not because I don't trust her, but because there's still that embarrassment. So I ask her to drop me off at the entrance.

She doesn't ask why. Maybe she's just happy to get rid of me.

Another car comes flying out of the entrance, going the wrong way on the one-way street through the park. Bethany slams on her brakes as the guy doesn't stop.

I twist around in my seat, thinking I can catch a license plate number, but my cracked ribs have other ideas. Ow-ow-ow. All I'm able to see are the fancy LED taillights of an expensive car.

Bethany eases over to the curb and takes a moment to put her hand against her chest and hyperventilate a bit.

"You okay?" I ask.

"Yeah. Where are the police when you need them?"

I shrug and reach for the door lever. "Thanks for the ride, Bethany. And the photo."

"You're welcome."

"Um. Drive carefully, right?"

"No kidding."

I should say more, but I don't know what. I smile and nod at her. Her lips move as if she's trying to smile back. Then she grips the steering wheel in both hands and stares at her horn. The smile peeks through in her profile. I've charmed her just a little. Which is enough for now. I open the car door and step out.

"Take it easy, now," I say.

Another tiny smile as I'm closing the door, and then she's rolling away. And despite our panic-stop moment, something inside me feels good. A sense of accomplishment. A tiny bridge of redemption crossed. It's all good. I walk past the trailer park sign and scuff my feet on the coarse pavement, like I could do a shuffling dance.

And then it stops. All the good feelings. All my internal blue skies and happy times.

The front door of my trailer is hanging open. Winston is barking like crazy.

I freeze.

Dad?

But his pickup truck isn't parked anywhere around.

"Noah!" Simon's mother is standing on the screened porch, holding the door open. She frantically waves me over.

What's going on? I cross the narrow street and ease past my house, staring at that open door.

A break-in?

Why me? I was supposed to be the uninvolved, impartial observer. Maybe I got too close to the truth.

"Noah!" Mrs. Walsh says, trying to yell softly.

What if the person is still inside? What if... The thought of violence and possible gunshots gets my feet moving. I bound up the steps of Simon's porch while his mother holds the door.

"I've called the police," she says, her hand on my back to usher me inside.

"Did you see anything?"

"Just the door hanging open and a car backing out of the driveway fast. I didn't see the driver."

A speeding car. Like the one that almost caused a T-bone wreck with Bethany. What kind of car was it? I struggle to remember, but it happened so fast. This is a real bad moment for my concussion to mess with my memory. Small. Dark. LED lights. Expensive.

Drake drives a pickup truck. That much I remember.

And Todd rides the bus.

"I have to call my mother," I say.

Mrs. Walsh turns around, without the use of her walker, and wraps me in a hug. I can feel her shaking.

"Oh, honey! I'm just so grateful that you weren't home," she says.

Yeah, me too. Although...

Why did the guy go rushing away from the house that way? Maybe he knew the school bus would get there soon?

Who knows where I live?

I take out my phone but do my deep breathing exercise first. Not for my lungs, but to calm myself down before I have to tell Mom what has happened. She is not going to take it well.

I call Mom, but she doesn't answer, which probably means she's away from her desk. I leave a message for her to call me *immediately*. While I wait, I wander to the bay window in Simon's trailer that faces the street. The front door of my house sways a little in a breeze.

I've got to get over there. I need to know what happened inside.

"Do you think I can..." I point my thumb toward my house.

"No," Mrs. Walsh says. "I think it's better if you stay here until the police arrive."

Probably a good idea, but my insides are jumping around like marbles dropped in a glass jar.

The two more minutes or so that it takes for the two squad cars to arrive feels like a whole lot longer. Mrs. Walsh goes out to her porch again with me, and she calls one of the policemen over. By his first name.

"Jeannie," he calls back. "Are you all right?"

Okay, that's a little freaky. Then from a dark corner in my brain comes a memory, and I grasp it gladly. Simon's father was a cop. It's been a long time since he was killed, but his mother probably still knows some people on the force.

"I'm fine," she answers. "I saw someone leave that house in a hurry. Small black sportscar, Georgia plates." She puts a hand on my shoulder. "This is Noah. He lives there and just got home from school."

As he comes toward us, I put together the man's first and last name with what's inscribed on his nameplate. Paul Meyers.

"Okay," he says. "Well, hang tight while we check out the house. Was there anyone inside?"

"Mom's at work," I answer. Or... she was supposed to be. Did she go in to work after she dropped me off at school? She couldn't be in there, could she?

The cop presses his lips together and nods, like he sees my uncertainty. He holds up a hand to make sure I know not to move, and leaves to talk to one of the other cops.

I call Mom again.

And again.

Mrs. Walsh rubs my back, looking toward my house with worried eyes.

Mom's van isn't there. That means she's not there either. Right?

Finally, on my fourth try, Mom answers. "Noah, what's the matter? I'm at work—"

"Mom! Someone broke into the trailer. I'm at Simon's house, and the cops are here. You need to come home."

"What? Oh, my Lord. Noah? Why can't anything go right?"

"It's not my fault, Mom. I just came home from school, and the door was open. Mrs. Walsh called the police before I got here."

She doesn't respond, but I hear her rattling around with something."

"Mom?"

"I'll be there as soon as I can," she snaps.

"But— Fine! I'll deal with it myself."

I hear my name spoken in anger the split second before I disconnect the call.

Okay, maybe I overreacted. Maybe that banging around I heard was her getting her purse out of a drawer or something. But she didn't ask if I was okay. Maybe she assumed, since I was able to call her, that I'm not hurt or anything, but... she didn't ask.

It hurts.

A cop comes out of my house and walks across the street. "All clear," he says. "You can come over now."

"Do you want me to go with you?" Mrs. Walsh asks softly.

I shake my head.

"I'll be here, then. If you need anything."

I walk down the wooden steps of Simon's porch and climb the metal steps of mine. Walking through the front door, I see devastation and my limbs go weak. Everything is torn up and tossed around. The lopsided chair in the living room is upside down. Stuff has been pulled out of the kitchen cabinets and dumped all over the counters and the floor.

"Did you have a television or a computer?" a cop says to me. "Anything look missing?"

I shake my head and numbly pick up one of Mom's new pillows at my feet. I step around random stuff, drop the pillow on the couch where it belongs, and to go toward the hallway.

There's a picture frame on the floor, the glass smashed. And not like it fell off the wall and broke, but shattered in a million pieces. Inside it is a drawing that I did for Mom a few weeks ago, ruined now with a bunch of little rips and a big black mark. Probably from someone's shoe.

The bathroom looks okay, but my room... my room. There wasn't much in here to begin with, but it's all thrown around. Like someone just wanted to make as big a mess as possible. My sketchbook is shredded, torn pages mixed in with everything else. My clothes are everywhere. My mattress was pulled off the bed frame.

"Son," a cop says. "Give me your name, please."

"Noah Dickerson," a voice that sounds like mine says.

"How long have you lived here?"

"Um."

"Are you okay?"

"Yeah. Uh. About a month. A little longer."

"Can you tell if anything has been stolen?"

I shake my head and wander away from him, toward my mother's room. There the devastation stops. Just... stops.

Maybe because the person knew the bus would be dropping me off and he had to get out of there.

"Could they have been looking for something?" another cop says.

"Noah," the one standing at my shoulder says. "I need you to be honest with me. You'll do yourself a big favor by telling the truth. Were there any drugs in this house?"

The question pushes the rage button in my brain. "No!"

But then I think... my migraine medication. I push past the cop to go to my mother's room again. She kept the medicine hidden away and gave me the pills at the prescribed times. Seven and seven. Parental precautions that I didn't think were worth arguing about. But now... where did she keep the stuff?

I turn and rush to the bathroom medicine cabinet. Just ordinary stuff in there. Toothpaste, deodorant, my shaving cream. Tylenol.

Hairspray. I slam the cabinet door.

"What are you looking for?" someone asks.

"My medication. I have a-a concussion. The doctor gave me medicine."

"Oxycodone?"

"No. Triptan. Something triptan."

No one freaks out at this partial name. I have no idea if there's any street value to the stuff.

"Noah!" Mom's voice bounces off the walls of the trailer.

I push past the two cops to go to her. She grabs me and squeezes me hard against her.

"Are you okay? Oh, baby. Baby. Are you all right?"

"I'm fine. The guy left just when I was on my way home."

"He?" a policeman says. Mrs. Walsh's friend, Paul.

I pull away from Mom. "I saw the car. And I think I know who it was."

Not Todd. He was on the bus that would take him to the lofts and couldn't possibly have made it here before Bethany and me.

Not Drake. He drives a pickup truck.

Not Jun. He wasn't in the state when the first break-ins happened.

And unless Kevin is skipping classes from his college, two-hours away, it's not him.

That leaves just one...

Later... After Accusing the Son of a Prominent City Councilman

Mom and I are across the street in Simon's trailer. Mom has been crying. Mrs. Walsh has been listening. And Mom spilled our entire family story that I'd been reluctant to tell Simon much about. She even moaned how she doesn't understand why I just can't stay out of trouble.

Simon looks at me now with sympathetic eyes, and I don't like it.

The mothers are sitting at the kitchen table, drinking coffee, and I'm sitting with Simon in a pair of throw-covered armchairs next to the bay window. I'm turning my phone over and over in my hands. Neither of us has mentioned texting Chloe yet. Simon said she'd still be at youth group anyway.

"Do you think the police believed you?" Simon asks.

I look across the street at the dark trailer where I lived until today. I'm not sure what we'll do tonight, since I don't think Mom is in any emotional shape to go back to the scene of the crime yet. At least not until daylight and when we can put the place back together.

"They said they'd look into it, but I don't know if they will. Kinda crazy, right? The son of a politician, who was named prom king and is going to Georgia Tech, decides to risk everything to get revenge on people from his high school for making fun of him. Why not just… move on?"

"He always did think highly of himself," Simon says. "Strutting around like a rock star. If his ego is bigger than his common sense, maybe he thought he wouldn't get caught."

I pull air deep into my lungs. Now that I've had a chance to settle down and think things through, doubts are creeping in.

Bethany was wrong. I'm no good at this kind of thing.

"How did he know where you live?" Simon asks.

I shrug. That part is easy enough to guess. "Followed me home from Starbucks last night."

"But you weren't even here when all that stuff happened last year."

"Guess he figured I stuck my nose into his business, so I'm fair game now."

Simon shakes his head. "I don't know, Noah. Would he trash his own house just so he wouldn't look guilty?"

Yeah, the cops reminded me of that too. They were interested in what I had to say about all the recent break-ins being connected to people who attended prom last year. After I mentioned a few names, I had their attention. But then one of them asked me how I knew so much and suggested that I should be taken in to be fingerprinted.

That's when my mother started crying.

She calmed down enough to show them the paperwork from my hospital stay and the doctor's visit today, and I guess that provided the benefit of the doubt that I deserved.

My phone vibrates. I look down at the text.

CHLOE: I've been thinking about you-know-who. Do you think he spray painted defective on O'Toole's to make it look like Bryce?

Interesting question, especially since we haven't told her what happened yet. But all the messages Todd's been putting on social media seemed to make the Kevin/Drake/Jun trio look bad. And his statement that a UGA football player would go down… What if Todd was just guessing too?

"Could we be wrong?" I whisper to Simon. "Could it still be Kevin? Not Bryce?"

He's looking at me kind of weirdly. After a moment he sniffs. "It's possible." He pulls his phone out of his jacket pocket. The screen is dark.

And suddenly I understand that look. Chloe texted me, not him.

"You want to text her back?" I ask.

He shrugs.

"Simon…"

"It's okay. If you like her. I understand."

"I don't. I mean, she's nice. But… I wouldn't do that to you."

He glances at the mothers in the adjoining room. "It's all good. She doesn't like me that way anyway."

"Have you asked her?"

"No. I don't have to. I already know."

I'm not sure what to say about this, because I suspect he's right. A girl who was crushing on a guy would text him first.

But why me? She hasn't given me any of the usual signs that she's interested.

Simon sniffs again, like he's trying to clear away the emotion. "Know what? Better you than Connor."

"The future valedictorian?"

"If he doesn't get busted for cheating."

"Whatever. I'm not interested in her, okay? In fact, there was this other girl at church. I'm hoping Chloe can arrange an introduction."

"So... you're not leaving?"

Simon has a way of getting right to the heart of things. Like what my mother said and left unsaid about going back to North Carolina.

I wish I could do the same. But all I can answer is, "Not yet."

Chapter 12

Thursday... Fallout

We spent the night in Simon's trailer, as I expected, because Mom just couldn't face the mess and the feeling of insecurity at our place. But Simon's house isn't exactly a hotel, and sleeping on the floor of his bedroom was not exactly comfortable. He offered me his bed, because of my ribs, but I turned that down. So I'm sore today and in a rotten mood, not saying much to anyone.

I'm waiting for the fallout from last night. Any second now, Drake is going to storm up to me in the lunchroom, bellowing because the police went to his house to question him. Or Daniel is going to want to defend Bethany's honor after I "flirted with her" yesterday. Or Todd is going to point across the cafeteria and laugh at me for getting everything wrong. Something... something is going to happen.

Instead of any of my dire expectations, Chloe comes rushing to our table, her cell phone clutched in her hand like she's got news. And here I'm faced with a dilemma that has intensified since yesterday. I need to back off.

The "let's just be friends" talk usually ends up with hurt feelings and the loss of real friendship. I've found that skipping that part gets to the ultimate result faster. And really, I'd rather have a girl mad at me than be brokenhearted.

It fits in with my sulking attitude anyway. I stare numbly at my fish sticks and peas, trying like anything to not pay attention to what she's saying to Simon.

Until he slaps me hard on the shoulder and thrusts her phone in front of my face, too close for me to see anything.

"What?" I snap.

"Read it, read it! They arrested Bryce!"

Exit angst, enter insatiable need to know. I take the phone from Simon to read.

> *Bryce Valentino, the 18-year-old son of Middleboro City Councilman, Anthony Valentino, was arrested Wednesday night after a traffic stop on Canton Road. Valentino was caught on radar driving 77 mph through the industrial district of Middleboro. Valentino's blood alcohol level was recorded at 0.10. While searching his vehicle police discovered several items of stolen property linked to a string of home burglaries around Middleboro in the last few weeks. The car, a new Jaguar XE, has been impounded by city police. Oddly enough, the home of Councilman Valentino was the site of one of the burglaries over the weekend. It is unclear at this time whether the councilman's son is directly connected to the burglaries at his home and others, or if other people are involved.*

I gawk at what I'm reading, to stunned yet to jump up and pump my fist in the air.

"You mean... we were right?"

Simon grabs me by the shoulders and shakes me. "You were right, dude. You were. I was betting on Drake and a borrowed car."

"And I was sure it was Kevin," Chloe says.

"Well, yeah, but I thought it was Todd until last night." As I say this, I still have that gut feeling that Todd has hidden himself in the events somehow. Just like he did with Ivan and George the Maintenance Man.

I rub my face, not exactly eager to do what I should do next. "Can I borrow this phone for a minute? I need to show this to someone."

Chloe says okay and grins at Simon, hunching her shoulders in giddiness. Good. Let Simon be her go-to guy for good feelings. I get up and walk across the cafeteria to the Manganites' table. They've apparently got a new partner in crime, some baby-faced guy who looks like he's a freshman. Daniel sees me first, and he bristles. Paisley gasps and pushes away from the table like she's about to run away.

"Relax, y'all. I just need to show you something."

I hand Danny Boy the phone, and he leans close to Paisley to read the article.

"Bryce Valentino stole my doll?" Paisley says, squeaking.

Bethany grabs the phone and reads. When she looks up at me, I nod, pointing at her. Then give her a thumbs-up. She hides her giggle behind her hand and stands to return the phone to me.

"Why? Why would that guy..." Daniel shakes his head, not making the connection.

I lean between him and Paisley. "One word. Vengeance."

"Vengeance for what?" Paisley says. "I don't even know him."

"No, but you apparently made an impression with your doll."

The pinched look on her face softens, and her mouth forms a little O. She gets it now. "But how did he know where I live?"

I shrug. I have a theory about that very question, but I'll keep it to myself now, until I have another face-to-face with my Moriarty. In the meantime, I walk away from their table feeling vindicated. More than that. Like Bryce's crimes actually helped me to extend an olive branch to my enemies.

It's good.

Heading Home... Looking Forward to Talking to Mom

Simon is off work this afternoon, so we ride the bus home together, and he spends most of the time talking about Chloe. I guess since our discussion last night, he feels free to gush.

Chloe told him she's hoping her camera equipment and laptop are among the items the police found in Bryce's car. Since we discovered his hiding place in the woods, maybe he was searching for another place to stash his booty. Somewhere in the industrial district? Or perhaps he knew the value of those things and planned to keep them.

Although I don't mention it to Simon, I wonder if there was anything in that car—a Jaguar? Seriously?—that came from my house. We don't have anything valuable, but since he'd just been there...

The bus rolls past the intersection where O'Toole's Formal Wear sits. The graffiti is gone. It's absence reminds me of a task I meant to do yesterday. I send a text to that unknown number I suspect is Todd's.

NOAH: Do you like graffiti?

That's the one missing piece for me, although both Chloe and Simon seem comfortable without it. What exactly was Todd's role? Why the subterfuge with me? Why was he sneaking around at both Starbucks and the snake pit? Even at Waffle House?

And exactly how did Bryce get the addresses of people he didn't know personally? Maybe with the help of a hacker?

The bus stops at the trailer park entrance, and Simon and I get off, along with the two middle school girls who live nearby.

It feels kind of eerie, walking up the street toward my house when twenty-four hours ago it was not a place of peace and security. Today my mother's van is in the driveway, which means she came home from work early to start cleaning the mess Bryce left us. She's going to be so happy the cops caught the guy.

I nod at Simon to say goodbye and cut over toward my place. As I do, the door flies open, and Mom comes out with a box in her arms.

"Good, you're home," she says. "Go clean up your room and pack whatever things you have left that isn't trash." She pushes past me and slides the box into the cargo area of her van.

Cleaning up I get. But packing? I glance toward Simon's trailer. He's standing outside the porch, his hand on the latch, watching us. I give him a little wave so he'll head inside. But I'm betting he'll sneak over to that bay window to see what's going on.

"Did you find us another place?" I ask Mom as she's strutting past me again.

"We're going back," she says without stopping.

"Back. Home?"

"Yes."

I follow her into the house before I confront her. "Why?"

She goes to the kitchen, starts stacking the plates she bought when we came here. The ones Bryce didn't break. "Because I made a mistake leaving with you in the first place. None of this would be happening if I hadn't panicked and left."

"But—"

"Don't argue with me, Noah." The plates, not wrapped in anything to protect them, go into another box.

"So I don't have any say in this?"

My phone pings. Probably Todd's response. But I don't care. I just don't freakin' care.

"We should never have left." Mom starts in on the bowls. One is cracked, so she pitches it into a big black trash bag. Crash.

"He nearly killed me!" I point in a direction that might be northeast, toward home.

Mom whips around to face me. Her eyes are red-rimmed, probably from crying. "I lost my job today. Because I was taking too much time off to deal with you. Because of *you*. So don't give me any more grief today."

"Mom—"

"No!" She goes back to packing stuff.

The blame game. I've seen this so many times before. I usually tell myself she's lashing out because she's hurting and she doesn't mean it. This time, though, she's doing more than lashing out. She's uprooting us again.

"You think you're so grown up, don't you?" she goes on, like she's talking to herself more than me. "But you're not. You're incapable of making rational decisions. Simple, reasonable actions that will keep us safe. So I've made up my mind. We're going back, and I'll let your father straighten you out."

"And you think *that* is safe? Or reasonable?"

"We're going to fix things and put this family back together."

"It hasn't been together in years."

She grabs the box off the counter and uses it to push me aside. "Go pack your things. We're leaving tonight."

"No! I'm not going back there. Not to him."

She stops at the door, lifting one knee to balance the box. "So you'd rather I got arrested for kidnapping you? You'd rather your father and I go through a messy divorce that's going to tear us apart even more?"

"Mom... you didn't kidnap me."

"According to his attorney, I did. His *attorney*, Noah. He called me at work, and that was the last straw for my boss."

I poke myself in the chest. "I have a right to decide where I'm going to live. And with who."

"Not until you're eighteen, you don't."

She's got all this determination now. All this strength. She's made up her mind. Not for my welfare, but for hers. So she won't be arrested. So she won't be divorced from the only man who ever said he loved her.

I don't have time to ponder this as she walks up to me, the box leading the way, to give me another command.

I beat her to it. "I'm not going anywhere."

She slides the box onto the countertop and jabs a finger toward the hallway. "Go pack your things."

"No. I'm not going."

She slaps my face.

She has never done that before.

It doesn't hurt. The slap was weak. But it snaps something inside me and I stagger away from her... so I won't hit her back.

I can't escape this violence. I know that if I go back to my father, the rage inside me will boil over, and the next time he hits me, there will be a fight. He might even kill me, because he's bigger and stronger.

This anger... now nearly turned against my mother.

I know what I have to do.

Darkness Falls... Fly, Fly Little Bird

It's not like I have a lot to pack, but Mom wants to leave the trailer in better condition than the way we found it. She gave me some plastic garbage bags to clear out any trash in my room and to stuff my bed linens into. My laundry basket will hold all of my clothes. Bryce left me a mess more than anything else. The white shirt I wore to Starbucks the other night has slashes through it.

Which meant Bryce sent me a message, *and* he brought a knife with him.

I can't think about that now. I've got a backpack with school stuff inside, which I could probably leave behind with Simon so he could return the books... if I was really leaving.

No plan. No clue. I can't go to Simon's house, because that's the first place Mom will look. I don't have any other close friends I can call. Not in Georgia, anyway.

If Mom said we were going back to get our own place in North Carolina, I'd be okay with that. If she said I could stay with Nathan, that would be all right. But no. We're going back to the person who is the real cause of everything that has happened to us.

While Mom is in her bedroom packing her things, I stuff my backpack as full as it will get with clothes. I yank my phone charger out of the wall socket and jam it into my pocket. I take the laundry basket with the rest of my clothes to the living room and set it down next to the door. Then I carry the bag of linens out too, along with the trash. My room is clear. Needs vacuuming. I'm not going to worry about it.

Mom is still in her room.

The backpack weighs a ton. I slip my left arm through the second strap so I won't drop the thing. Then I turn and survey the trailer. It's bland and ancient looking... just like when we moved in.

There's a business card on the kitchen counter. Karen Dupree, Department of Family and Children Services. Did Mom talk to her today too? Maybe to see if they would tell her how not to get arrested?

Did they talk her into going home?

I can hardly breathe. It's like I'm trapped somewhere deep inside my body, my soul screaming, while my arm reaches out to take the card and stuff it into my hoodie pocket.

"I'm ready," I call out, no enthusiasm whatsoever in my voice.

"I'll be out in a minute," she yells. "Take that trash to the dumpster for me."

That's an order. But I see it as opportunity. With my backpack stretching my shoulders backwards, I grab the garbage bag. It's even heavier. I half-drag it out of the trailer, my ribs adding to my internal screaming. I close the door loud so she knows what I'm doing and then lug the bag to the dumpster at the back of the trailer park.

Then I keep going.

A path behind the trailer park leads to some industrial buildings. I pause next to one and send a single text.

NOAH:	I love you. I know nothing I say will make you change your mind about going back to Dad. I guess it makes sense. I don't want you to go to jail. But I can't go back there. I'll be okay. Don't look for me. Just go home. I'll be in touch when I can.

I use my phone to light my way until I reach the industrial area. Is this where they caught Bryce speeding? I'd wonder what he was doing here, but I really don't care. I really, really don't care anymore.

I stay away from the main road. I get to an old neighborhood where the houses are close together. Some people on a porch are speaking Spanish. One of the houses is completely dark and looks really rundown. The weeks are thick around it. I go around the back.

The rear door is locked, and I don't want to risk making noise and attracting attention by smashing a window. I've never broken into a house before, but I've seen on television where they slip credit cards between the door and the frame.

I almost laugh. Bryce Valentino could have given me some tips.

Karen Dupree's business card is thin cardboard. I shred one edge trying to get it into the lock. I don't have anything like a credit card... except for my student ID.

After some wrangling and hushed cussing, I get the door open. Inside smells like dirt and mold and rotten food. I find a room upstairs, away from the front or back windows.

This is home. For now.

Midnight...

What have I done?

Chapter

Friday... All On My Own
Until They Catch Me

A police siren wails behind me. I keep walking, trying to look like I'm not freaking out inside and about to dive into the kudzu and hide. My backpack weighs me down, since every muscle and joint in my body is crying in agony anyway. Hard, filthy floor, stinking of God only knows what. No sleep. My phone pinged every few minutes as Mom, and then Simon, and even Mia and Chloe, tried to get me to respond and tell them where I am. I sent one identical text to Simon and Mom. *I'm fine. Don't worry.*

Like that would stop them.

I refused to read their messages after that. Turned my phone off. Not just to silence the constant reminder that I'm an idiot and people actually care about me, but also just in case they could do that GPS location thing and find me huddled in a crumbling hell hole.

I tried to rest, but every little sound jerked me to full alertness. The old house creaking. Something skittering across the floor. Cars going by on the street. Police sirens in the distance.

Looking for me?

This morning's screaming cop car passes by, and I breath again.

As much as I tried to think about the future and what I could do next, nothing seemed clear except that I have made things worse. But there's no way to reverse course and make it better. Mom needs to go home. And I need to figure out what I'm going to do now.

I'm walking along a four-lane road, heading in the direction it seems like most of the traffic is going. It's cold out, but I'm sweating, and my throat hurts.

A school bus rumbles past, leaving a wake of diesel fumes. I look ahead. A group of kids wait at the corner next to a subdivision sign.

School. Principal Manning. Karen Dupree. Will they help me?

I run, or plod along as fast as the backpack will let me, waving my arms and yelling, "Wait!" The bus stops and the kids load onto it, and I'm still running. A girl, the last in line, looks toward me.

"Tell the driver to wait! I yell.

She gets on... and the bus doesn't move.

I nearly career past the open door but catch the handle and pull myself up the steps. The driver looks at me like a homeless person has just boarded her bus.

Well... yeah.

"Sorry," I croak, huffing. "Thanks for waiting."

"May I see your student ID?" she asks. The door behind me is still open, so she can shove me out if she has to.

Fortunately, I have my ID handy, since I tucked it into my hoodie pocket after I picked that lock last night. I show her. She still looks skeptical, but finally jerks her thumb toward the seats behind her.

I take the first seat I find with no one else sitting there. At the next stop, some big dude plops down next to me, and I have to slide closer to the cold window so our legs aren't touching. I stare out the window, and he does me the favor of not acknowledging my presence. The bus comes to a stoplight, and I realize we're on the main road through town. There's the drug stores and O'Toole's Formal Wear. We make the turn onto the main road, and it's just a minute before the school comes up on our left.

My normal bus is sitting two lanes over from where we've stopped. I hang back, hoping the crowd around me will be enough to hide me as

Simon gets off.

He looks unhappy. He turns toward the door of the school without seeing me, and then he's inside.

I wait a few moments longer, then trudge into the building and straight to the administration office, where I collapse into a vinyl armchair and wait for the secretaries to get through helping the usual morning crowd of parents, students, and teachers coming in and going out.

No one notices me.

The first bell rings, signaling six minutes until class time. They must have timed how long it takes for someone to walk from one end of the building to the other, because six minutes doesn't make sense. Why not five? Or ten?

I'm kind of dizzy. My brain is going weird places. My throat hurts.

I glance toward the hallway in time to see two policemen—city cops, not school—coming toward the office. Crap. I shield my eyes, like I'm rubbing away a headache—which I've had since last night anyway— and sit tight while they enter the office and approach the secretary's desk. Impossible to stop my knee from bobbing. But they'd expect a kid sitting here would be waiting to see the principal or a counselor, right? Nothing suspicious here.

Except they're talking about me. I hear my name. And because the secretary has been too busy to notice me and ask my name yet, she says something about looking up my schedule to see where I'm supposed to be for my first class.

Moving as silently as a person can while freaking out inside, I reach down beside the chair where I set my backpack, snag one strap in my hand, and glide out of the chair. Head down, no fast moves. I walk out the door and turn, like I'm going to class. Except I head for the side entrance next to the student parking lot instead.

Just a guy who forgot something in his car, right?

Outside. Along a line of cars. Past the place where I saw Drake and Kevin fighting days and days ago. Almost to the end of the lot. I hear that second bell ring, signaling the start of class. It chills me, and I have to stop and get a grip. I find a beater pickup truck with the obligatory deer head sticker on the rear window. I lean against the side door, close my eyes, and hyperventilate.

God. God. What am I doing?

Prayer isn't my thing. I doubt the Deity would listen to me anyway. After all, I'm not one of His lost sheep. I'm a *runaway*.

"Noah?"

I lurch upright, almost dropping my backpack. My shoulder bumps the truck's mirror. I try to move the mirror back to its original position but give up.

Bethany stands a few feet away, her head tilted with concern. "Are you all right? What are you doing out here?"

A Manganite would be among the last people on this earth I'd want to confess my problems to, but Bethany lingers like she's the answer to my prayer that God sent. Pretty, innocent looking, genuinely concerned.

"What are you doing here?" I counter. "You're late."

"Yeah, I know. Stuff at home made me late. Noah... you don't look so good."

"Hey, thanks. That's good to know."

"No, seriously. You look like you might be sick."

No kidding. "Stuff at home," I say and then smirk at my own stupid joke.

Bethany hugs her arms and looks down at the ground, a sign she's not ready to hurry on to class. "Noah, I'm really sorry... about everything that happened."

This again? I'm over it. And Bethany shouldn't be the one to apologize to me. I don't think she knew that one of her manga friends raped a girl, and I'm pretty sure she had no clue that his father tossed her into the river. To be fair, I'm not even sure of that. The attorneys haven't contacted me yet, and they're probably not going to clue me in on their investigation because I'm such a great detective. Right.

What were we talking about?

"You're not like them," I say. "Daniel and Paisley. You could have lots of other friends."

She does a big, girly shrug that says she doesn't want to answer.

I lean back against the truck again, not wanting to offend her but just wishing she would leave.

"Noah, do you need help? Really, you look like you're about to pass out. Is it your concussion?"

I huff a laugh at myself. Concussion. Medication. I don't have it.

"Noah?"

"No! I'm fine. Just... go to school, Bethany."

The compassion fades from her eyes. "Fine. I tried to be nice. It's probably drugs anyway."

I chuckle at this. Drugs. More like the lack of them. "I wish," I mutter.

She doesn't respond, but finally walks away. For a moment I feel relieved, until it hits me that if she sees the police inside the building, she just might connect their presence to me, hiding out here in the parking lot.

Time to move on.

I head to the park. That might be the first place the cops will look for me if Bethany says anything to them, but everywhere else is too open, too close to the main road. Maybe I can find a place to hide until I figure out what I'm going to do.

Everything feels heavy. The daylight hurts my eyes, even though it's cloudy. I'm sweating like crazy and freezing at the same time. I find the regular entrance to the park, because no way I'd be able to climb a fence. My backpack seems to weigh twice what it did last night. I trudge up a gravel path, but soon I'm walking sideways more than forward.

This isn't good. Migraine. Exhaustion. Pain. Throat hurts. Pneumonia... And when was the last time I ate anything?

I'm going down.

The Grass is Greener... Somewhere Else. Not Here.

There's a metallic smell to Georgia red clay. Like a moldy copper penny. That's what I notice first. And then that it doesn't taste like the pennies I used to suck on in kindergarten. It tastes like dirt. I spit and push myself away from the ground. I've been lying on top of my right arm, and my ribs are complaining.

"He's coming around," someone says.

I try to roll onto my back, but something's in the way. My backpack. Gritty stuff covers one side of my face. I blink at a man hovering over me. All I can see is his silhouette. Has a hat on.

He puts a hand on my chest. "Take it easy, son. Help is on the way."

Help? That means police. I shake my head and immediately regret it. "No, I'm... okay."

"Like heck, you are. You got a cell phone? Someone we can call?"

Mom? It just keeps getting worse. I can't think clearly, which means I have no control over this situation.

"What's your name?" he asks.

Are you kidding me with this? For a second, I can't even remember my own name. But then it comes. "Noah."

Maybe I shouldn't have told him.

Nah. It's done. Give it up. I let my head drift down and close my eyes. A fleeting idea comes to me. Just an image. The Great Cloud of Concussion tries to drive it away, but I grab it long enough to take action. I slip my right hand into my hoodie pocket. After fumbling around with my school ID, my fingers find a bit of thin cardboard. I pull it out. My hand shakes as I give it to the man.

"Karen Dupree. This lady gonna help you?"

"Yeah," I whisper.

Tires popping on gravel. The help has arrived. I breathe in and out, unable to do it deeply like I'm supposed to. Trying to get back to reality.

"Noah," a man says. I can tell from the direct tone of his voice that he's a cop.

I've got to come up with an excuse why I'm lying here in the wet grass and clay and not in school where I belong. "Migraine," I mutter. "Throat hurts."

"Ambulance is on its way."

"No! No hospital. Please." I grab someone's arm. My stomach muscles contract and pull the rest of my torso upward. "I can't go to the hospital."

"You were found unconscious in the park, son. You're going to the hospital."

An image shocks my brain. My father walking into my hospital room after that car accident. They'll call him again, and this time I'm sure he won't leave Georgia without me. I can't let that happen. Big problem, though. At the moment, I don't have the strength to run or the wits to argue.

I blink up at the man in the blue uniform. "Call Karen. Please."

"He gave me this card," the first guy says.

I can see him more clearly now. He's wearing a khaki uniform. A patch on his breast pocket says Sanderson. He hands the business card to the cop, who nods and slips the card into his breast pocket. No name there, but a gold-colored badge above it. The cop squats down next to me, taking Sanderson's place.

"Noah, we're here to help you, but you need to be straight with me right now. Have you taken any narcotics?"

I can't remember the name of the stuff the doctor prescribed for me. Doesn't matter, because my problem is that I haven't had any of it since yesterday morning.

"Concussion medication," I say. "But not today."

"You have a concussion? Is that why you passed out?"

A bunch of numbers come over his radio in a garbled voice, followed by my first and last name, which I hear quite clearly. The cop touches the radio and says, "10-4."

I relax. There's nothing I can do. I'm too sick.

For the next ten months I'll be controlled by people who think they know what's best for me.

What's best for me? How about a normal life? Without concussions. Without yelling and cussing and smashing things into walls. A girlfriend would be nice. Someone who thinks I'm good looking and talented. Okay grades and making plans for whatever comes after graduation. That's normal. Can any of them give that to me?

The truth is, I probably don't even have the right to ask for it.

My father always said I don't have rights in our house, no matter what I might see at my friends' houses. Ultimately, everything belongs to him, and I have it, or not, based on his good will. So often I've heard him rant about entitled kids and how he was doing us a favor by keeping us on the edge, having to earn whatever he gave us. In his more sober moments, he explained the world doesn't hand out blessings, and we all should learn to work hard to get whatever we want in life.

There's one big problem with that idea. It doesn't work. He didn't feel that he had to work hard to keep his family together. Nathan and Naomi both left as soon as they could do it legally. I will too. Just... not today.

Afternoon...Seems Like I've Been Here Before

There's a needle in the back of my right hand, dripping fluid into my vein. The ER doctor made a diagnosis. Dehydration and complications from a concussion. Waiting on a strep test.

I'm feeling a little bit better and sitting on the side of the bed. I don't want to relax. Lying down is like the ultimate sign of surrender, on my back with my belly exposed to predators. I want to be able to move if I have to.

I swing my feet above the floor, choreographing the kicks in patterns to use up the time. People are outside this curtained room, talking about me, although the police left when they were certain I wasn't going to run away again. Mom is here. And Karen Dupree from DFCS. They're arguing. Quietly. But I hear Mom's voice squeak numerous times.

Mom wants to take me home to North Carolina. Are they arguing because Karen is telling her she can't? Maybe Dad is on his way, and they're afraid Mom will actually run somewhere else with me.

The curtain hangers zing against the rail and a nurse comes in. She looks serious. She doesn't call me "sweetie" like she did when she stuck me with the needle. *"Little stick. Good job."* Mom is behind her, and Ms. Dupree comes in last. I'm surrounded by stern-faced women, and I don't know if any of them are on my side. Maybe the nurse.

Mom is a mess. It's obvious she didn't sleep. Her eyes are swollen and bloodshot. Her skin seems to be hanging a little looser over her facial bones.

"Here's the situation, Noah," Ms. Dupree says, all business-like. "Your father wants to have your mother prosecuted for kidnapping. Your mother says he abused you and caused a concussion. The other night y'all convinced me that there was no kidnapping, in the sense that you, Noah, were not being held against your will. That you wanted to stay in Georgia. I believed you. But last night, you ran away from your mother."

She holds up a hand to stop the excuse that's about to fly out of my mouth.

"I understand that she intended to take you back to North Carolina. Just in terms of the legalities, that certainly would be a solution. But my concern is for you, what's the best situation for you. Your mother has told me that she has everything packed in her car, ready to go. Now, I want you, in a moment, to take a bit of time to think about what *you* want. No one is going to argue. No one is going to punish you for whatever you say. However, I do need for you to understand the consequences first."

I nod, swallow hard against the dry knot in my throat, and wait for the consequences.

"If you do not go with your mother and return to North Carolina, then you will stay here and be taken into protective custody by the State of Georgia. We will arrange for temporary housing until such time as things are resolved between your parents and the authorities in North Carolina confirm that the house is approved for you to return."

I wish they would do that. Not take me into custody but lay down the law with my parents so they would straighten up and the house would be *approved.*

Good luck with that.

Really, I'd give anything to go back home, to see Naomi and Nathan, to be in school with people I know, and to have my own room with stuff that is actually *mine,* not on loan from my dad.

"If you decide to go with your mother," Ms. Dupree says, "then your case will be transferred to DHHS in North Carolina, and they will monitor the situation with your family. If it comes to their attention that the abuse is continuing, you will be taken into custody there, and your parents may face prosecution."

Which is probably what would happen. And DHHS would step in too late, because someone would be dead. Probably me.

I swallow again. Try twice before I find my voice. "What happens to them if I decide to stay here?

"They have to register with authorities up there and prove the home is safe for you to return home. Our ultimate goal is to keep families together, as long as standards of care are met."

Right. She already told me that. My brain is still fuzzy.

"One thing I need you to keep in mind, Noah. Running away is a very, very serious thing. You cannot legally live on your own, and the streets are not safe havens for anyone."

I have another question, and I can't look at my mother as I ask it. "What about... emancipation?"

A gasping sob escapes Mom. Yep. That's why I couldn't look.

"That's certainly a legal option, but it isn't easy," Ms. Dupree says. "You have to go to court and prove that the situation with your parents warrants your separation from them. This isn't like taking a break for a while so you can do your own thing. It's legal and complete separation. You can't just go back if you decide you made a mistake. That's another court case. You also have to prove that you have a means of supporting yourself."

Complete separation. And she wants me to decide this today?

I can't. I can't.

But I also can't go back to North Carolina. I don't care what Ms. Dupree says about DHHS doing whatever they do. As soon as I go back, Dad will blame me for everything that happened, for being a *baby* and coming between him and his wife. For convincing Mom to stay away this long when he's been pleading with her to come home. None of that is true, but the truth amounts to a load of bull squat with my father.

I look at Mom, and it's hard for me to breathe.

She's waiting.

She knows.

I'm about to break her heart.

"I can't go back," I say, with almost no volume in my voice.

My mother breaks down. I slide off the bed and put my arms

around her. We cry together. The nurse and Ms. Dupree give us some space and time. Mom asks me why. Why? Will she even understand?

"He'll kill me. And if he doesn't, I might kill him."

Mom buckles beneath me. The nurse comes in and helps her. I may be trying not to kill my father, but I might have just ruined my mother.

I'm the worst kind of person in the world.

A part of me has also just died.

I retreat to the bed and let myself lay back now, because I have no energy for anything else.

Mom leaves the room.

No goodbyes.

Goodbye would be too hard.

Ms. Dupree comes back in. She doesn't say anything and looks as sympathetic as I've seen her so far. She waits until I heave a long sigh, blowing it out toward the ceiling.

"Your mother told me she has your things in her van. I'll get them for you. The nurse will stay here with you. And I'll call the office and have them make temporary arrangements for where you'll stay tonight. It will probably be for just the weekend, while we arrange something more permanent."

I barely hear what she's saying. She's talking about what happens next, about my future. Thing is... I don't feel like I have one.

I exist. But I'm dead.

The doctor informs us that my strep test came back negative, but he keeps me a little longer to make sure I'm hydrated and the medicine for my migraine has worked with no ill effects. I check my phone for messages and anything interesting on social media. Not because I want to be entertained or informed. Not because I care anymore about stolen prom dresses or a humiliated rich guy. I just need a distraction. Relief from the torture that's going on inside me.

Agatha Cross High School is buzzing with news that the prom king was arrested. And a couple of people again suggest that I'm really in league with the Georgia Bureau of Investigations.

Did I really just agree to stay in *this* place?

Todd McCaffrey, my "Moriarty," is silent. His answer to my text question yesterday was just unrevealing cryptic banter, asking if I'd done any artwork lately.

Simon has sent me about ten messages since last night. I guess I owe him some kind of explanation, since my mother obviously went over to his place and got him all worried that I'd been abducted by human traffickers or something. It's hard for me to put words together, but not because of migraine or medicine fog. I just don't know how to explain to someone else that my family has fallen completely to ashes.

NOAH: Hey. Sorry about last night. I'm okay. Won't be coming back to the trailer park, though. DFCS is working out a new place for me. I'll let you know where later. Maybe see you at school.

Maybe. If I'll even be at the same school.

The other messages on my phone are from Mom, Mia, Chloe, and Naomi, who Mom apparently contacted to see if she could get my attention. I delete them all without reading.

Self-preservation.

Ms. Dupree comes in, and she's got a clean shirt and a jacket for me. "Cold outside," she says.

The nurse removes the IV needle from my hand. I'm being discharged from one authority and handed over to another.

How did this happen to me?

I'm able to dress myself without assistance. Physically, I feel a lot better now than I did earlier. In a weird way, I'm starting to separate myself into different parts, the physical and the emotional, and a part that almost feels external, like my omniscient self that analyses everything else. I push the emotions to the side, still there for me to observe and analyze, while I focus on the physical. Actions, movements, following directions.

Paperwork is signed, and I'm ready to go.

Ms. Dupree stands before me and takes a deep breath, her chest rising and falling. "Noah, please, for your own sake, don't try anything that will only get you into more trouble. We're going to walk out to my car, and I'm going to drive you to where you'll stay tonight. At this point, if you try to bolt, it will be the police coming after you.

I close my eyes for a moment and nod. "Ten months. That's all I'm giving you of my life. Then it's my own."

A small smile touches her lips. "I'd say that's the spirit, but that cocky attitude can also get you into trouble."

Good to know that one thing hasn't changed, anyway.

She takes me to her car and then drives, through rush hour traffic—which clogs up this town not built to handle it—to Riverbend Estates. Where a lot of the burglaries happened. Where the rich people live "up the hill." How ironic.

We turn into a showcase type street, with a landscaped median and fancy signs with home prices listed. Starting in the low 300s.

I can't even…

The first section of the subdivision is called "Birch." The houses are already bigger than the one my parents rent in North Carolina. They've all got big porches and identical mailboxes. Sidewalks and manicured lawns. Maybe ten feet in between each house.

Then we move to another section with a sign saying, "Dogwood." Here we turn off the main road and head along a curving road, where the houses are a little bigger, but still situated close together and with identical features. Muted pastel colors. Two-car garages.

My house in North Carolina doesn't even have a carport.

We pull into one of the cement driveways. If anyone is home, the car must be parked inside the garage.

I follow Ms. Dupree up the stairs to the front porch, where cushioned wicker furniture looks like something out of a magazine. She rings the doorbell. A dog barks, and through the beveled glass door I see some kind of terrier running so fast that its feet rumple a throw rug on the hardwood floor. A woman follows, shushes the dog, and calls for a kid behind her to put the dog outside. Finally she lets us in.

She already knows Ms. Dupree.

I'm the stranger here.

"This is Mrs. Radcliff," Ms. Dupree says. "She's one of our volunteers to take in children with temporary needs."

Radcliff. The name is familiar.

"Noah," the woman says, extending her hand to me. She's nice looking, slender, and maybe around forty years old. Her grip is stronger than I would have guessed. "It's very nice to meet you."

Is it? What a weird thing to say, considering my circumstances. Or any circumstances that I would imagine a kid like me to be in. Temporary needs. Meaning nothing is permanent. Nothing is secure.

I find I'm unable to say anything to her. I just nod and look away from her sympathetic eyes.

The other kid, in a second living room at the back, is leaning over the top of a chair and peering at me down the hallway. Big windows behind him, and I see the railings of a deck. Nice furniture all around. The hardwood floors are polished, not scratched and worn dull like the floors at my house.

Not my house any more.

I push down the emotional side of me again. The women are talking. Mrs. Radcliff turns to me once more. "You'll have your own room upstairs. I hope it will be comfortable for you. You'll address me as Mrs. Radcliff, and my husband as Mr. Radcliff. We expect you to abide by our rules which, I assure you, are not strict but necessary. You will not be able to come and go as you please, and our doors all have additional locks to prevent this. You will eat your meals with the family, and no cell phones are allowed at the table. We have set times in the evening for homework, and you will go to your room at a reasonable hour at night. No loud music. I understand you're already enrolled at the high school, but if you'll be here for more than the weekend, I'll take you to school Monday morning to handle the necessary paperwork."

I don't respond. It's all so unreal. I don't know what to say.

"Please take your shoes off. We'll put them in the mud room. Then I'll show you around and take you to your room so you can rest and clean up before supper."

Mrs. Dupree touches me on the arm, gives me another business card, and slips away. The hand-off is complete.

I take my shoes off—my bloodstained Converse sneakers—and follow Mrs. Dupree to the "mud-room" at the back of the house.

Although I can't imagine that tidy room, with it's nooks and hooks and shelves, has ever seen any mud.

My mother would gush over this place, especially the kitchen. It's big and shiny, with lots of cabinets and countertops and appliances. The first living room, in which I stood with Mrs. Dupree, was small and cozy looking. Across from it was a formal dining room. Gleaming furniture, glistening chandelier. The second living room is huge, with a big-screen television and floor-to-ceiling bookshelves. Those windows look out on more homes in the neighborhood. Rolling hills beyond them are in full fall color.

The terrier is jumping at the windows, it's little head popping up and disappearing.

The boy, who's seven or eight years old, doesn't say anything when his mother introduces him as Phillip. He's scrunched up in the chair now, one hand clutching a squirming foot, the other giving me a circular wave. I get it. I'm the intruder into his house. He doesn't have to talk to me.

Mrs. Radcliff takes me up a double flight of steps to the rooms upstairs. Yet another living room with another big screen television.

They trust me around all this stuff?

I'm in the foster care system now. I could be anyone, do anything. They don't know me at all. But this woman is showing me around like I'm a special guest.

Although... there are *rules*.

All the bedrooms are up here, but Mrs. Radcliff doesn't show them to me. She points at one closed door and says, "That's Phillip's room." Then, "That is mine and Mr. Radcliff's." And then, "That is Connor's room, and this one is yours."

I don't even look where she's pointing. I stare at the door of Connor's room, which is slightly ajar.

Connor Radcliff.

The coincidence is staggering.

Didn't Simon say something about the dude's family taking in foster kids?

"Noah?" Mrs. Radcliff says.

I get ahold of myself. Okay. Fine. My room. I follow her in there.

This... can't possibly... be mine.

I've never lived this way my whole entire life. None of my friends back home live this way.

More big windows look out over those hills, and bright daylight floods the room. The walls are pale sage green. No ancient, dark paneling. There's a wide bed with pillows that match the blanket, a dresser and a mirror, and a desk where I can do homework. A big closet—not that I'll need it. An entrance to a bathroom that I'll share with Connor. Not with four other people.

It's too much. It's extravagant and wasteful and fabulous. I stand in the middle of the room and don't quite know which way to turn.

Mrs. Radcliff rubs my arm. "I know it's hard. You're not our first foster. It's always strange and even scary at first. Take whatever time you need. I know you've had a rough day and you're not feeling well. I'll have Connor bring your things up for you. Get some rest."

She leaves me alone, gently closing the door behind her. I stare out the window, then peer into the bathroom, run my hand over the soft, thick blanket on the bed. I stare because I'm completely lost.

My phone pings, and I pull it quickly out of my pocket, because *this is mine* and is a part of me that I still understand. It's a text from Simon, who has probably heard by now that I've been found and am still alive. I open the text to read.

SIMON: Noah, this is Simon's mom. I hope you're okay and we'll see you soon. Please know that I've been praying for you. But I have some bad news to tell you. Simon had an accident while he was walking to work today. He says someone tried to shoot him. He ran away, and a car hit him. He's hurt very badly and in the hospital. Please, Noah, tell me if you have any idea who could have done this to my baby. Please.

I feel sick. I have to sit on the bed or I'll fall over. Someone tried to shoot Simon? *Simon!* Why? He's just a quirky kid. And who could have done it? Yeah, I think I have an idea. Maybe who and why.

Because they can't get at me now. So they went after him.

I can't breathe. I stand and pivot around the room, feeling trapped and helpless.

Simon is hurt, in the hospital, because of me. Because he's my friend. Because I got the prom king in trouble.

Rage boils inside me, building and building until I can hardly see.

There's a wall.

And my fist.

Slamming into it.

Because I need to hurt somebody.

"What are you doing?" someone yelps.

I grab my right hand and press it against my stomach. I've probably broken it.

Connor stands in the doorway, a laundry basket and my backpack in his hands. He drops the basket to the floor and grabs my arm. I want to jerk away from him, maybe even punch his face instead of the wall. But I'm going numb.

Numb.

Escaping deep inside myself.

My fault. My fault. Simon is hurt. I should have been with him. I should have protected him. He's just a shrimp kid...

Connor moves my fingers around. "Don't think it's broken, but it's probably going to hurt like crazy. Should put some ice on it." He lets go. "My dad will make you repair that wall yourself."

He takes a step back and judges me.

"You're not making a good first impression, Noah Dickerson."

I don't freaking care. My only real friend is hurt, and I'm trapped here.

Someone, somehow, is going to pay.

TO BE CONTINUED...

Acknowledgements

NaNoWriMo stands for National Novel Writing Month, and it takes place in November every year. While most sane people in the United States are thinking about the upcoming holidays and family gettogethers, many—who would probably agree with me that the activity is somewhat less than sane—are pounding away at their computer keyboards to write 50,000 words in 30 days. This year I have five new novels coming out, and all five of them were either birthed or raised up during NaNoWriMo. The craziness allows creativity free reign, and it also allows me to brainstorm with other people who are— they would probably agree—just as crazy during that month as me.

And so, for this novel, I have to thank my fellow North Georgia NaNoWriMo peeps for the laughter, the brainstorming, the competition, the word wars, and the steady flow of our favorite caffeinated drinks, that helped me with the creation of this novel. Thank you, Jesse, for always being there and giving me something to laugh about or think about. Thank you, Cassie, for nipping at my heels, so to speak, that pushed me to word counts I never would have thought possible. Thank you, Rose, for dropping your own project to brainstorm with me when I had gaping plot holes to fill. Thanks to all of you for your continued friendship beyond November madness.

But there is one person who was there at the beginning, when I was just planning out what adventures would consume Noah in this novel. A guest in our house, staying for a few weeks while he traveled to and from a new job. While he is not a writer, he is a man of quick and sick wit, and he is directly responsible—he would definitely agree—for some of the weirder elements in this story. Including... Green Bean. Yes, we can all thank my buddy Wes for that bit of high class humor! But seriously, I loved the enthusiasm and out-of-the-box thinking you leant me while you were here, and I am very grateful.

I also have to thank my friends, Ardith and Mark, for their help in my research of matters related to social work and police matters. Thank you for being so generous with your time and your expertise.

As always, to my husband, who is my rock, and my daughter, who is my inspiration, and my Lord, Jesus Christ, who makes all things Good. All my love.

Here's a brief excerpt from book #3
in the Because... Series.

Because...Paranoid

Available August 15, 2018

Hospitals Come ... Hospitals Go

I've seen enough hospitals lately that I could become an aficionado of them. The one Mrs. Radcliff brings me to is the same one I walked out of just yesterday. Same polished floors and potted plants, and everything that goes into making the place look inviting. We stop at a tall, curved desk and Mrs. Radcliff asks where we can find Simon Walsh. She directs us to an elevator and the fourth floor.

It all looks so familiar. Not that I've been to this part of the hospital, but like every other hospital. Rooms with carts sitting outside them. Nurses' station. Doors into the rooms that are wide enough for beds with rails to pass through.

I see Simon's room and outpace Mrs. Radcliff to get there.

She stands outside the room, allowing me to see him alone.

Simon looks like a little kid lying in that bed. He isn't wearing his glasses, and his sleeping head is turned to one side, green-tinted hair splayed across his pillow. Even with a huge purple bruise covering one cheek, he has that angelic look of a child.

So wrong that he should be here at all. Why would anyone want to intentionally hurt him, even kill him?

His hospital gown has slipped off one shoulder, revealing bandages, and the lump beneath his blanket looks like his arm bent stiffly at ninety degrees.

"Simon?" I say softly, thinking if he doesn't answer, I'll leave him to sleep.

His eyes open and he blinks at me. "Oh…" He fumbles around for the controller on his bed.

I step closer to him. "Hey…"

Now that I'm here, I don't know what I can say. *"I'm sorry I left you alone so someone would shoot at you instead of me."*

"Noah." His voice is scratchy. "What happened to you? You just went away."

I shake my head. "I'm still here." My throat tries to close up on me. "I'm sorry. I should have been here with you."

"Don't be stupid. It wouldn't have mattered."

"Your mother said someone shot at you."

He lifts his left hand—which is bruised in all the places nurses would stick with needles—and rubs his eyes. "Yeah, but the police don't believe me."

"What?"

"They said they couldn't find any evidence, and it was probably just a car backfiring."

I blow out a long breath as relief settles in. No one actually shot at Simon.

"But I know they shot at me," he says. "I'm sure of it. I looked back, and I saw a guy in a black pickup truck. I saw this cloud of smoke."

Smoke? Do guns put out clouds of smoke?

"And the bang I heard wasn't a car backfiring. It wasn't, Noah."

His eyes are pleading with me to believe him. Maybe no one has believed him yet. I try to remember exactly what the message from his mother said. Did someone shoot at him or did he just say someone shot at him?

Simon rubs his good hand over his bruised face. "The doctor said it's possible I don't remember everything clearly. But I remember that noise. So loud. And the smoke. I could smell the gunpowder."

I move closer to his bedside and keep my voice as soft as I can. "Do you know who did it?"

"That's the thing. I can't remember the face. All that smoke."

"You know everybody, Simon." I grin so he'll think I'm teasing him.

He shakes his head. "Not this time. Not an old guy, that's all I can say. But I did get a good look at the hood of the red car I ran into, just before I dented it with my face." He smiles too, but like mine, there's little humor in it.

I reward him with a huff. "What about the pickup truck?"

He sighs. "I don't know. I am having a hard time putting everything together."

"It'll come back to you," I say, from experience.

"Mom kept asking me if I was sure. It's like she doesn't believe me either."

I know how that feels, too. "Where is your mom? Is someone bringing her to see you?"

His turn to huff. "Yeah. That cop she knows. Paul. I guess he knew my father."

"Is that... a bad thing?"

He doesn't answer for a moment. "He probably told her there wasn't any evidence, and she believes him more than me."

"Ouch."

"I've been laying here thinking about it. Like, what kind of evidence would they expect to find? A shell casing could have fallen out inside the truck. A bullet could have flown all the way into the empty lots behind Grumpy's."

"Simon, don't worry, dude. I'll do whatever I can to figure out who did this to you."

His eyes go wide. "No!" He shakes his head back and forth. "No, Noah. Leave it alone, okay?"

"But—"

"Leave it alone!"

"Okay. Chill, dude. Relax. It's okay."

Maybe it was a car backfiring. Maybe someone had a cherry bomb and was trying to scare him. One thing I know, anyone at our school that has a black pickup truck is going to hear from me.

And one name immediately springs to my mind. Drake Ogletree.

I thought we had that burglary thing all wrapped up since the stolen goods were found in Bryce's car. I was also pretty sure that Bryce and Drake hated each other. But... could I have been only partly right?

"Where did you go Thursday night?" Simon asks.

I suppose I owe him an explanation. He was probably scared for me while my mother was freaking out after I disappeared. So I shrug and give him part of the answer.

"Spent the night in an empty house in that old neighborhood behind the industrial park."

He winces, probably picturing the place. The neighborhood didn't look much better when I walked through it the next morning than when I was slinking through it at night, trying to find a place to hide.

"Why?" Simon asks.

I shake my head. My mother already laid out our entire family drama for Simon and his mother, so I've got nothing to hide now. Except... being in the foster care system. I can't quite bring myself to talk about that yet.

"I'm not going back to North Carolina," I say. "Mom is gone, but I'm still here."

"In the trailer?"

I shake my head slightly. "Just... here."

Want more from Noah?
Sign up for Diana Sharples' newsletter to receive news and free content, including a short story with Noah and Stacey, coming soon!

www.dianasharples.com

Coming in August, 2018,
Book #3 of the Because... Series
Because...Paranoid

Now it's personal, and despite the total collapse of his family and being thrust into foster care, Noah needs to find out who is trying to hurt his best friend and why. The problem? There's no evidence of a crime, and Simon isn't talking.

Other Books by
Diana L. Sharples

Running Lean
(Available wherever books are sold)

Equilibrium. That's what Stacey and Calvin found in each other. He is as solid as his beloved vintage motorcycle and helps quiet the constant clamor in Stacey's mind. She is a passionate, creative spirit—and a life-line after Calvin's soldier brother dies. But lately the balance is off. Calvin's grief is taking new forms. Voices of self-loathing are dominating Stacey's life. When struggles with body image threaten her health, Calvin can't bear to lose another person that he loves. Taking action may destroy their relationship, but the alternative could be much more costly.

Running Strong
(Coming June 29, 2018)

Flannery Moore rides motocross bikes and can't remember the last time she wore a dress. She's also in love with one of her riding friends. Although nothing else could make her do so, Flannery decides to redefine herself into the kind of girl Tyler Dorset might fall for. Tyler, however, has dreams of his own... dreams that will take him far from sleepy and safe Bentley, North Carolina. When Flannery's mother is diagnosed with cancer, Flannery is compelled to make sacrifices, some easy, some that break her heart. Will this mean settling for "less than" with Tyler when she longs for so much more? For the sake of staying true to themselves, both Tyler and Flannery are pushed to make the choice between running away... or running strong.

Finding Hero
(Coming September 11, 2018)

Daniella Cooper just wants to audition for a leading role in her new school's production of *Much Ado About Nothing* ... not because she has something to prove, but because she wants to remember who she is.

Devon Jones just wants to play high school baseball and graduate next year and get his life back on track after running with some of the wrong people.

But one night, Devon's cousin is arrested, and his Cherokee grandmother confesses that there's blood on her hands. That same night a severe storm washes out land on the Cooper farm to reveal human remains, and Devon and Daniella are thrust together to discover details of a fifty-year-old murder case—details that could send loved ones to jail—as well as uncover the secrets to Devon's heritage.

CPSIA information can be obtained
at www.ICGtesting.com
Printed in the USA
LVHW03s1235200618
580950LV00001B/26/P